The Envious Nothing

The Envious Nothing

A Collection of Literary Ruin

Curtis M. Lawson

Hippocampus Press

New York

Published by Hippocampus Press
P.O. Box 641, New York, NY 10156.
www.hippocampuspress.com

Cover art by Rebecca Clegg, facebook.com/RebeccaCleggArt.
Cover design by Dan Sauer, dansauerdesign.com.
Hippocampus Press logo designed by Anastasia Damianakos.

First Edition
1 3 5 7 9 8 6 4 2

ISBN 978-1-61498-365-1 (paperback)
ISBN 978-1-61498-366-8 (ebook)

Contents

This book about Nothing is for Christine,
who gave me everything

Angrboða

In the hollowed husk of an ash she dwells
Surrounded by tribute of blood and bones;
With tragedy and death her belly swells,
Her unborn howl and growl in hellish tones.

She sees the future, scrying dying moans,
And shares secrets with those by madness kissed;
Her dark, burning eyes reflect flaming thrones,
Her laughter is the world's last chapter hissed.

Her love is black hate, her breath poison mist;
Her touch can drive men and even gods mad;
She beds flame and lusts for naught to exist,
She writhes upon chaos, sky-and-blood-clad.

And when the ember of life and light dies
Dread Angrboða will laugh where she lies.

You and I and the Envious Nothing

Clay Nichols trembled as he stared out the observation window of the space station, only vaguely aware of Zoya's wavering screams. His mind couldn't accept what his eyes perceived. The Earth was gone—not shattered into debris by some enormous meteor, not bathed in nuclear fire by man's love of war; it was just gone as if it had never existed.

"Commander!" Futoshi shouted.

In the void left by the Earth there was nothing, not even empty space. Clay's eyes twitched as he tried to wrap his head around the presence of the nothing before him—this planet-sized anomaly, devoid of light and matter—this ink spot on space-time, so dark that it couldn't truly be described as black.

"Commander!"

What he was seeing was impossible, of course. He grasped at reasonable explanations—an eclipse or a problem with the polarization on the glass. Neither of those made sense, and he knew it.

"Clay!" Futoshi screamed louder. "We need to sedate her before she kills someone!"

Clay turned to his crewmate, still in a daze. Futoshi bled from his nose and ears. His eyes were full of fear.

Zoya floated in the zero gravity, flailing and screeching, despite Futoshi's attempts to hold her in place. With the maddening vision of the absent Earth behind him, Clay's shock faded and he became grounded in the more immediate crisis. Only now did he become cognizant of the pain in his frontal lobe.

"Priscilla, dispense ten milligrams of haloperidol IM to observation module 1."

"Yes, Commander Nichols," the AI replied. A pleasant chime followed only seconds later, and a small door marked with a red cross opened in the wall opposite the glass dome, revealing an autoinjector.

Clay grabbed the sedative and pushed off the wall toward Zoya. The closer he got, the more fiercely the psychic waves radiating from her mind battered him. Vertigo seized him and his brain pulsed with agony. He jabbed the autoinjector into her leg, even as his capillaries burst and the whites of his eyes ran red.

Clay lost his grip and fell weightlessly away from Zoya. The stars outside the observation module twirled around him, and crimson droplets danced like will-o'-wisps in the air.

Zoya's screams faded into hoarse moans and her psychic barrage weakened. Clay closed his eyes and wiped his bloody nose on the sleeve of his uniform.

"What the hell is going on, Commander?" Futoshi's voice quivered.

Clay opened his eyes. Futoshi held Zoya's sedated form with one arm and a grab bar with the other. His expression was stoic beneath the blood streaking his face, but his eyes held a look of deep concern.

The commander turned back toward the clear dome of the observation deck. A drop of blood splattered against the glass, dead in the center of where Earth should have been—dead in the center of that gaping vacuum.

"I don't know."

After checking Zoya's vitals, Clay and Futoshi maneuvered the unconscious psychic through the narrow corridors of the space station and to her cramped quarters. Once they had Zoya secured in her sleeping bag, which hung in what was essentially a closet, the two men took a moment to breathe.

"I told you she was bad news from the start, Commander," Futoshi said, blunt and forthcoming as always. "Psychics are dangerously unstable. Bringing one on a space station . . . Sir, it's just foolish."

Futoshi's criticism brought a flush to Clay's cheeks. He agreed with the man, rationally, but he also cherished having Zoya onboard. It was nice having a woman around, especially one so exceptional in both her beauty and her insight.

Clay was an old hand at hiding his emotions. None of the crew knew that he'd fallen head over heels for her, except for maybe Zoya herself. He wasn't completely sure how her talents functioned. If she had plucked this secret from his mind she had never called him on it, which he both lamented and appreciated.

"I honestly had no say in the matter. Someone above my pay grade wanted to see the effects of orbital isolation on the psychic mind. Also, Zoya is a decorated military officer, not some street-corner oracle."

"A decorated military officer who is still a major creep," Futoshi replied, pointing to a wall covered with ink drawings of chimeric beasts and fantastic monsters. "I asked her about those once. She said they were her dreams. Well-adjusted people don't have dreams like that."

Futoshi was right. Zoya wasn't all that well-adjusted, despite her military accolades. It was that hint of insanity that made her so irresistible to him. What that said about his own character, he was unsure.

"Regardless, I think we have a bigger problem than Zoya. We've lost visual contact with the entire damn planet."

Futoshi shook his head. "Bullshit. That was a side effect of Zoya's psychic breakdown. She messed up our perception. If we go back to the observation module we'll see our shining blue home, right where it should be."

"Yes . . . You're right. I mean, you have to be right."

Nothing else made sense. Clay felt foolish for not coming to the realization himself.

"Priscilla!" Clay shouted to the station's AI. "Send a request to ground control for a medical evac."

"I'm sorry, Commander Nichols, but communications are down. Please try again later."

"Damn it," Clay hissed.

"Futoshi, I need you to check on the others—make sure Zoya didn't fry their brains. Bales is working with the bees in the bio lab and Singh should be in his bunk. I'll check on our visual and use the shortwave to request a medical evac for Zoya."

The Earth was still gone, replaced with the yawning nothing. Tendrils of unlight stretched forth from the void, so much blacker than even the emptiness of space. The fabric of the universe seemed to ripple where they touched.

Clay couldn't turn away at first. The nothingness had a special kind of gravity to it—one that sucked at his consciousness, threatening to devour his mind as a black hole devours light. Steeling himself against its draw, Clay turned his back and fled the observation module. His heart pounded and his breath came in nervous gasps as he propelled himself along the narrow corridors of the space station. The disorienting effects of zero gravity prodded his equilibrium, and panic pressed upon him like a boulder on his chest. He had been living in a world without up or down for months, but now his mind spun like a broken compass desperate for true north.

Clay gripped a handrail, paused, and took a deep breath. He was trained for this. Leaders did not give in to the anxiety of their panicked animal brains. He closed his eyes and exhaled in a slow, deliberate manner. His heart rate began to normalize.

A sound came from farther down the corridor: a furious tapping, like heavy rain on glass. Clay's eyes shot open in time to catch the merest glimpse of a terrible shadow—a monstrous shade scrambling across the far wall on a dozen hinged-needle appendages.

The shadow was gone before Clay could gasp. The skittering sound of those horrible appendages echoed faintly for several moments before fading away. He floated in the silence that followed, mouth agape. He wondered if it was real—if any of this was real—or if he was losing his mind.

He called out but was met with no response.

"Priscilla, did something just run through this corridor?"

"My motion sensors did not detect anything, Commander."

Clay let out a long, relieved breath. That settled it. Whatever stress-born hallucinations he was suffering, he had to power through them. Once he secured a medical evac for Zoya he could figure out his own issues.

Futoshi flicked the light to Singh's quarters, but they wouldn't turn on. Even in the dim illumination, he could see that room was a violent mess. The LED wall panels were shattered. Plastic debris and unmoored objects floated around the room like so much space junk. The walls were painted with crimson streaks, and beads of blood danced in the air like tiny red balloons.

An arrhythmic tapping echoed faintly from the darkness. Futoshi chalked it up to loose debris banging against the walls.

"Singh?" he called out, his voice cool and steady, even as his body trembled. There was no answer.

Futoshi crept into the room, doing his best to avoid the sanguine orbs that floated all around him. The door to Singh's sleep station hung on broken hinges, casting a shadow across the red-stained sleeping bag within. He approached the sleep station and retrieved a penlight from his pocket. The beam of the light revealed the lifeless face of Singh, still secured in his sleeping bag.

Blood smeared Singh's cheeks and ears. Futoshi cursed Zoya's name, instantly blaming the unstable psychic for his crewmate's death. Zoya's breakdown couldn't explain the ragged hole in his esophagus or the numerous bloody puncture marks in the sleeping bag, however. Futoshi examined the torn fabric and the pierced tissue beneath. It was as if someone had hammered dozens of nails into his legs and torso, then pulled them out.

"Kowai!"

The clicking sound from the shadows of the room grew in volume and tempo. Futoshi gasped and pushed himself away from Singh's corpse, his mind reeling. He scanned the darkness, no longer convinced that the noise was the clanging of broken plastic and Singh's unsecured effects.

Futoshi focused his gaze on the source of the nerve-racking skittering. The corner it echoed from was darker than the rest—blacker than anything he had ever seen, save for that void where the Earth had once been.

Something rushed forward from the utter blackness of that corner. It moved so quickly that Futoshi couldn't process what he'd seen until it was upon him. He stared into its chitinous, charcoal underbelly as all too many legs stabbed into him like sharpened pistons.

Clay called out over the shortwave radio, trying one frequency after another. His only answer was static. Internet communications were still down as well. He rebooted the communications array, desperate for some evidence that his eyes had betrayed him. He needed to know that someone was still out there. He needed to know that the Earth had not simply vanished.

And then of course there was Zoya. She'd never freaked out like that, not in all the months she'd been on the space station. Something was wrong with her and she was a danger to herself and the rest of the crew. He was worried for them all, they were his responsibility—they were like family— and he'd failed them. His secret love for Zoya had compromised his judgment.

As he waited for the computer to restart, a burst of sound like the buzzing of hornets escaped the speakers. It startled him, then faded, and Clay decided it was simply a squelch of static or feedback.

The communications array powered back on, but there was still no connection. He had no contact with Earth—not radio, digital, or visual.

"This can't be real," Clay muttered. "There's no way this is happening."

The buzzing came again, this time over the station's intercom. The speakers rumbled in the walls and Clay could feel the air vibrate against his skin. Uneven gasps and pained cries broke through the bee-buzz cacophony.

"Bales," Clay muttered, propelling himself off a wall and out of the communication's module. "I'm coming, Bales!" Clay cried as he pulled himself through the narrow corridors of the space station.

The screaming on the intercom stopped and the buzzing receded before he reached the biology laboratory where Bales did most of his work. As he entered the module, his fears were confirmed.

Dr. Bales floated lifeless amid shards of broken plastic and strands of golden honey. The sterile LED lighting left no doubt as to the grotesque cause of his death. Dozens of swollen, pink bumps riddled his bloated, puffy corpse. A couple of bees from the hive he'd been studying—the hive that was now shattered—still meandered on his dead form. A few others tumbled helplessly in the zero gravity or floated dead in the air.

Clay surveyed the room, trying to piece together what could have happened. How had the hive been broken? Had Zoya's outburst shattered it? Had she made the bees more aggressive? And where were the rest of them? Spread throughout the station, wreaking havoc on the delicate infrastructure?

Clay cursed at God and fought to hold back his tears as he looked into Bales's lifeless eyes.

"Priscilla, open intercom."

"Yes, Commander,"

"This is Commander Nichols. All personnel, lock yourselves down where you are. Several critical risks are threatening the station. I'll make an announcement when the situation is under control."

Clay hated making such a statement over the intercom, especially without offering further information, but it was necessary. He didn't need Singh and Futoshi running into an aggressive swarm of bees, and he didn't need them panicking about Bales's death.

"Priscilla, keep trying to contact Ground Control. We need that medical evac."

Clay smashed the bees that sat on his friend's body, partly out of anger, partly out of pragmatism. He grimaced as he wrestled with Bales's corpse, securing it to the wall so that it didn't float freely through the station. With that grim job taken care of, Clay retrieved an autoinjector of epinephrine from a first aid kit on the wall, a countermeasure in case he ran into the released swarm.

Taking a moment to calm himself, Clay retracted the plastic shade from the window and stared into the endless black. He didn't know what to do. Sometimes gazing at the stars inspired him, but the infinite sea of space was no comfort to him now. It swam with amorphous shapes, darker than the surrounding space. He no longer felt like a scientific pioneer or a galactic frontiersman. No, he felt like a man adrift far from shore, watching the water ripple with unseen predators.

The sound of rapid clicking drew Clay out of his grim reverie. It echoed through the cramped space. He whipped his head from side to side, trying to pinpoint its source.

The lights flickered, then burned out, leaving Clay blind in the darkened laboratory. He fumbled for the penlight in his breast pocket as the unnerving clicking grew louder. The light slipped from his grip. He grasped blindly for it as the skittering drew nearer.

Catching hold of the penlight, Clay clicked it on to find a mandibled face with two massive compound eyes. He bellowed and kicked at the beast, sending himself backward. The beam revealed more of the monster as he retreated—a long segmented body with dozens of needle-like legs and an exoskeleton the color of ash. It clung to the walls, contorting the front portion of its body upright like a charmed snake.

The creature snapped at him, nearly catching his leg in its dripping mandibles. Clay dropped the penlight and cursed as he scrambled to escape the laboratory.

The pen spun lazily in the air, casting its beam in wavering circles. Clay nearly vomited from the combination of fear, vertigo, and disorientation.

He pulled himself out of the laboratory and into the corridor beyond. The monster pursued him. It ran across the walls, vanished into shadow, and re-emerged in the spinning illumination of the penlight. Clay slid the door to the laboratory shut behind him. The nightmare creature battered the door, puncturing it with its mandibles and lancinating appendages.

The corridor was dim, illuminated only by low-light LED strips. Clay scrambled forward, desperate to put distance between himself and the insectoid beast on the other side of the door.

"Priscilla, turn on the damn lights."

"We are in power-save mode, Commander. The solar array has been compromised. Overriding power-save mode may jeopardize life support. Do you wish to override?"

"God damn it!"

"I'm sorry, I don't understand your command. Do you wish to override power-save mode?"

"No!"

Clay stuck close to one wall, propelling himself from one handhold to the next until he came to a cross-section of the corridor. To his left was the airlock used for spacewalks. Straight ahead was the kitchen. Zoya's quarters were down the corridor to the right.

Before he could decide which direction to go, a figure emerged from the darkness ahead of him. It was a human figure—a heavy-set woman with stringy ashen hair and parchment skin. Glistening amber oozed from cuts and sores on her pockmarked flesh. Her eyes were bits of honeycomb, crawling with bees.

Clay screamed and lost his grip on the wall. Bees hummed from within her and the woman gurgled as honey dripped from her mouth. She grasped his leg and he kicked her with the other. His blow caved in her chest. Honey oozed out from the wound and angry insects swarmed him.

Stinging sores erupted across Clay's body. He weathered the agony and scrambled from one handhold to the next. He was so racked with pain that he didn't know nor care where he was headed, so long as it was away from the monstrous woman and her swarm.

Each breath became a greater labor than the last as the venom from the stings began to close his throat. Reaching the edge of the next module, Clay fumbled with the door, nearly passing out before making it through. Across the threshold was a fire extinguisher, as there was in every module. Clay sprayed himself down with the fire suppressant, killing some of the bees and scaring off the others.

He retrieved the autoinjector from his pocket and jabbed himself in the leg. Epinephrine coursed through his body, counteracting the anaphylaxis induced by the venom. He took a deep and much-needed breath as he slammed the door closed.

Only now did he realize that he was back in Zoya's quarters. She floated in the air, her legs crossed. Loose, wild hair, unhindered by gravity, framed her face like a golden halo. Tears dripped from her eyes and hung in place.

"Zoya?"

"The world is gone," she whispered, casting a sad glance at Clay. "We're all that's left."

"That's not true, Zoya." He took a step toward her. "I'm not sure what's happening, but the Earth is still there. Planets don't just vanish."

"It's gone, Commander. I felt it. Ten billion human minds just . . . poof. Do you know what that kind of silence feels like to me? Can you imagine the emptiness?"

Clay wanted to reassure her. He wanted to reassure himself, but words escaped him.

"All gone." Her words were slow and drawn out. "All but you and I and the envious nothing."

Her use of the word "nothing" made his skin crawl. It invoked the image of that void, blacker than black, where the Earth should be. It made him think of the empty, insectoid eyes of the monstrous centipede and the hollow honeycomb witch.

"Nothing can't be malevolent," he uttered, knowing full well she would detect his insincerity.

"Nothing can't be envious. Nothing is just . . . nothing." She laughed and her eyes gleamed, almost aglow in the dim light. "It's envious of our form and function. It's envious of our will and imagination. It wants me to give it those things—to be its conduit from nothing to something."

Clay shook his head and caught a glimpse of one of her drawings—the sketches of her nightmares. Rendered on the paper was a huge millipede with serrated mandibles and legs like sabers. Another sketch depicted a crone with honeycomb eyes and viscous fluid bubbling from her mouth.

"The monsters! They're just psychic manifestations!"

"I'm the conduit of the nothing. I give it form and function."

Clay placed his hands on Zoya's arms and looked into her eyes. They both wept.

"Zoya, none of this is real. You're making all this. The Earth is still there, you're just blocking us from seeing it. The creatures in the station, they're only manifestations of your nightmares. You can make this all go away before anyone else gets hurt."

"Before anyone else gets hurt?" Her lip quivered. "There is no one else. I told you, Commander, it's just you and I . . . you and I and the nothing."

A dull thud startled Clay. He turned to see the door to Zoya's quarters shaking. Another thud sounded, this time louder. Something was in the corridor, trying to break in. Clay scanned the pictures in the room, his eyes darting from one monstrous illustration to another. What nightmare creature had Zoya given form to now? Faceless demons with midnight flesh and bat-like wings? Cybernetic cherubs with murder in their crimson eyes?

"Zoya, you need to focus. You can stop this. You're the only one who can stop this."

Zoya leaned forward and kissed Clay on the mouth. Her lips were soft, her kiss firm and fatalistic.

"You're right. I am the only one who can stop this."

She placed her lips against his forehead, and the world retreated around him.

Sleep. The word echoed in his mind.

"Zoya, don't . . ." He struggled to finish his command.

Zoya floated along the corridor, crying and laughing all at once. The emptiness she felt was so much worse than any pain she had ever known, so much colder than the black ocean beyond the meager walls of the space station.

To feel the great nothing channel itself through her, to know the antithesis of light and life in such an intimate fashion, and to be its tool—it was too much to bear. Her grasp on sanity had always been tenuous, as was the case for all those with psychic gifts, but now her mind was broken. Worse still, she was just lucid enough to realize it.

Her nightmares chittered and scurried in the shadows. The ashen centipede stalked her. Threats buzzed from deep within the honeycomb crone. Blank-faced demons growled from nonexistent mouths. None of the monsters dared strike Zoya, though. They needed her, and their threats reflected their nature—mere echoes of nothing.

Zoya opened the door to the airlock as her nightmares screeched and gibbered. She looked down the corridor, hoping to catch one last glimpse of the commander, but it was too dark to see back to where she'd left him. She didn't love him, not the way he did her, but she was fond of him. He was a good man—a responsible man. Stretching her consciousness, she reached into his mind and blessed him with sweet dreams of love, lust, and respite.

A low thud sounded from the airlock door as she sealed herself in. She looked out through the window and smiled at the distant stars—the billion somethings that stood in defiance of the dreadful nothing. There were worse fates than joining those bright spots in the cosmic sea.

"Priscilla, open the airlock."

Zoya's nightmares screeched and clamored at the door as she was sucked into space. They seized as her lungs ruptured and her eyes boiled. And when death overtook her, the monsters retreated to the shadows of nonexistence.

Clay was all alone. No walking nightmares. No Futoshi, Bales, or Singh. No Zoya. Even Priscilla hibernated in the digital aether of a dead computer.

Worst of all, the Earth was still gone. Zoya had not blocked his perception of it as he had suspected and hoped. That gorgeous hunk of iron, rock, and water was simply no more.

Clay looked out at the gaping nothing where his home should be—that rip in space and time that even cosmic darkness could not abide. There was a gravity to it, enough to keep the station in a decaying orbit around it. Perhaps even more unsettling, the nothing was expanding. Solar flares of unlight reached out from that planet-sized umbra, giving birth to formless ghosts. He could almost hear the silent screams of those jealous anti-beings—those expressions of that which lies beyond the boundaries of existence.

He pulled his gaze away from the observatory window and looked back into the darkened space station. The solar array was damaged; it looked as if it had been ravaged with monstrous claws—undoubtedly the work of one of Zoya's nightmares, one that Clay was happy not to have come across.

The power reserves were fading without the array to recharge them. The station had gone completely dark and the useless communications equipment sat without power. Life-support systems would be the next to go.

Death would for him come soon, just as it had for Futoshi, Singh, and Bales. Just as it had for Zoya. Just as it had for the Earth. Soon Clay would join them. Soon he too would be nothing.

The Witch of Rock Hollow

C*lint Avery—*

"Is Elmdale haunted? What town isn't?"

He takes a drag from a cigarette clutched in cracked and coarse fingers, tobacco-stained at the tips. Faded, angular runes are tattooed across his knuckles.

"Shit." He lets the word drag out as he exhales. "What *person* isn't haunted, for that matter? You are. It's written all over you, lady. Why else would you have come back to these parts to sift through the ash-es?

"But sure, maybe Elmdale is a touch more haunted than most places. Things were always fucked up there, long before the smoke drove everyone out of town . . . before your old man and his drinking buddies went after Deidre . . . before Deidre's great-great-great-aunt started that coven of theirs.

"All that tragic shit that went down when we were kids—that wasn't anything new. You ever look through the old newspapers? Elmdale has a long tradition of misery. It started as a coal town—ghastly conditions. The miners used to tell stories about ghosts and demons luring men deeper into the tunnels—whispering secrets, mak-ing promises—right up until the mine caved in on those poor bastards.

"Then there was the slave uprising of 1826. Eli Jackson, a twenty-four-year-old slave, just had enough one day and killed his masters—the whole family, kids and all. Vengeance against his own masters wasn't enough for Eli. Dude rounded up a posse of slaves and broke into ten other homes and slaughtered those families as well. The white folks in charge of Elmdale at the time claimed Eli had made a pact with a dark power. They burned him and his crew as witches, but that wasn't the end. No, they went all Old Testament and slaughtered the first-born son of any slave in town—a reminder to the other black folks that there was no path to freedom, not even in the darkest corners.

"Back in '73, way before Columbine, a seventh-grader named Billy Eames brought his pop's shotgun and a lunchbox full of shells to school. Blew the torsos out of three kids and a teacher before he got lit up in a shootout with the sheriff's department. They later found notebooks filled with ramblings about voices in the woods urging him to kill."

Clint taps the ash from his cigarette into the rim of a Coors can. He takes another long drag, then stares at the glowing tip of his Marlboro. The slightest trace of a smirk crosses his lips as he exhales.

"So yeah, I think it's fair to say that Elmdale is haunted."

Sean Porter—

"I wouldn't say it's haunted. That whole concept is pagan nonsense. It's heretical. The souls of the deceased cannot be anchored to the physical world. The dead go to heaven, or they go to hell. End of story."

His voice is weaker than I remember it being. The swapping of holy vestments for an orange jumpsuit diminishes his presence. Still, there's something menacing about his timbre and something dark within his eyes. We speak through a piece of glass, just as we spoke through the confessional screen in my childhood. It occurs to me that I've never talked to Sean Porter without a barrier between us, a fact that I'm grateful for.

"That being said, I do believe that Elmdale is cursed, or perhaps even possessed. There's no denying that now. The place is choked with toxic smoke and reeks of brimstone. Natural fires don't smolder for decades on end.

"I'm sure you've researched the troubled history of our hometown for this little project of yours. Surely you can see that Elmdale's tragedies stem from a supernatural source—some agent of hell that exploits the sin inside the human heart—greed—wrath—lust. Whatever devil resides beneath Elmdale, it's no beast to trifle with. I'm a man of the cloth—er, was a man of the cloth—and even I couldn't resist its whisper in my ear.

"Don't get me wrong, I tried to fight against the demonic forces in that place. I led the charge against Deidre Pierce and her unholy works. I smashed her idols and that slab on which she made her wicked sacrifices. It was my congregation that sent her to hell for good, but you know that. Your father was there that night, doing the Lord's work, God rest his soul.

"I understand that some people lament about what happened there, but I'll be damned if it wasn't the best thing for everyone. Was there a cost? Yes, a terrible one, but at least the evil isn't hidden beneath the ground anymore and it's no longer gestating like worms in our hearts. It's out in the open where anyone can see it and give it a wide berth."

Curtis Walker—

"Elmdale ain't haunted. There's no such thing. I've worked in law enforcement for thirty-six years now, and I can tell you that no make-believe monster can hold a candle to the vileness of man."

There's a hardness to Walker's brown eyes as he speaks. His brow is creased and I imagine that each line on his face has been chiseled there by tragedy.

"People like to lean on bullshit like ghouls and hexes because they can't face the evil next door, or worse, the evil in the mirror. Sure, a lot of bad shit went down in Elmdale over the years, but ain't none of it a mystery.

"The animal sacrifices out by Rock Hollow, we all know that was the Pierce family. Sure, it was some wacko cult shit, but it was still just humans being sadistic pricks. The missing kids? Well, we figured out who took them, and it wasn't some witch playing pied piper or an angry spirit from the old mines. Even that poison mist that fell over the town after the tragedy with Deidre Pierce and that lynch mob, there's no magic to it. Elmdale was built over a collapsed coal mine, for Christ's sake.

"Now would I go back there? Hell no, and I highly recommend you keep out of there, too. Ain't no reason to go back. It's a ghost town. There's nothing in Elmdale for anyone, unless they're looking for a case of emphysema."

Clint Avery—

"Deidre never used the term witch." Clint lets out a small laugh followed by a trail of smoke. "I suppose you could call her that, but she always made a sour face whenever the word was uttered. I think she associated it with mass-market New Age occultism—the kind of shit you find in self-help paperbacks masquerading as grimoires.

"She wasn't into that earth-mother, moon worship hippie shit that's so popular these days. She wasn't even a pagan, really. The spirituality she followed—a path laid out for her by her forbears—was a kind of non-denominational Gnosticism, if that makes sense. She studied all different myth cycles and was versed in dozens of magic systems, always trying to uncover some element of the deeper truth that might be hidden in each.

"We can only view the divine through tinted lenses. Looking through one, we might pick up just a single detail. Another may show us one or two more, but none offer the full picture. If we looked right upon unfiltered reality, if we stared God right in the face without a set of shades, our eyes would burn from our skulls and our souls would follow suit. That's how she explained it to me.

"If I had to define her, I wouldn't call her a witch. I'd say she was a truthseeker. She was born with an insatiable lust for knowledge. I always thought she knew everything because it damn well seemed like she did. Not just arcane shit, either. How to tend a garden and how to play guitar. How to chart the stars and how to fix a carburetor. She could quote as easily from *The Hermetica* as she could from *London Calling*.

"I learned some of her methods. Deidre taught me how to find visions in wavering flames and how to divine hidden knowledge in the arrangement of tossed bones. I've never found it as useful as she did, but I suspect I'm not asking the right questions."

A smile creeps across Clint's face as he stares at the burning tip of his cigarette. "I lost my virginity to her in a tantric sex ritual. I must have been sixteen, and here was this gorgeous, grown-ass woman offering her body to me and showing me the secrets of the universe.

"As wise and as learned as Deidre was, it was never enough for her. The need to know was a compulsion to her. She wanted to crack reality open and see its bloody innards. She wanted to touch the spirit of God."

Sean Porter—

"A witch. A sorceress. A succubus. Deidre Pierce was all those things.

"I know, I know. Such ideas are scoffed at by the rational." He pauses to make air quotes at the last word. "But what more evidence do you need?

"Do you think it was a coincidence what happened to the crops and the cattle after we cleansed the cursed land where her family performed their blasphemous rites? And the terrors that befell those children? I don't care what anyone says: it was all her fault . . . it was her influence. How much misfortune can simply fall on a community by chance?"

The former priest's eyes glaze over, and his voice takes on a performative aspect as if he's at the pulpit again. He's old and feeble, and I'm sure that prison has broken him down in many ways, but his heart still burns with the embers of zealotry.

"People act like she was a victim in all this. I tell you, she was not! Even if you're of a secular mind and don't believe in anything deeper than your senses, you can still see how dangerous she was. Her perverse influence was rotting our town. She sold drugs to children and lured young men into her bed. She undermined and mocked our most cherished institutions—the very bedrock of our community.

"Her very presence was a magnet for evil. Are you aware of the kinds of people who would come from afar to visit Deidre Pierce? Outlaw bikers, pervert Thelemites, and rock-'n'-roll sissy-queers. Those were just the visitors we could see. Imagine what invisible abominations she may have been in league with. Heck, you don't need to imagine. Go back to Elmdale and wander around in that mist. Stories say that the demons and familiars she summoned still roam that cursed land!

"So yes, Deidre was a witch, and her vile magic ruined Elmdale. It poisoned the land and the air. It ruined the people . . . It ruined me."

Curtis Walker—

"Deidre may have fancied herself a witch, but that don't make it true. A scapegoat is what she was. People don't want to accept that sometimes bad things happen for no good reason. They need someone to blame, and you better believe they'll find someone.

"A plague rips through Fred Hillman's livestock? Evil spirits must be at work. Millie Patterson's peaches wither before they ripen? Gotta be black magic, right? Kids across town start vanishing? Surely a witch is dragging them out to some sacrificial sabbath.

"And what better person to blame than the crazy lady with the Siouxsie Sioux makeup?" A smirk crosses his lips, though there seems to be no joy in it. "You're probably too young to know who that is, but you get the point.

"There were the rumors about the weird shit the Pierce family had been into for generations—sacrificing animals and dancing naked 'neath the moonlight. How much of that was true? Well, that don't really matter; the point is, Deidre was an easy mark.

"She was the last surviving member of an outcast family. The only friends she had in town were a few bikers and the kids who bought weed and mushrooms from her. She even had motive.

"Your daddy was a churchman, so I'm sure you remember how hellfire and brimstone Porter's sermons were. He couldn't stand the idea of witchcraft going on in his town, under his watch. A little while before we had that bad year with the farms, and before young boys went missing en masse, Porter and a bunch of holy-rollers went out to Rock Hollow, which was on Deidre's plot of land.

"They took sledgehammers to a slab of granite that the Pierce clan used as an altar going back generations. The stone was smeared with rusty stains from a hundred sacrifices, if you believe the stories. I guess there were these stone idols they trashed as well—gargoyle-looking things engraved with occult symbols, set up in a semicircle around the altar and the cave mouth. Once they were done smashing up Deidre's place of worship, Porter sprinkled some holy water in the dirt and said a prayer to consecrate the ground, as if some tap water and a few words mumbled in Latin would keep Deidre from rebuilding.

"So yeah, Deidre had motive, and hell, she might have tried to magic up some revenge, but her spells and hexes were about as powerful as Porter's prayers. If she was a witch, the genuine article, she sure wasn't any good at it, or else she wouldn't have met her end at the hands of pickup truck lynch mob."

Clint Avery—

"Sure, Deidre was fucking livid after those ignorant cocks trashed her ritual space outside of Rock Hollow. It was a damn shame. Most folks think that Deidre's great-great-grandma or whoever carved runes into that stone altar and sculpted the idols around the cave's entrance, but Deidre always claimed that it had been old when the first white folks showed up in these hills—old when the first Native Americans crossed the land bridge and started populating the continent.

"So yes, there was an element of anger toward Father Porter and his boys for trashing a sacred place—a spot with such rich history and tradition. And sure, Deidre was also pissed on a more personal level. You would be too if folks trespassed on your property and destroyed something of yours, especially if that something was intimately tied to your faith and your family.

"As pissed as she was, it wasn't her anger that stuck out to me back then. It was her fear. I'd never seen her scared before that. That look in her eyes and the way her lip trembled when she stared into the black depths of Rock Hollow . . . Fuck, man, it was chilling.

"I asked her what was in there . . . what could be so scary.

"'I don't know, but it's free now,' she said. And of course, she was right. She always was."

Sean Porter—

"Deidre couldn't sit back after what we did to that unholy patch of woods. The heart of a witch is a black thing, ruled by hatred and fueled by resentment. As such, she did what any witch would do: she sought out revenge.

"I should have seen that coming. My biggest failure as the shepherd to the people of Elmdale was suffering that witch to live. If we had smashed her to bits with the same hammers we'd used on her blood altar and those cursed idols, maybe we would have spared the town a whole mess of misery. You know what they say about hindsight, of course.

"First, she struck out at the good Christian soldiers who had accompanied me in the raid on Rock Hollow. The soil on their farms might as well have been ash. The nutrients were all gone, as if they'd just evaporated out of the dirt. No amount of cow shit or calcium could nurse the land back to health.

"Needless to say, almost nothing grew that year. What few crops did sprout up from the earth were sad and emaciated. On the rare occasions they lived long enough to yield a little something, it was always shriveled and dehydrated . . . nothing that could be sold or eaten.

"Livestock didn't fare any better. Fred Hillman's pigs went mad. They started killing and eating one another. They'd lash out at the Hillmans and their workers like they were wild boars. One of them hurt Fred's boy real bad—gnawed off a few of the kid's fingers. After that, Fred put the whole mess of swine down.

"Luke Turner's horses met a similar fate. Half of the beasts stopped eating and wasted away until they just fell over. A few others got wildly spooked for no good reason and freaked out until their hearts gave.

"Luke called me over once his favorite horse, a chestnut mare named Ulysses, smashed its own skull against an ash tree. He'd tried to stop the animal, but there's no stopping a horse like that. The poor thing just kept running headlong into the tree. With each hit, it left more of itself on that ash—shreds of skin and fur lodged in the rough bark.

"Luke was sure the poor animal had been bewitched, along with the others. I had to concur. Animals don't act that way without the Devil's guidance."

Curtis Walker—

"The phone at the sheriff's department wouldn't quit ringing in those days. People would call up with absurd complaints and demands, almost always tied to Deidre Pierce, to witchcraft, and to the damn

Devil himself. It got to the point where we couldn't focus on real crime because of all the time we had to waste on mass delusions.

"Fred Hillman wanted us to raid the Pierce property to find proof that he'd been hexed. Millie O'Connor was breeding French bulldogs at the time and tried to press charges against Deidre over a litter of stillborn puppies. The best might have been when Sara Ryan called us in a tizzy because her boy had blamed the crusty stains in his undies on Deidre visiting his dreams.

"When the first boy went missing, they tried to blame that on Deidre as well. None of us deputies bought into the Witch of Rock Hollow shit, but we drove out there and combed Deidre's property for signs of the missing kid because the town demanded it.

"We got nervous when we saw the structure she was building around the mouth of Rock Hollow—the same spot where her altar had been. I reckon she meant it to be a temple, but it looked more like a tin hut extending out from the mouth of the cave. The plywood walls on the inside were painted with odd symbols and the support pillars looked like morbid totem poles, but there were no signs of foul play in the hut or the cave—no blood or hair or clothes. It was just a weird little shack being built by a weird little woman.

"We went back when the second kid went missing and again for the third. Deidre never gave us a hard time and gave us free rein of the property. Never asked for a search warrant or anything. She didn't even hide her drugs from us, probably because she understood that we had limited resources and missing kids took priority over busting someone for weed and mushrooms.

"I wonder if we could have saved those boys if the people of Elmdale weren't so fixated on their witch. Of course, putting all that attention on Deidre was intentional, and it had nothing to do with whatever New Age drug and sex stuff she was doing in the woods. It was just a way to distract the town from the real monster that was hiding in plain sight."

Clint Avery—

"While most of the folks in town were busy tending to their dying farms and searching for their missing kids, Deidre was obsessed with rebuilding her sacred space.

"First thing was to find a new altar stone. She spent days wandering the woods around Rock Hollow until she found something that was accessible and the right size. We hooked it up to the tow hitch on my beat-up Jeep and dragged it back to where the old one had been.

"Once the altar was in place, I helped her build the structure at Rock Hollow. Calling it a temple would have been a stretch. It was a shack really—little more than plywood and studs built up around the cave entrance. Even that would have been beyond my skill level, but Deidre knew her way around tools, and a biker friend of hers helped secure the three walls and the roof to the natural stone around the cave."

Clint takes a drag from his cigarette, then stares at his hands, calloused and scarred. A smile crosses his lips.

"Come to think of it, that's where I learned about tools and carpentry. If I had to nail down where I got my love for building things and for working with my hands, I suppose it all started when we built that temple. I guess that's another thing I owe to Deidre.

"Don't get me wrong: we did our best to make the place suitable for Deidre's workings. We painted up the walls with runes and glyphs. She carved the support beams into totemic guardians to replace the statues that had been destroyed. There's only so much you can do on a budget, though, you know what I mean?

"I figured that maybe we'd put some sort of decorative façade on the outside, or at least paint it, but instead we just covered the thing in ugly sheet metal. At the time I figured it was supposed to be an extra layer of armor against anyone who might try to disturb the ritual site.

"Looking back, I don't think the sheet metal was there to keep people out. Hell, none of it was meant to keep things out. It was meant to keep things in."

Sean Porter—

"Now those boys . . . those poor, poor boys . . ." My stomach turns as Porter licks his lips and strokes one ring finger with the other. "It was Deidre who killed them. It was Deidre who consigned them to such a terrible end, and that's the truth.

"I admit, shamefully, that I played a role in it. If not for my sinful impulses that witch would not have found a tool for her evil work. But I had those impulses under control. I'd gone through conversion therapy. I'd given myself to God. It was her that awakened the evil in my heart and coaxed it into action.

"I hadn't touched another man in that unholy way since I'd been in high school, and I certainly hadn't thought about touching a child like that . . . not until Deidre Pierce bewitched me."

His ring finger moves up to his palm. He makes tiny circles on the back of his hand as he speaks and stares through me as if I'm not there.

"Elmdale was a small town, and most of the folks came from good Christian stock. Those boys knew me. They trusted me. I was their shepherd . . . I loved them all.

"I never wanted to touch them. I never wanted to use their flesh and break their bodies. You have no idea how much it hurt me to do what I did to them, but I wasn't in control of myself. It was the witch, exploiting the sin in my heart and using me like a puppet.

"People still say I tried to use Deidre as a patsy . . . that I tried to shift the blame for my crimes to her. She was to blame, though. What good would it have done to admit that she had used me as her tool? No one would have believed me. The modern mind is too poisoned by rationality."

Venom drips from the last word.

"The parents would have strung me from a tree, and I was the worst victim of all. Worse still, Deidre Pierce would still be out there, working her vile sorcery. But the Lord came through. Deidre faced justice that the law was incompetent to dole out, and I was brought here, where I may live a monastic life and preach the gospel to those who need it most."

Curtis Walker—

"I remember almost everything about the day that it happened—the day your daddy died—the day Elmdale died. It was a Saturday and I was making breakfast with my wife and my son—maple sausages, scrambled eggs, and cinnamon buns, the kind that come in the cardboard tube. That's when I got the call that the Hatcher boy had been found alive.

"The boy had shown up at home, spooked and damaged. All he did was cry in his momma's arms for the first few hours. He wouldn't say a word to the sheriff or any of us deputies. Eventually we got Rochelle Miller from social services down there, and I guess she was easier to open up to than a bunch of gruff men with guns.

"The boy told her how he'd come out from Griff's Variety to find his bike tires slashed. How Father Porter had been there and offered him a ride home. Where Porter had taken him and what the bastard had done to him.

"Hatcher was something of a troubled kid and a bit rough-and-tumble for a twelve-year-old. He'd had more than his fair share of schoolyard brawls and carried around a switchblade he got from his uncle. Porter didn't know any of that, of course, so he never saw it coming when the kid stuck him with his blade and took off.

"By the time we got to the rectory Sean Porter was gone and so was his truck. We sent out an APB and had every lawman in the county looking for the bastard. Word got out pretty quickly that we were after the beloved local shepherd, which didn't sit well with certain folks. They were sure we had the wrong man, so they decided to go after who they saw as the real danger."

Clint Avery—

"Deidre had been getting weird . . . weirder. She was almost always in the temple, talking to unseen forces that I couldn't hear even when I was tripping—voices that she claimed echoed from the depths of Rock Hollow. She would ramble about the voices . . . about how her family had been wrong in trying to keep them sedated below the town . . . about the secret wisdom they held and the gifts they could bestow.

"When she did spend time at home, all she did was gaze into the fireplace or the gas range of her stove. Just as I couldn't hear the voices from the cave, I couldn't see whatever visions danced in the flames for her. I didn't have the skill or the patience yet. I wasn't ready to see what she saw.

"It got to be kind of a drag after a while, but I hung around because I was in love with her. She was everything to me—a mother, a lover, a friend, and a mentor.

"She called me on the morning that it happened—the same day the cops figured out that Father Porter was a big fat pervert. She knew those holier-than-thou motherfuckers would be coming for her. She needed my help.

"I showed up at her house, my old man's shotgun slung across my back. Deidre laughed and kissed me on the lips. She called me crude but sweet and told me that the gun wouldn't be needed. We made love and ate mushrooms, then headed to Rock Hollow.

"We stood in the woodline, staring at the temple of plywood and sheet metal. Deidre told me what she needed from me. She made me promise to do as she asked and assured me that I had the will to do so. I gave her my word that I would, even as tears ran down my face."

Clint takes a drag from his cigarette and shakes his head. He looks upward and exhales slowly before speaking again.

"She kissed away my tears, then pressed her lips against mine. She told me this wasn't the end . . . that there is no end. Without another word she left me in the woods and strode toward her temple."

Sean Porter—

"I know that the Hatcher boy hates me, but I hold no ill will toward him. I thank God each day for saving the child's life. I only hope that someday he forgives me, not for my own conscience, but for his spiritual well-being. Anger is a poison.

"I owe that boy a debt. When he stabbed me and ran off, it woke me from the spell that Deidre Pierce had placed upon me. I was awake and in control for the first time in months.

"The police weren't going to see it that way, of course, so I had no choice but to run. I couldn't let that witch keep a spiritual stranglehold on Elmdale, though, especially if I wasn't going to be around to guide my herd. So I rounded up the most strong-spirited Christian men I knew, men like your father, and told them that the witch had framed me. I told them that I had to leave—that I couldn't go away for a crime that wasn't mine—and I implored them to execute the Lord's justice on my behalf."

Porter frowns and presses his hand against the glass between us. My disdain must be written across my face.

"I know that might seem dishonest to you, miss, but it's the truth, at least in a manner. True, I didn't tell your daddy or the others that she had used my flesh to commit those crimes, but that was a factor of little importance. It was still her will—her evil—that did those terrible things to those boys, and she aimed to pin it on me.

"Now what happened to those men when they caught up with Deidre Pierce—well, that was just tragic. I never meant to put them in harm's way, and I am so sorry that you lost your father like that. But know this: he died doing God's work."

Curtis Walker—

"Like I said, every available man in the county was out hunting for Porter. That bastard betrayed our trust and broke our community. We'd set up roadblocks and patrols. We went to the homes of every member of his church. We wanted him so bad it was like acid in our mouths.

"As focused as we were on bringing Sean Porter to justice, well, we didn't find out what happened at Rock Hollow until long after it was done. By the time we got there, we could barely see through the smoke. Little did we know how far that toxic cloud would penetrate—how it would overtake Elmdale and send us all packing.

"It was tough to put any sort of reliable narrative together, especially with no survivors or witnesses. There was a pickup parked in the dirt, a Jeep with no plates, and the charred remains of Deidre's temple.

"First we looked at the pickup. It had a good long length of rope in the bed—the kind of rope you might bring to a lynching. The truck was registered to Fred Hillman.

"The Jeep, which the VIN would reveal belonged to a kid named Clint Avery, was parked in front of where the temple door had stood. Clint would later tell us that he'd been there in the morning, but left his truck with Deidre and went home before everything went down. His story never quite sat right with me.

"The temple itself had collapsed into a heap of ash and charred sheets of metal—a burnt offering at the mouth of Rock Hollow. Black and gray smoke billowed from the cave beyond the remains of Deidre's temple.

"We waited for the firefighters, who told us that a fire in the temple had ignited the abandoned mines beneath Rock Hollow. There was no way to fight it, but they hoped it would go out on its own in a day or two.

"What's it been now?" The hardness in Walker's gaze diminishes. He lets out a heavy breath followed by a mirthless laugh. "Twenty years and change?

"Once the wreckage was cleared we pulled out the bodies and did our best to identify them. Fred Hillman, Millie Patterson's boy Jacob, Hank Jackson . . . your dad. Deidre's body was never recovered—which, of course, spawned a hundred urban legends and conspiracy theories.

"None of that stuff they say is true. Deidre Pierce wasn't saved by the Devil. She didn't take over the minds of those men and roast them alive in her temple. She didn't transform herself into the toxic smoke that covers the town to this day. I don't know exactly what happened, but I guaran-damn-tee you it was simpler than all that.

"If you ask me, those boys probably decided to get all medieval and set Deidre on fire. Sure, you can ask why they brought the rope if they were just gonna burn her, but that'd be applying rationality to a mob. Folks don't think straight when they got murder on their minds. That's why we catch them.

"So yeah, I reckon they lit Deidre up. Burning, scared, and in agony, she ran off into the cave and fell down some crevasse, setting off the fire in the old mines. No hocus-pocus. No occult conspiracy. Just plain old human malice.

"Like I said, I've been doing this for over thirty years, and crime always comes down to people being shitty to other people. It's as simple as it is ugly."

Clint Avery—

"What did I do? Well, like told the cops a hundred times, I went home. What Deidre asked me to do—well, that would have been criminal.

"But let's say I had stuck around . . . let's say I kept my promise. How would it have gone down?

"I imagine that them church folks would have roared down the dirt road to Rock Hollow in a big white pickup, hooting and hollering about Christ and demanding that Deidre come out and slide her neck into a noose. Of course, she wouldn't have come out. No sane person would.

"So next they would have chugged down a few beers and gone into the temple to drag her out. Once inside, I suppose I would have started up my Jeep and driven it out of the woods and up to the temple. I would have parked against the doors to barricade the bastards in there, just like Deidre had asked me to.

"From outside I wouldn't know how the fire started, but I would have seen the smoke. I would have heard the screams . . . the begging . . . the pounding. But I wouldn't have moved the truck, because Deidre said not to, no matter what I heard, or smelled, or saw.

"I would have felt the heat radiating off the sheet metal siding and realized that we hadn't built a fortress or even a temple, but an oven."

Clint stubs out his cigarette. He clears his throat and wipes at his eyes with a knuckle. He's not crying, but his bloodshot eyes are shining with wetness.

"Tears would have poured down my face and ugly sobs would have echoed from my chest as the smartest and most beautiful person I had ever known burned to death with a bunch of small-minded, small-town slobs. But part of me would have known that she was ascending to a new state of being . . . that she was becoming one with the flame and learning its secrets.

"And as much as it would have hurt, I would have stayed there until the temple collapsed into ash and embers. I would have waited to make sure nothing walked away—to make sure it all burned—that Deidre's final sacrifice was complete."

Clint laughs, then smirks. He looks into my eyes as if he's trying to take measure of me . . . trying to see if I'm my father's daughter or my own person.

"But I'd have been an accessory to murder if I'd done any of that, now wouldn't I? So like I said. I just went home."

Clint flicks his lighter and gazes into the tiny fire. A smile crosses his lips and he runs his finger along the curves of the flame. His eyes glitter like those of a man in love.

I drive through the empty streets of cursed Elmdale, my headlights barely cutting through the smoke. Even with my respirator, the air smells acrid and ashy. The fire started at Rock Hollow, but it spread through all the old tunnels beneath the town. It wasn't long before cracks erupted in sidewalks and basements. Now hot smoke belches through sewers grates and gaping holes in the asphalt streets.

It's been so long since the last time I was here, but the details come flooding back. I pass by Griff's Variety on my left, its windows plastered with yellow newspapers—twenty-year-old headlines and funnies. I turn the corner onto Beaumont Street, past the barbershop where my dad used to get his hair cut. I can almost smell the talcum powder and aftershave.

Saint Anthony's looms a few blocks ahead. That's where Father Porter would preach his hellfire gospels and where he would take the young boys he preyed upon. It's smaller than I remember—less grandiose—but the ever-present smoke enveloping it lends a sense of awful dread to the decaying façade.

I pass my old house, thinking about the man who played games with me in the backyard, the man who fed me and tucked me in . . . the man who died while lynching a woman because she looked and acted differently.

Eventually I make it out to past Deidre Pierce's house and all the way to Rock Hollow. The remnants of Deidre's temple have been carted away, but the ground outside the cave is still blackened and charred. Not a single weed or blade of grass grows there.

The cave is a dragon's maw, breathing out hot smoke. I stare into the haze, hoping for answers, though I'm not sure to what questions. Was my father truly a killer? Did Deidre Pierce deserve to die? Did she even die?

I hear noises from deep within Rock Hollow . . . the smoldering of burning coal and the creaking of hot stone. Sometimes it sounds as if there are voices . . . the voices that Clint Avery couldn't hear . . . the voices that Deidre Pierce did.

So you seek the truth?

The question is posed by a choir of voices, my father's among them. The words echo, perhaps from the cave, perhaps from my mind.

"I do. That's all I ever wanted."

Ash clings to my sweaty skin as I step into the cave. I toss aside my respirator and breathe in the blistering smoke, just as I breathe in all the answers I have ever sought and all those I never thought to wonder about.

Tears roll from my burning eyes as I collapse, but I'm not afraid. This is not the end . . . there is no end.

Orphan

Ian sat at the red light on the corner of Ripley and Walton. The night was silent, save for the music on his stereo and the sounds of nightbirds. Streetlights bathed the empty city with sodium radiance. He scanned the rows of tightly packed houses on either side of the street for any sign of life. The stoops and porches were vacant despite the pleasant, springtime weather, and no light shined from any of the windows.

While Ian had never been to Ironwood, Minnesota before, he knew its story just the same. He'd seen places like this in his travels—parts of Flint and Detroit, the whole town of Thurmond in West Virginia—towns that were propped up on a single industry, then buried under its collapse. He didn't know what business Ironwood had been built upon and it didn't matter. Paper mills, coal mines, or manufacturing plants—once that staple industry dried up, the story always ended the same.

The map on Ian's phone showed that he was still about a mile from St. Teresa's. Maybe the area around the church wasn't so dead. He'd driven out of his way to make this show, and he was going to be pissed if no one was there. Then again, the promoter promised him four hundred bucks just for showing up. What did it matter to him if he played for an empty room?

Four hundred dollars—it seemed too good to be true. Ian rarely made that much money from a single performance, especially since he'd gone solo. There wasn't a whole lot of money in punk rock. Most of the time he made just enough for gas to the next show and a few days of food and beer.

In the days following the breakup of Negative Space, Ian had considered trying to reinvent himself. He started writing new songs—

more mature and complex tunes but still with a strong hook. They were good songs, marketable even, all the A&R people who heard them said as much, but they all agreed that Ian was not marketable.

A series of physical deformities meant that he was too ugly to be anything but a punk rocker, or maybe the frontman for a gothy industrial act. His eyes were too far apart and completely black, as if the pupils had ruptured and leaked like ink across the iris and sclera. The tips of his knees and elbows were pointy and over-prominent. His chin and nose were too angular, his face too gaunt and narrow.

A few labels had offered to buy the new songs from him, but he turned them down. The thought of losing ownership of his music made him queasy. He imagined some pseudo-deep corporate rock guitarist playing his melodies and sexpot Disney Channel alumni singing his lyrics. Whatever money a label might pay for his songs, it wasn't enough.

The light stayed red and Ian wondered if it was broken. Confident that no cruisers were hiding in the shadows and sick of waiting at an empty intersection, he drove through the light. Two blocks up, his GPS instructed him to take a left onto Kerrigan Avenue, where the vacant colonials with sagging vinyl siding gave way to long strips of crumbling row houses.

Ian slowed down as he approached another intersection, though he intended to treat the red light as a stop sign. Something stirred in his peripheral vision. He held down the brake and glanced over. A twig of a man in ill-fitting clothes watched him from the open doorway of one of the row houses.

The details of the man's face were lost beneath the shadows of a hood, but long, stick-like arms shot out from the too-short sleeves of a voluminous sweatshirt. The guy was too tall and thin for his jeans, which were bound around his waist with a piece of rope.

Smack or meth? Ian found himself wondering. His money was on meth. The man was fidgety, his movements quick and erratic.

An eerie feeling, like that static-electricity vibe of being watched, caused the hairs on the back of Ian's neck to stand as he blew the light and continued down Kerrigan Avenue. In his side mirror he could see the guy watching him. Then again, there wasn't much else to watch out here, so who could blame him?

Turning off of Kerrigan Avenue, Ian could now see St. Teresa's off in the distance. It was a plain church, by Roman Catholic standards, a whitewashed façade, dotted with stained-glass windows that stretched toward the roof. Still, the light gleaming from its open doors seemed almost supernatural next to the miles of darkened windows. The steeple stretched high above the boarded-up shops and condemned restaurants that made up the rest of the defunct downtown area.

Ian spotted a few more meth-heads as he drove toward the church. One twitched on the ground at the mouth of an alley, the brim of a soiled Minnesota Twins cap covering his face. Another smoked a cigarette while pacing between the husks of wrecked cars in a gravel parking lot.

Ian began to worry about his van. The vehicle was his whole life. It was where he lived and slept. It got him from gig to gig. It held all his gear, his merch, and his few meager belongings. The last thing he needed was some tweaker smashing a window or prying off his rims.

Ian parked right outside the church and patted his front pocket, feeling for his switchblade. He knew it was there, it always was, but it was a nervous tic of his to double-check on the knife whenever he felt unsafe. He hoped he wouldn't have to use it, but he'd have no issue stabbing some meth-head if it came to that.

Three crust punks—two dudes and a chick—sat on the steps of the church, passing a joint back and forth. They all wore the same uniform of nonconformity: asymmetrical haircuts interspersed with dreadlocks; black denim vests covered in silk-screened band patches; face piercings and prison-quality tattoos.

Ian watched the group from his van. He studied their faces: at least two of them were moderately attractive beneath the rebel façade and the layers of grime. They went out of their way to make themselves ugly . . . to make themselves outcasts, but they were just tourists. All it would take for them to rejoin society was a shower and a haircut. They had no idea what it meant to be forced to the fringes of society.

The crust punks looked up as Ian stepped out of the van. One of the guys nodded in his direction. The girl arched her back and pushed out her tits. She made an effort not to let her eyes linger on him, playing as if she either didn't recognize him or didn't care who he was. It was an annoying bit of theater that always seemed to work on other band guys, but Ian had no interest in chicks or sex and even less interest in head games.

"Ian fucking Abyss!" the other dude shouted. Ian waved at them as he retrieved his guitar case from the back of the van. He locked the doors and made his way to the stairs of the church.

"Thanks for coming out," he said, stopping to shake hands with each of them. The girl, still feigning aloofness, offered him a hit from their joint. He took it, inhaled deeply, and held the smoke in his lungs. It had a strange taste—a subtle chemical complement.

"Man, I saw you on the last Negative Space tour, just outside Cleveland," the most openly excited of the group said. "It was my first punk show. Fucking changed my life."

A twinge of guilt ran up Ian's spine at the words. He looked at the story of hard living etched across the young man's face . . . the track marks on his arms . . . the scars from streetfights and DIY piercings.

He found himself wondering what the lives of these people would be like if they had never heard of him—if he hadn't turned his own misery into a musical pathogen. Would they still be with their mothers and fathers, however imperfect those families might be? Would they be happier with a shitty nine-to-five and an apartment full of consumerist refuse?

Ian shrugged off the train of thought and pushed the smoke out from his lungs. He handed the joint back to the girl, now noticing speckles of emerald in the glowing, orange tip.

"Is it laced?"

"Maybe," the girl shrugged. "We got it from the chick inside, the one who put the show together."

Ian nodded and continued up the stairs. St. Teresa's was sparsely decorated, aside from architectural design elements like stained-glass windows and cherubs carved into the molding. The pews had been neatly pushed to one side or the other, leaving a huge open space. On the wall above the altar was the ghost of a massive cross—a T-shaped space where the paint was a bit less faded.

A girl was fumbling with the wires of a PA system set up in front of the dust-covered altar. She wore sunglasses with massive lenses and a shock of thick green hair framed her narrow face and angular features. Presumably, this was Tia, the girl who had booked the show. Ian cleared his throat and she turned toward him.

"You must be Tia."

"Fucking A!" she squealed, ignoring his question. "You really came!"

Tia rushed toward him, the clomp of her boots echoing throughout the church. Ian offered his hand to her, but she pushed it away and pressed her body against his. Gazing up at his face, she caressed his cheeks. If the girl outside had been trying to play it cool, Tia was the polar opposite.

"You look just like your pictures."

Tia ran fingertips along his sharp jawline, up to his cheeks, and across the bony ridges of his deformed eye socket. No one had ever looked at him with such an expression before. Most people took great effort not to look at him at all.

"No, you're not like your pictures," she corrected herself. "You're even more beautiful."

Tia kissed him, gently biting his lip and giving it a playful tug. Her body felt good against his. He wanted to kiss her back . . . he wanted to pull her closer.

This was something new for him. Sure, he'd experimented with a few girls, as well as with a few guys, but he'd never enjoyed it. He simply had never been attracted to other people. But this girl—she felt different. Maybe it was her smell or the timbre of her voice. Maybe it was the compliments she'd thrown his way.

"Whoa!" Ian said, reluctantly pushing her away.

Between her makeup and her clothes, he couldn't be sure how young she was, but he knew she was too young.

"How old are you exactly?"

"Do you give a shit?" she asked with a tilt of her head. "That's not very punk rock."

She was right. He didn't care how old she was, not really. Neither laws nor rules mattered much to Ian. Tia kissed him again, and this time he let it happen. He returned her affections, grabbing her by the hips and kissing her back. She pushed against him, grinding herself against his growing erection.

"Tia?"

Ian pushed Tia away and turned toward the voice. A man in the black vestments of a priest stood by an open door toward the back of the church. He wore dark glasses and carried a white cane.

"I—I—um . . ." Ian scrambled for some excuse for being caught making out with a potentially underage girl until it hit him that the priest was blind. "I—I'm Ian. Nice to meet you."

The priest began walking toward Ian's voice, waving his cane back and forth to find his way. Ian rushed forward to meet him. He placed one hand on the priest's shoulder and shook his hand with the other.

"Father Lucas. And the pleasure is all mine."

"I'm guessing this is your place. Thanks for letting me play here."

Ian was always exceptionally polite with the people in control of venues. He'd learned early on that playing up the *I'm punk rock, fuck you* attitude was not conducive to getting shows.

"Thank you for coming, and sorry for the state of things. Attendance isn't what it used to be and the church decommissioned us, so it's kind of a DIY congregation now."

"I can appreciate that," Ian replied.

The priest placed his hand on Ian's shoulder and seemed to look him right in the eyes. His expression was earnest for a few moments, and then a smile crept over his face. The strangeness of a blind man holding his gaze creeped Ian out in a way he couldn't fully understand.

"You should grab the rest of your gear," Tia said, taking Ian by the hand and pulling him away from Father Lucas. He nodded in agreement and excused himself.

Ian loaded his gear into the church. Aside from the beat-up Gibson SG he'd been touring with for fifteen years, there was just a Marshall half-stack, a few pedals, and a box of merchandise. It had been more complicated back in the Negative Space days when he'd been touring with a full band. Setup was simpler now that it was just him.

Tia stood nearby as Ian ran the wires between his amp and pedals. She stared at him with unapologetic admiration. Ian found it almost unnerving. He wasn't used to that manner of attention.

"Who else is playing?" he asked, trying to diffuse the awkwardness.

"It was supposed to be Surf Hearse and The Vengeful & Godless. They both bailed at the last minute. It's hard to get people to play shows in Ironwood. There's not a lot going on here."

"I'm guessing you didn't offer them the same money you offered me."

Tia smirked and pulled out a chrome cigarette case from her pocket. She retrieved a joint from the case and patted her pocket, looking for a lighter. Ian retrieved a Zippo from his jacket and flicked the wheel. Tia smiled and leaned over the flame.

Tiny dots of emerald glowed within the orange ember at the tip of the joint. The colors grew more intense as she sucked in the smoke. Ian wondered again what the weed was laced with.

Familiar music swelled outside the church, accented by excited howls and loud engines. Tia's smirk faded and she shot an angry glance toward Father Lucas before turning her attention to the open doors.

"Sounds like we might have more than three people show up," Ian said.

"Seems like," she agreed. The words fell flat and lifeless from her lips.

Tia sucked on the joint, causing the tip to glow hotter—burning orange mottled with kryptonite green. She held the smoke in and pressed her lips against Ian's. He opened his lips, letting her shotgun the smoke into his mouth. She pulled away and headed for the front door.

Ian's head swam as he hooked his phone to the mixing board and tuned his guitar. Whatever was in the weed was hitting him hard and fast. The lights on his tuner glared like shifting starbursts. They exploded and wavered every time he hit a string. Finally he closed his eyes and brought the bridge up to his ear. Plucking two strings at a time, he listened for dissonance between notes and adjusted the machine heads until it was resolved.

More people filed in as Ian finished setting up. The crust punks from the stairs were followed by a couple of old metal guys and a group of high school kids in baseball caps and mall punk shirts. Ian could hear the crust punks making jokes at the expense of the high schoolers. The kids carried on their own conversation, pretending not to hear the jabs.

Ian looked up, a slight feeling of vertigo gripping him. Tia was walking back into the church. Several of the local meth-heads followed in behind her, their cowed faces covered by greasy hair or shrouded by hoods and hats.

Their lanky bodies looked even stranger in the light of the church. Their proportions were off and they walked with jerky movements. Ian shook his head, trying to gain control of his paranoid thoughts. It had to be the drugs he'd smoked. They were screwing with his perception and making him nervous.

Tia closed the door to the church and Ian could see her fiddling with something, though he couldn't tell what she was doing. The meth-heads slumped against the back wall of the church as Tia strode down the center of the chapel.

"You ready?"

Ian nodded. Tia smiled and turned toward the small crowd. She tapped the mic, eliciting a pop and a wave of feedback.

"Hold on to your cocks, motherfuckers! Let's hear it for Ian fucking Abyss!"

Ian smirked at the animated introduction as he hit play on the drum track on his phone. The recorded sound of drumsticks clicking together played over the speaker, and Ian broke into a series of manic downstrokes as the drum track kicked in.

The song he played was a stripped-down version of *Orphan* from Negative Space's self-titled debut EP. It was their first hit, as far as you can apply the term "hit" to an underground punk band. The crowd was already hollering and slamming into one another. They were into it, even without Fungus on bass to fill up the low end and without Luna's manic stage presence behind the kit.

"Left in the gutter by my mother, never fucking wanted by another!"

Ian was sick of playing *Orphan*. He'd only been fifteen when he wrote the song, and he'd composed much better music since then. Still, he screamed the words into the mic with as much vitriol as he had the first time he sang them.

"Grew up in group homes, found my escape in a pair of headphones!"

One of the crust punks was inches away from him, screaming the lyrics in unison. Ian wondered if the guy could honestly relate to the song or if he just thought it sounded cool. Was he the real deal—a gutter punk with no way off the street—or could he go home to his parents in Connecticut or L.A. or where the fuck ever when he got bored with playing squatter?

"Ran away at the age of thirteen, just me and my this guitar in the streets of Racine!"

Ian's dizziness worsened. The floor seemed to shift beneath him and the rowdy crowd looked as if it was spinning in the narrowing tunnel of his vision. It reminded him of the shifting tubular passageways in a carnival funhouse. He closed his eyes, hoping the disorientation would fade.

"Stayed on my own, too ugly to love, too weird for friends, I was bereft of . . ."

Ian could feel his knees buckling. He willed himself not to fall and focused on the rhythm of the pre-recorded drums and the feeling of the strings beneath his fingers.

". . . any connection to man fucking kind! I grew a black hole heart, a malignant mind!"

He ran his pick down the low E, then let a diminished D chord ring out. A feeling of nausea welled up in his stomach. He tried to fight it, giving himself to the music . . . letting his consciousness dissolve into the sound, just as he always did when he was hurting.

"Just an orphan with no fucking place! An orphan with a fucked-up face!" He screeched the lines of the chorus. "An orphan screaming at the stars, cursing the world for his shitty cards!"

Something hit Ian's guitar, knocking him backward and screwing up the song. He fell on his ass and the guitar let out a squeal of feedback. Ian opened his eyes and tried to keep the church from spinning for long enough to make sense of what had happened.

The crust punk who'd been singing along with him was seizing on the floor. His two friends stared at him with dazed expressions. It looked to Ian as if they were unsteady on their feet, but then again the whole church seemed a bit shaky.

The rest of the crowd gathered around Ian and the seizing crust punk. Some gawked and pulled out their phones to document the scene. Others yelled for someone to call 911.

One of the high school kids pushed his way through the crowd, shouting that he knew CPR. As he knelt beside the older punk who'd been teasing him earlier, the female crusty collapsed. Her head hit the marble floor with a dull thud.

The last of the trio staggered to his knees to check on the girl. He muttered something about blood, then his body went limp on top of her.

Ian looked toward Tia, who stood calmly to the side. The locals and the priest were grouped behind her. She raised her arm above her head and brought it down in a sweeping arc. The emaciated creatures behind her lunged into the small crowd of Ian's fans. They skittered on all fours, their movements inhuman and their speed incredible.

Ian watched in horror as one of the seemingly demonic wretches tackled a high school kid and bit chunks of meat from his neck and face. Another grasped one of the aging metal guys by the waist and burrowed into his stomach with gnashing teeth.

A few of Ian's fans managed to avoid their insane attackers and rush for the exit. The door of the church shook and clattered as they tugged and pushed, but it never gave.

Tia strolled through the carnage, her stride cool and confident. She took off her sunglasses, and Ian shuddered as she stared at him with bulbous, jet-black eyes—eyes just like his own. An exclamation of fear traveled from his brain to his lips, but it drizzled out of his mouth like a drunken whisper. Tia pressed her bony finger to his lips, hushing him.

"Don't worry about those posers, Ian. They'll never understand us."

Tia took another hit from her joint. Ian stared transfixed by emerald specks that glowed at its burning tip. She leaned over and pressed her lips against his and exhaled the smoke into his mouth again. He tried to back away but found himself too weak to crawl or even to keep his eyes open.

Ian's head pounded in rhythm with a chorus of croaks. The noise reminded him of crickets or swamp toads but amplified through movie theater surround sound.

A single voice sang an ugly melody beneath the rhythm.

"All praise the witch of Ironwood! The daughter of naught who lay with flame."

The meter of the singing was awkward, and the words fit ill in the space. It reminded Ian of psalms he'd been forced to sing at one of the group homes he'd lived in as a kid.

Bony hands clutched his arms and his boots scraped against the ground as he was dragged along. His eyelids were too heavy to open and his mouth too dry to form words of protest.

The croaking grew louder as he was dragged farther along, as did the song of prayer.

"All praise the mistress of the end, she who birthed death itself!"

Ian moved his tongue around, hoping to coax some moisture into his mouth. A tiny bit of spit formed. His body was beginning to respond to his commands.

It was a struggle, but he managed to open his eyes now. He found himself being dragged through a massive basement with rough concrete walls and an earthen floor. The walls were decorated in angular runes and knotwork monsters—rust-red sigils and beasts painted upon a hard, gray backdrop.

The locals—the men he mistook for meth-heads—were gathered here. All but a few stood still as death, save for pulsating bulges at their throats.

Ian shuddered upon seeing them, unshrouded by hats or hoods. Each of them possessed the same deformities as he. Some were more pronounced, some less. Regardless of how exaggerated their unusual features were, each of the men (they all appeared to be male, save for Tia) had the same black, insectoid eyes and gaunt limbs.

Tia stood at the back of the room. Dim light from bare bulbs in the ceiling illuminated her naked form. Her knees and elbows met at sharp points, the bones threatening to break through her skin. The space between her breasts was marked with a series of horizontal ridges. Her waist was waif-thin—a narrow dividing line between her upper and lower segments. Without her sunglasses, Ian could see the bony ridges around her obsidian eyes. He'd never known such beauty could exist.

Several of Ironwood's emaciated men rubbed her down with dark oil. Father Lucas, who had dispensed with his ruse of blindness, waved a smoking censer around her. The embers inside the censer gave off the same emerald radiance as the laced marijuana had.

"Praise the mother of monsters, who loves all her terrible children!" the priest sang.

The two men holding Ian came to a stop. They forced him to his knees and held his arms tight in their grips. He wondered how they could be so strong, given their slight physiques. Then again, he was stronger than he looked as well. Appearances could be deceiving.

The rhythmic croaking suddenly stopped. All eyes were on Tia, and hers were on Ian. Her skin glistened beneath a haze of incense, her visage like that of a terrible goddess. She took a step toward Ian and his heart stuttered.

"Dread Angrboða, hear our prayers," the priest shouted, no longer singing. "Bless our sister Tia, so she may birth a hundred young! Place the crown of our race upon her brow!"

"Let him free," Tia commanded. "Ian Abyss is not a prisoner. He is our guest. He is our salvation."

The two men released their hold on Ian, and he slumped over without their support. Tia knelt beside him and cupped his face in her hands. She locked his gaze, and he could almost feel the gravity of her black hole eyes sucking him in.

A tear streamed down Tia's face.

"You're crying," he said.

"You're just . . ." she whispered. "You're just so beautiful."

Her words mirrored his own sentiments toward her. Tia was the most incredible creature he had ever laid eyes upon.

Ian wiped the tear from her face. Tia kissed him on the lips. She gripped Ian's shirt at the bottom seam and lifted it over his head. She pushed him onto the dirt floor, where she unbuckled his belt and pulled his pants down around his thighs. Ian didn't resist as she climbed on top of him and lowered herself onto his erection.

The strange congregation formed a circle around Ian and Tia as they made love in the dirt. The priest muttered soft prayers as he watched. Ian was so caught up in the ecstasy of the moment that he was barely unnerved by the cultish audience.

"I have waited so long for you," Tia moaned. "*We* have waited so long."

Ian watched her, finding such profound beauty in her writhing form that it made even his favorite music seem mundane in comparison. What was the wailing anger of *Earth A.D.* or the dark, sovereign spirituality of *Sonic Mass* compared to the vision and the touch of the woman atop him?

Ian grasped Tia's hips as he approached climax. He held onto her tightly, as if their connection tethered him to existence . . . as if his whole life had been leading up to this moment.

Euphoric chemicals exploded in Ian's brain as he climaxed. He lay on his back, his eyes closed, drowning in a sea of oxytocin. It was the best feeling he'd ever known. Better than booze. Better than playing music. Better than the few times he'd shot dope.

Tia collapsed on top of him; her breasts pushed against his chest, and the bony ridges between dug into his sternum. He moved his hands up from her hips and wrapped his arms around her. This was everything he'd been missing his whole life. This was home.

A sharp burst of pain shot through Ian's collarbone. He screamed and opened his eyes. Tia's face was pressed into his neck, her head moving back and forth in tight jerking motions. It took him several long seconds to process what was happening. She was biting him—tearing bits of flesh away with her teeth.

Ian balled his right hand into a fist and punched Tia in the ribs. She flinched at the blow and a guttural noise bellowed up from her chest. Ian swung again, hitting her in the same spot. This time she pulled her face away from his neck and smiled at him through a crimson veil.

Something was happening to Tia's face beneath the wash of blood. Her jaw pulsed as if the bone had split down the center and was trying to break free from the skin that bound it.

Ian moved to punch her again, but Tia gripped his face with both hands and slammed his skull into the dirt, not once but several times in succession. He looked up at her through the haze of pain and the retreating fog of inebriation. Her eyes were full of love and lust.

Tia smiled, wider and wider, until the skin at her jaw tore apart and her lower jaw split into two bony mandibles. Blood drizzled from her raggedly bisected lip, landing on his chest, warm and wet. She rapidly clicked her mandibles together, like the machine-gun fire snare drum from one of his songs. The gathered men of Ironwood responded, joining together in a chorus of maddening croaks.

Ian thrashed and screamed beneath Tia, as Father Lucas shouted out prayers and invocations that were surely not directed to the Christian God or his saints.

She parted her mandibles and lunged down at Ian. He struck her in the throat before she could bite into him. She reeled back, gasping. A slimy, crimson mist sprayed from her split jawbone as she struggled for air.

Ian pressed his advantage, sitting up and shoving Tia off of himself. Scooting away from her, he drew his legs in tight and retrieved the knife from his pocket. The blade trembled in his hand.

Father Lucas knelt beside Tia, stroking her and whispering soothing words. Tia's wheezing slowed, her breath normalizing. The priest's gaze shot up to Ian and his expression went ice-cold.

"How dare you!" the priest exclaimed. "How dare you lay a hand upon her!"

Ian clumsily pulled his pants up and got to his feet. He spewed a string of curses as he waved the blade back and forth, hoping to ward off the men surrounding him. None of them had any reaction. They stood still and dispassionate, like machines waiting to be turned on.

Tia sat up and nudged the priest away. Her tongue darted out, licking blood from one mandible, then the next. It was longer than it had been when they'd kissed, and thicker—a wet, ropy muscle.

Panicked by the sight of Tia's metamorphosis, Ian scanned the area for a means of escape. At the far end of the basement was an unlit passageway—a brick arch framing utter darkness.

Ian gave Tia and Father Lucas a wide berth, then ran forward. Tia screeched and one of the men stepped in front of Ian, blocking his path. Without a second thought, Ian plunged his knife into the man's stomach and shoved him aside. The blade slipped out, red and slick.

His heart thundering in his chest, Ian ran for the passageway. He didn't turn around to see if the mad locals pursued him, but he could hear their rapid footfalls behind him.

He lunged forward, succumbing to suppressed instincts, and his hands slammed against the earth. Suddenly, he was running on all fours, his pace exponentially faster. The act brought back flashes of forgotten memory—caregivers and foster parents yelling at him to walk like a human being and nuns speculating that he was possessed.

A hand grasped Ian's ankle and pulled him back. He kicked with the other foot, the sole of his boot smashing into the face of his pursuer. The hand let go and Ian skittered across the ground and through the brick archway.

Ian careened through the darkness, brittle debris breaking beneath his boots and his palms. His foot caught on something unseen—a root growing out from the earthen floor perhaps, or a rock jutting up from the dirt. He stumbled headlong. In a bid to maintain balance, he flailed his arms and grasped blindly.

His hand found purchase on something in the dark and he was able to control his fall to a certain extent. His knees still hit the earth hard, but at least his face was spared.

The object Ian caught himself on was roughly half his height. He ran his hand against it, wishing he could see. The thing felt like a cluster of orbs, each smooth and rounded, but the texture was interrupted by jagged lines like cracks in leather.

Ian knelt on stinging knees, half expecting the stampede of maniacs to descend upon him while he caught his breath. At that moment he realized that the terrible sound of their nightmarish locomotion had ceased. The drone of their croaking, or whatever the hell you might call the noise they made, still echoed through the darkness, but they hadn't followed him beyond the brick threshold.

In the space between the rhythmic croaks, Ian heard footfalls so soft that they might have been in his head. It was Tia. It had to be. Tia, naked and monstrous, stalking him in the darkness.

Ian reached up and grasped onto the cluster of orbs. He gripped a rounded surface and tried to pull himself up, but his fingertips ruptured the orb. A watery substance rushed out, followed by a more viscous sludge that reeked of sulfur.

An involuntary utterance of disgust shot from Ian's lips as he pulled his hand back and shook the slime from it. He wiped his fingers in the dirt and pushed himself to his feet, not seeking support this time.

Ian reached into the pocket of his jacket and grabbed his Zippo. He flicked open the cap and rolled his thumb across the flint wheel. The small flame didn't give much light, but Ian had always had excellent night vision. He'd never needed much light.

The cluster of orbs stood before him, visible in the glow from the lighter. Ian studied the yellow slime that oozed from the ruptured orb like liquid sunshine, and bile rose in his throat. It was an egg. He was standing before a mound of huge, leathery eggs.

"It's okay," Tia called from beyond the reach of the Zippo's modest radiance. "Those aren't viable. None of them are."

Ian stepped around the clustered eggs and shined his lighter back and forth. The light fell upon mound after mound of leathery orbs. He swallowed hard and moved away from Tia's voice, careful not to stumble into any of the clusters.

"That's why we need you, Ian. There's something wrong with our bloodline. Maybe there's too much inbreeding, or maybe it's just the opposite. Perhaps we've tainted ourselves with too much human blood. That's what Father Lucas believes."

Ian picked up his pace, desperate to find an exit before Tia caught up to him and finished what she'd begun. The mounds of eggs became more densely placed the farther he moved. Some were already broken, lines of white and yellow crust dried open their leathery surface. Others were deflated and desiccated.

"Whatever the root of the problem, our males had lost the vitality to fertilize new young."

The light from Ian's Zippo fell upon a waist-high wall of eggs that stretched out into the darkness on either side. There was nowhere else to go. He grimaced, pushing through the mass. Sulfurous yolk soaked into his clothes and bits of leathery husk clung to him. The slimy feeling on his skin was nearly as sickening as the stench of rot and death that hissed out from each ruptured orb.

Ian held his arm out, hoping that his flame might fall upon an egress. Instead, he found a monster. There was no other word for it—none that he knew at least.

"I think the stress of that—the tragedy of staring at all this unrealized potential—that's what killed our mother."

The creature was perched on a wooden dais that was engraved with interlaced runes and knotwork monsters. It rested on a segmented coil of countless insectoid legs. From that sinuous lower half sprung the body of a woman with gray, brittle skin, the texture of a wasp's nest. Her stomach looked as if it had once been distended but now lay sunken in and bony ridges shown between her shriveled breasts.

Ian stared into the monster's face, framed by long locks of brittle, white hair. Its lifeless eyes were as black and wide as his own, but she had so many of them—four sets going down her long face. Serrated mandibles sat where her jaw should have been—the same kind of terrible maw that he'd seen Tia's mouth morph into.

Ian's mind was flooded with a series of unmoored emotions: sadness and homesickness—nostalgia and yearning—love and fear.

"I knew there had to be others like us out there." Ian jumped as Tia's hand grazed his shoulder. "Other hives hidden among the children of Askr and Embla."

"This isn't real." Ian shook his head and backed away from Tia. "That's some sort of fucked-up taxidermy idol."

"And what about me, Ian?"

He considered Tia with her bisected and serrated jaw, the Zippo flame reflected in her eyes, a wavering flicker of amber against a backdrop of obsidian. She was terrible. She was beautiful. She was inhuman. For this he had no answer.

"We need to finish what we started. I need you inside me, fully and completely, so that I might sit as the new queen.

"Don't you want to be inside me, Ian?" Tia asked, stroking his cheek.

Part of him wanted that. He wanted to be consumed by her in every way. In her eyes and touch he felt the home he had never found elsewhere.

Tia gripped Ian by the hair. She spread her mandibles and pulled him toward herself. Oily, viscous fluid ran from her mouth; Ian found it sexy, the way one might yearn for the glistening mouth of a seductress.

The hormonal spell broke as Tia's pincers bit into Ian's face. Ian flinched and squirmed at the pain elicited from Tia's bite. He tried to back away, but her mandibles tore at his cheeks and scraped at the bone beneath. The pain from the lacerations was terrible, but worse was the crushing pressure threatening to cave in his cheekbones.

The Zippo fell from Ian's slackened grip. A dull thud echoed through the chamber as the lighter hit the dirt floor. The flame stayed lit and caught the debris on the ground, spreading from the lighter to the husks of the dead, dried eggs.

Tia's grasp loosened. She backed away from the flame, and Ian fell to the earth among the burning debris. Ancient curses dripped from her tongue and her mandibles clicked together.

"Nei!" she screamed, watching as the fire spread throughout the chamber and licked at the rune-laden dais where the dead and terrible queen sat enthroned. Her voice regressed into desperate croaking and the gangly men of Ironwood poured into the chamber.

Father Lucas was the first among them. He scanned the room, awed and appalled. Whispered prayers fell from his lips as he made complex, somatic gestures.

Tia motioned and clicked, speaking in some language that defied human speech. The men responded to her commands and rushed toward the fire. Some stripped off their jackets and shirts to smother the flames. Others tried to extinguish the fire by throwing themselves upon it. It didn't matter: the blaze spread faster than they could combat it.

Ian batted flames from his jeans and hopped to his feet. He ran back the way he'd come, giving Tia and her people as wide of a berth as he could manage. None of them even glanced his way.

The room on the other side of the archway was empty now, save for the discarded effigy of Christ who peeked out with one eye from under a yellowed tarp. Ian looked back through the passageway, at the panicked monsters battling the growing inferno. Nausea set upon him as he tried to make sense of the current surrealness—the inhuman cult and their ghastly, burning queen.

Fighting to keep his stomach from flipping, Ian stumbled toward the basement stairs but stopped as he noticed the water heater tucked against the wall. His eyes fell upon the black iron gas line that fueled the water heater. His body was already trembling with adrenaline, and it only took a few strong kicks before gas began to hiss from one of the damaged joints.

As the smell of gas reached Ian's nose, he ran upstairs and emerged in the church's sacristy. No Christian symbol decorated the room. No Bibles or scholarly religious texts lined the shelves, but rather aged leather tomes with faded, angular writing on the spines.

Most disturbing were the pictures of him—clippings from zines and printouts from punk rock websites. These were pinned to a corkboard, and someone had scrawled notes in red ink across each photo. Some of the writing was decipherable, written in Latin script, albeit in a tongue that Ian didn't speak. The normal writing was interspersed with occult nonsense—Nordic runes, astrological symbols, and alchemical formulae.

Ian only spent a few seconds staring at the serial-killeresque shrine to him. He didn't need to understand this place or these people; he just needed to escape.

The door of the sacristy opened into the chapel, which was littered with human offal. A few corpses lay eviscerated beside his amplifier, which still hummed with feedback. Others had fallen into bloody heaps by the heavy front door. Ian's fans glared at him with dead eyes wherever they lay.

Ian unplugged his SG and let the cable fall into a pool of blood. The amp let out a static hiss as he stumbled away, avoiding the corpses strewn across the floor.

Guitar in hand, he ran for the front door. Ian remembered Tia messing with it before commanding her lunatic army to attack. She'd locked them in. He rattled the door, desperate to escape before the place blew up or the cultists came clamoring after him, but it wouldn't budge.

Cursing and trembling, Ian scanned the chapel for some other exit. His eyes fell upon the tall, stained-glass windows that ran the height of the walls on either side. He approached one of the windows: it was a mural of Adam and Eve. At their feet lay what must have been a serpent, but its body was segmented and it looked more like a millipede than a snake.

Another figure lurked in the background of the mural. Delicate channels of lead formed angular tattoos across her glassy, ice-white skin. Her eyes were cut from obsidian, rather than translucent glass.

The figure had to be an angel. That was the only thing that made sense—a grim medieval seraph holding judgment over Adam and Eve. Even so, that didn't seem quite right to Ian. This woman in the background, even rendered in stained glass, seemed much older, wiser, and far more terrible than any angel dreamed of by man.

Ian gripped the neck of his SG with both hands and swung the guitar into the window. Chromatic shards of glass rained down, like bits of a crumbling rainbow. Lead channels bent and broke beneath the force of the blow.

The mural was ruined, and the window now looked like a gaping mouth, with sharp and wicked teeth. Ian swung the guitar back and forth, clearing away jagged glass and barbs of lead. He tossed the guitar outside, then laid his jacket over the window frame to protect himself from the remaining bits of glass and metal.

A loud croaking echoed through the chapel, over the hiss of Ian's amplifier. Father Lucas stumbled out from the sacristy. A revolver hung loose in his grip. His neck bulged in rhythm with the animalistic sound he uttered. Scarlet spittle leaked from his mouth with each croak.

The priest raised the gun with an unsteady hand and fired at Ian, but the shot went wide. Ian flung himself out through the shattered window. He landed on his back and the wind was knocked out of him. A string of vulgarities formed in his mind between each gasp as he tried to catch his breath.

Ian got up, despite the breathless sensation in his chest. He left his jacket and guitar behind and ran from the church as fast as he could. Once again, instinct urged him to lurch forward, and his palms slammed down against the dead lawn. He raced away from the church on all fours, more like a beast than a man.

Gunshots echoed in the night. Father Lucas cried out guttural exclamations between each shot. Venom dripped from every harsh syllable.

Ian didn't look back. He prayed to whatever gods or spirits might be listening that Father Lucas would keep missing him and he scrambled for his van. Crouched low, Ian reached up and swung open the passenger side door.

A slug grazed Ian's left shoulder as he tried to crawl into the van. He fell against the wheel well, groaning and gritting his teeth. He looked toward the church. Father Lucas stood framed by the jagged remnants of stained glass in the shattered window and drew a bead on him.

Ian tried to get up and into the van, but his legs were like jelly. Tears welled up in his eyes, which shone like polished obsidian. The priest had him dead to rights, but a petite, blazing figure shoved the holy man aside before he could pull the trigger.

It was Tia, her aberrant body aflame. She leaped through the broken window and galloped toward Ian on all fours, amber fire trailing behind her, and the ground left burning in her wake.

Ian turned and gripped the passenger seat with a shaky hand and pulled himself up. He could hear Tia's hands and feet slapping against the ground. The sound of her sizzling skin pricked the hairs on his arms. He flung himself over the seat and shut the door behind him.

Ian shimmied over to the driver's side and slid his key into the ignition. The van roared to life. He shifted into drive and peeled away from the church as fast as he dared. In his side mirror, he could see Tia gaining on him, outpacing his vehicle.

The RPM dial hovered around 2000, regardless of how hard Ian pressed his foot down on the gas pedal. The van crept up from 30 miles an hour, reluctant to accelerate. Ian swore and punched the steering wheel, eliciting a series of honks.

Without warning, a sound like a hundred thunderstrikes filled the night. Safety glass splintered and spiderwebbed as the van spun out to the side. Ian gripped the wheel and tried to straighten out, but the vehicle flipped and rolled across the asphalt.

Ian would only remember the succeeding moments in blurred mental snapshots: the smell and the sound of gasoline dripping from a ruptured fuel line; the ruins of the blazing church against the lifeless, black cityscape; the abrasive pain of crawling through shattered glass; Tia's still and lifeless corpse, burning in the street like a demonic effigy.

Ian strummed the opening chord to *Orphan* for a crowd of eighteen fans gathered in a basement in some dying Rust Belt town. The small crowd hollered and cheered. He barked out the first line of the song, and they all sang along with him, but he knew none of them got it, not on any level that mattered. They were fair-weather freaks—normal people who could go back to the vanilla world of their parents any time they chose.

He'd been sick of playing *Orphan* for a long time, but it held a renewed meaning for him ever since that night in Ironwood. It conjured images of sad and desperate creatures who looked so much like him. It made him think of beautiful women with eyes that gleamed with the blackest hunger. It made him wish he'd stayed and given himself to that hunger.

Ian scanned each face in the crowd. He looked for familiar deformities—gaunt, elongated limbs or bony ridges around the eyes—but found nothing.

That was okay. There was another hive out there somewhere—another forgotten town of monsters like himself. He'd play gigs in every shithole and ghost town across the world if that's what it took. Someday he'd find them, and he would be an orphan no more.

White Night and Black Stars

She sang beneath the white noise of an old UHF band;
She beckoned from the static of a broken Magnavox.
Atonal, yet alluring—her song a siren's demand.

Her monochrome beauty spoke of a far, exotic land
Or long-forgotten races, living in oceans and lochs.
She sang beneath the white noise of an old UHF band.

Sweet, discordant notes and nothings formed my lady's command
To lay my lips upon the screen, to bow before that box;
Atonal, yet alluring—her song a siren's demand.

Her electric caress coursed through each finger and each hand;
Her outré lips and copper kiss gave playful static shocks.
She sang beneath the white noise of an old UHF band.

She urged my face through liquid glass, into that shifting sand
Of black and white cathode ray light—a realm heterodox;
Atonal, yet alluring—her song was a siren's demand.

One last kiss and she vanished into white night and black stars.
The glass reformed leaving my soul and face within that box.
Atonal, yet alluring—her song was a siren's demand;
She sang beneath the white noise of an old UHF band.

The Happiest Place on Earth

Nathan couldn't count the hash marks. There were too many of them—countless rows of five. Regardless, he scratched another onto the wall with his pencil. It was force of habit now to mark the days, and there was a bit of comfort that came from the routine. At one time he would have gotten into trouble for drawing on the walls, but there were no adults here anymore. There were no people here at all, except for him.

The radio played in the corner. Every morning it was the same song—a cover of "Wild Horses." It was his favorite part of the day.

Nathan got dressed, moving his head along with the music. The song ended as he slipped on his sneakers and the news followed. It was bad news, as it had been for a while. The world was coming apart at the seams. People were getting violent over things he didn't understand—politics, race, and religion.

The voice on the radio explained that the violence wasn't really about any of those things. It was about people losing their jobs and food shortages. It was about the threat of war. It was about gangs, governments, and corporations exploiting tragedy. Nathan didn't understand any of that either, but he liked hearing that voice, even when it sounded afraid.

The news report always ended with the voice backpedaling, talking about how everything wasn't really as bad as it seemed. Things would get back to normal soon. Cooler heads would prevail. There was nothing to be afraid of.

Nathan was young, but he knew a lie when he heard it.

The radio went silent, save for the soft hum of static. Nathan left it on, as he always did.

He wasn't sure how long he'd been squatting in the happiest place on Earth, but he remembered that he used to love going outside and exploring the grounds. This place was a dream—an empty amusement park all to himself. He'd ride the rollercoasters and go-karts from dawn to dusk and binge on cotton candy and funnel cakes. At some point, though, the rides stopped working and the food went rotten. A shroud of darkness hung over the park now, even in the day, and it was not an empty darkness.

Phantoms lurked in shadowed corners and sea monsters growled from the cavernous recesses of dark water rides. Dead presidents with vinyl skin and steel bones screeched hate from their podiums in a language of static and feedback. And then there was the obsidian fog surrounding the park—that dark and terrible mist that consumed all it touched.

The monsters rarely attacked in the day, but the days were getting darker and shorter, and the terrible creatures in the park were growing bolder. He couldn't stay hidden away in the castle forever, as much as he might like to. He needed to salvage supplies. He needed to move his body—to stretch and run and leap.

Nathan pulled the curtain aside, exposing a set of three arched windows. From this vantage point, he could see from the leafless trees and desiccated bushes outside the castle, all the way down the main thoroughfare. There was a time when the front gates were visible, but the ring of heavy black fog that encircled the park had grown tighter by the day.

The fog didn't concern Nathan this morning, however—not as much as the things that haunted the park. He watched from the window, looking for shifting shadows or lifeless objects that moved with unnatural power. Everything looked dangerous from up in the castle. It was impossible to tell if a shadow moved because of shifting light or because it possessed a life of its own.

He grabbed his spear—a kitchen knife fastened to a broomstick with a zip-tie—from the side of his bed and hung it across his back with a harness made from window-shade cord, then slung his backpack over one shoulder. Nathan left the castle suite and descended the stairs, running one hand across the smooth mahogany railing and the other hand across the rough faux-stone wall. He concentrated on their textures, appreciating the contrary sensations. He'd always taken such simple sensations for granted, but now Nathan made a point to focus on little details he would have previously overlooked.

The front gate opened to an overcast day. Ragged standards fluttered in the wind, their colors faded. Shadows of flags danced across the ground. Nathan avoided the shadows, fearful they might transform into black serpents or amorphous phantoms.

In front of the castle was a bronze statue of a well-dressed man holding hands with a cartoon mouse. The man's arm was pointing out toward the horizon, a smile on his face, as if he were gazing out over all the wonder and magic that the future held. Nathan stood beside the statue and tried to see the same thing—some promise on the horizon. There was only shadow and fog.

Nathan didn't bother with the main thoroughfare: it had been picked clean some time ago. Instead, he walked to a small pond near the castle. There were fish here in the shallow water and they were easy to spear. Some of them were ugly prehistoric-looking creatures with jagged underbites. Others bore rich, crimson stripes, warning of their toxicity. Others still were adorable and cartoonish with big, sad eyes.

Nathan took off his shoes, rolled up his jeans, and stepped into the water. With his spear poised above the surface, he watched for any fish he might catch. One of the ugly ones swam toward him. It was a silver-scaled beast with teeth like needles and a body like a javelin. A barracuda—that was the name that came to mind. He'd written a report on them for school once, and this sure looked like the same thing.

The monstrous fish rushed toward him, leaving rippling trails in its wake. Nathan tensed, fearing that if his spear missed the beast might bite off one of his toes. He stabbed at it and felt his spear tip cling against the concrete bottom of the artificial pond. His eyes closed instinctively, and he waited for the inevitable pain from its snapping jaws.

He felt no pain. Nathan opened his eyes and saw the barracuda flailing and struggling in the water. His spear had pierced its back fin and held it pinned. An audible sigh of relief escaped his lips.

Careful not to let the fish free, Nathan backed away to shore. He kept the tip of his spear pinned against the concrete and dragged the barracuda along while keeping a safe distance. His prey's rage turned into panic. It tried to turn and swim the other way. The fish flailed and tugged until its fin ripped free from the spear tip. With a ruined fin, the barracuda couldn't make it far, however. Nathan stabbed the crippled fish again, this time in the center of its body.

The fish lost its fight, and Nathan brought it to shore. He was careful to drop it far away from the pond so it might not flop its way back into the water. It seized on the ground, bleeding out and unable to breathe.

Nathan smiled. It was a big fish, and it would be enough food for him and Baba. Truthfully, Baba never had an appetite, but Nathan felt guilty showing up without enough food for both of them.

The multi-tool in Nathan's backpack had all the accessories he needed to clean the fish—a sharp blade, a fish-scaler, and a pair of pliers. He stabbed the barracuda once more, putting the creature out of its misery, then went about the work of cleaning and gutting it. It wasn't something he enjoyed, but his father had taught him how at a young age and he was able to disassemble his prey with a cool detachment.

Focused on his blade and the fish, Nathan didn't immediately hear the ticking behind him. Even when he did, his subconscious shrugged it off as ambient noise. Only when the ticking gave away to a brassy alarm bell did Nathan realize what was happening.

He turned, nearly dropping the fish, and saw a massive crocodile crawling out from the pond. The monstrous reptile regarded him with cold, black eyes. A guttural growl played like a sustained bass note beneath the ringing sound that came from inside the beast. It shook its head back and forth until the alarm stopped. Both Nathan and the crocodile stood silent for a moment, the only sound the echo of ticks and tocks from deep within the reptile's belly.

The crocodile charged. Its speed was scary, even on land. Nathan tossed the flayed fish at the beast. It paused to devour his offering. Nathan grabbed his backpack and spear and ran off before it could decide it wanted him as dessert.

Nathan didn't dare to try another fishing spot. Instead, he raided a hotdog stand—one of the few that wasn't overrun with feral cats. The freezer had thawed out long ago and the meat inside was rotten, but he managed to salvage a package of stale rolls and a few packets of relish.

Baba didn't seem very thankful for the meal. He stood still and silent, never even glancing at the food. This was the monkey's way, though—ever quiet and stoic.

"Sure, the fish would have been better, but I don't see you getting off your butt and finding us lunch," Nathan said to the monkey.

One side of a bun broke off as Nathan squeezed relish into the slit. Once it was slathered with the green spread, he pushed the broken piece back on. The relish held it together like paste.

"This is why you're so sluggish. You never eat."

The filthy, man-sized monkey sat in the chair across from Nathan and stared blankly into the distance. It showed no reaction to his words.

"It's not so bad," Nathan said after taking a bite.

The first bite hadn't tasted like much of anything, so Nathan concentrated on the next one. He tried to remember the smell of pickles and the hard chewiness of old bread. The taste and texture of both intensified with each chew.

"Okay, maybe it is pretty bad," he said with a laugh.

Nathan took his time with lunch. In between bites, he told Baba about his run-in with the crocodile, exaggerating the encounter to make himself sound more heroic. In this version, the reptilian monster had sneakily stolen the flayed barracuda and then run off. Nathan told Baba that he pursued the beast with his spear, ready to carve it into crocodile steaks, and that it narrowly escaped into the water. Baba was unimpressed, his expression never changing.

"Okay, maybe it didn't happen exactly like that," he admitted, then changed the subject.

Nathan reported the mist had overtaken just a little more of the park, the same way it did every day, and that things were getting even worse outside. That's what the man on the radio said, at least.

"This place might not be what it used to, but hey, it was still the happiest place on Earth. I suppose that's something, right?"

Nathan forced a smile, but it was short-lived. Despair pulled at the corners of his mouth like gravity. He reached across the table and placed a hand on Baba's matted paw.

"And, hey, we have each other."

He wished Baba would say something to reinforce his optimism—a single utterance or even a reassuring wink. He couldn't, of course. Baba wasn't a real monkey or even a person in a monkey costume. He was just an empty mascot. Even so, Nathan left him with a hot dog bun and a few relish packets, in case he changed his mind and got hungry.

Nathan returned to the castle, weary of the shadows and the monsters within the park. What little light penetrated the gray skies dimmed into blackness, and night enshrouded the park. Nathan closed the curtains and waited for the radio static to give way to the sound of an acoustic guitar.

There were different songs at night, not just that Stones cover his dad used to sing to him. It was all acoustic stuff, though, accompanied by a melancholy voice. The singer always sounded on the verge of crying, as if the music were the only thing keeping him together but also threatening to break him apart.

Nathan went to bed with the radio playing. The music was his talisman against the things in the dark.

The mist had rolled in further overnight. Nathan looked out the window: there was less to see today than there had been yesterday. He wondered how long it would be until the black fog swallowed the castle and him along with it.

Music swelled beneath the radio static as Nathan marked another hash mark on the wall. He closed his eyes and concentrated on the sound of "Wild Horses." He never sang along, even though he felt the urge. The man on the radio only played or spoke in the morning and night. Singing over that would ruin it.

A news report followed the song. Stuff was still bad outside, but help was coming. The government had a plan.

"We just need to make it a while longer," the voice on the radio proclaimed. "By the time you're back, everything will be normal again."

Nathan didn't want to leave the castle. The hotdog buns and relish could sustain his hunger, but he still needed batteries. He feared the radio might go dead at any moment, and he couldn't bear the thought of being without it, even for a day.

He crept out from the castle and made his away across the eastern bridge to the futuristic section of the park. The water below the bridge had once been clear and blue, but now it was gray and brackish. Nathan was careful not to let his mind wander, always listening for the *tick-tock* sounds of crocodiles in the water or trolls growling beneath the bridge. His eyes scanned for malevolent shadows that might peel themselves off the ground and take on a third dimension.

The section of the park across the bridge was a 1960s B-movie utopia, or it had been at one time. Now it was like an abandoned human colony on an alien world. Double arches supported a huge sci-fi sculpture of armored cable, cathode tubes, and mad science arrays. An unnerving hum came from the sculpture. Electricity arced between the metal arches at random intervals and stray lightning bolts shot down from the array. The pathway beneath was painted in black carbon and riddled with cracks.

Nathan veered off the paved road and gave the sparking archway a wide berth. Still, he flinched with each snap of electricity. Somewhere close by a radio broadcast played in a shop or café. He could hear the man on the radio giving soft assurances that everything was okay.

The entire section of the park was blanketed in the shadow of Mount Cosmos, an enormous structure that extended into the sky like a snow-white peak. Its design reminded Nathan of a bio-dome city-state on some far-off world. Dark fog engulfed more than half of the building, the black mist in stark contrast with the sprawling ivory architecture.

There was a rollercoaster in there. Nathan had gone on it once when he was younger—when he and his family had come here before the bad times. The ride had scared the hell out of him. It was huge and fast, and spooky synthesizer music played in the darkness beyond the rails of the track. Even now he could hear the faint echo of that music and the clicking of a rising coaster.

Nathan stepped through the shattered glass door of a nearby shop. A feral cat sat upon the counter, eating astronaut ice cream from a chewed and torn package. It let out a warbled mew, warning Nathan to keep his distance. He took the animal's warning and kept to the aisles, searching for anything of use.

There were plenty of clothes—plenty in his size even. He stuffed a few T-shirts and a pair of flip-flops into his backpack, along with a pair of swim trunks.

The cat mewed at him angrily, raising its hackles. Nathan imagined it yelling at him for shoplifting.

"Oh yeah?" he asked. "Did you pay for that astronaut ice cream?"

The cat hissed, then went back to its snack. Nathan turned away from the animal and rooted through shelves full of toys, looking for anything that might have the batteries he needed. He ripped open package after package, only to find battery compartments crusted with white corrosion. Every battery was swollen and leaking.

He cursed and moved to another aisle. Flashlights, ray guns, and laser swords hung from pegs. Nathan unscrewed their handles and popped open their battery compartments. Each time he was met with disappointment.

The feral cat hissed and cried at the counter. Nathan ignored it at first. The cats only got violent when you challenged them for food. Otherwise, they were just loud. He yelled for it to shut up, then turned around to see what it was mewling about.

His mouth hung open and a toy ray gun fell from his hand. The mist had rolled into the store. It pushed through the broken front door, then poured across the floor and climbed the walls. Racks of clothes and shelves of toys vanished into its nebulous dimensions.

The feral cat arched its back and hissed at the ebony fog. Dark and wispy tendrils reached out like probes and the cat swatted at them with its claws. The mist wrapped around the animal's leg and snatched it off the counter. A loud, discordant mew was cut short as the cat vanished into the wall of fog.

Nathan grabbed as many of the laser swords as he could manage and ran for the emergency exit of the shop. He slammed his body into the push bar and kept running out into the street.

Up ahead Nathan could see the double archway before the bridge. It sparked and barked in an erratic display of electrical chaos. He didn't know how close the hungry mist was and he didn't dare turn around to find out. Could he make it around the archway before those black tendrils dragged him into oblivion?

Nathan decided not to chance it. He ran straight through the double arches and beneath the sci-fi sculpture array. The hair on his arms stood on end and electricity hummed in his ears. Lightning bolts rained down all around him, and the ground shook with the force of their impact. Crisscrossing blue sparks arced across the outer arch like a gate.

All but one of the laser swords slipped from his grasp as Nathan dove beneath the wavering lines of electricity that barred the outer archway. He rolled to his feet and stumbled onto the bridge. His body trembled with adrenaline and tingled with electricity.

He thought back to the time he'd been dared to lick a nine-volt battery—the shock, the metallic taste. He dwelled on the recollection as he raced across the bridge.

Halfway across, Nathan dared a backward glance. The tidal wave of fog had come to a stop, but it had devoured nearly half of Futureland. Even Mount Cosmos, that titanic ride that scraped at the heavens, had been lost to the terrible mist.

Nathan ran back to the castle. He didn't bother to listen for the ticking of approaching crocodiles or the jerky movements of living shadows. He didn't keep an eye out for food or supplies.

When he made it back to the castle, Nathan raced upstairs to his suite and slammed the door behind him. He dropped the toy laser sword on the floor and stared out the window that overlooked the park. The mist had rolled in as fiercely on all sides. Half of the park was gone, lost to the oblivion that lay behind that black veil.

Nathan collapsed into bed. He cried in silence and waited for the radio to play its goodnight songs.

White corrosion leaked from the bloated, ruined batteries in the laser sword, just like all the others. Nathan cursed as he tossed them into a trash barrel near his bed. Static played in the background and he wondered how many days of power the radio had left.

The opening notes to "Wild Horses" came over the speakers. Sobs broke up the vocals and the music would pause as the singer took deep, audible breaths.

News from the outside world followed the music. The man on the radio sounded desperate and afraid—worse than Nathan had ever heard him. He muttered a string of bad news.

People were killing one another over canned food and gasoline. The hospitals had shut down and the doctors had all gone home. The pharmacies had been raided and there was no medicine to be found. Neither the police nor the military were responding—it was every man for himself.

Bad news was usually followed up by backpedaling. The man on the radio would gather his composure and assure that everything would go back to normal soon. This time, though, he didn't do that. A crying apology ended the transmission instead.

Nathan added a hash mark to the wall and looked out the window. The mist had rolled further in overnight. Not as fast as it had while he was scavenging the day before but more quickly than usual. Most nights it encroached upon the park by inches, but this time it was by yards.

A terrible thought occurred to him. What if the fog had claimed Baba?

Nathan got dressed and hurried out of the castle, taking only his spear for protection. He rushed down the steps, nearly tripping on his flip-flops, then ran past the dead bushes and toward the western half of the park. He raced across the bridge, shouting Baba's name.

A ticking sound brought Nathan to a halt as he stepped off the bridge. A low growl accompanied the mechanical ticks and tocks. Nathan readied his spear and turned around slowly.

The monstrous crocodile that had nearly killed him two days prior hissed and snapped in the water, the back half of its enormous body lost in the fog. Smoky black tendrils lashed around its neck and its front legs. Terror shone in its primal eyes as it clawed at the cement riverbed.

From where Nathan stood, he could see it was a losing battle. With every thrashing movement and snap of its terrible jaws, the crocodile was pulled deeper into the nothingness behind the black fog. It growled and bellowed, and Nathan wondered what it was trying to say. Was it raging with anger, making violent threats to the end? Was it asking for his help? Did it want him to save its life, or was it begging for the mercy of death before it succumbed to whatever terrible fate awaited it in the mist?

Nathan didn't move to help the crocodile. He stood stricken with fear and watched as its scaled flesh and gnashing teeth fell behind the obsidian veil. Its bassy growls went silent and the constant mechanical ticking from its stomach ceased.

The mist lurched forward, its dark volume staining the water and the air like black ink spilled onto a drawing. Nathan turned and ran.

His throat and lungs burned by the time he made it to Baba. The monkey was still there, sitting at the same bistro table as always. Nathan hunched over, grabbed his knees, and took a moment to catch his breath.

The fog was rolling in quickly from the west and the rust-colored mountains that rose so high just two days ago were gone. Baba seemed oblivious to the approaching doom. He just sat there wearing the same expression as always.

"We need to get out of here, buddy."

Baba didn't move.

"We'll go back to the castle," Nathan said, pointing toward the white and blue spires in the center of the park—the place farthest away from the mist. "We'll be safe there."

Nathan placed his hands under Baba's arms and pulled him out of the chair. He dragged the monkey away from the approaching fog, Baba's limp legs scraping against the ground.

"You gotta help me out, Baba! You're heavier than you look."

The monkey did nothing. He didn't stand and walk on his own. In fact, he stopped moving altogether.

Nathan tugged at Baba, but it was as if he were nailed to the spot. He pulled again, then saw that Baba's own shadow held him in place. It had come to life on the ground, acquiring depth and some facsimile of mass. Its paws gripped Baba by the ankles and pulled against Nathan.

"Let him go!" Nathan screamed.

The shadow did not concede. It pulled harder, dragging both child and monkey toward the rolling wall of fog. Nathan dug his heels into the ground, but his flip-flops had little traction.

"Let go of my friend!"

The shadow monsters never made a sound, but this black mockery of Baba threw its head back like a laughing mime. It pulled even harder, and Nathan's feet skidded across the pavement. The distance between them and the fog eroded.

Tendrils darted out from the mist like the probing black tongues of some terrible alien. Baba's shadow reached its tail out to one of the tendrils. It became one with the fog and then dragged Baba's legs through the dark veil.

"I can't do this alone, Baba."

Nathan pulled at the monkey, trying to wrestle him away. The mist would not relinquish its grasp, though. It held Baba tight and slowly rolled forward, overtaking the monkey inch by inch. Baba smiled a static grin at Nathan, even as the fog devoured it.

"I can't do this alone."

The black mist rolled over Baba's face. Nathan dropped the monkey's hand and backed away. The monkey's outstretched arm vanished into the great nothingness.

Nathan's bottom lip trembled. His face was wet with tears. At first, he couldn't remember what that felt like—the warm and wet feeling of ugly crying. He concentrated on it. It was important to feel, even the bad stuff. He willed the sensations—the weight and warmth of fat teardrops and the saltwater taste as the tears ran into his mouth.

Nathan ran from the mist, through the receding streets and byways, and back across the western bridge. He stopped outside the castle, in front of the statue of the well-dressed man and the cartoon mouse. He looked up into the man's eyes, desperate for some assurance or comfort, but there was only madness within the man's gaze. The statue stared out at the encroaching fog with a look of insane wonder and happiness—a look of sublime hope, as if he saw God on the horizon. The mouse grinned from ear to ear. There was something sinister and suspicious in that smile, as if it knew just what horrible thing came their way—as if it had been waiting for it.

Nathan left the well-dressed man and the cartoon mouse to their fate. He raced through the castle gates, up the steps, and into his suite. Praying it might make some sort of difference, Nathan locked the door and pulled the curtains shut. He fell into bed and waited for the radio to play its nightly transmission. It did, but this time it skipped the music and didn't bother with the news.

"Things are bad, little man. Really bad. If it was just me . . ." The man on the radio broke into a sob, and it took him the better part of a minute to regain his composure. "If it was just me, I'd stay here right next to you. I'd die by your side if that's what it took."

Nathan had never heard his father sound so sad. It broke his heart.

"I have your sister to worry about too, though. I can't help you, anymore. I've tried . . . God, I've tried . . . But I can still help her. I can try to get her someplace safe."

Nathan reached out and stroked the radio. The red indicator light faded in and out.

"We need to leave in the morning, So I need you to find your way back to us. I need you to wake up for me, Nate. Okay, buddy?"

Sobs and sniffles crackled over the radio static.

"I don't know the way home, Dad," Nathan whispered. "And I can't do this alone."

"I love you, Nathan. I'll always love you."

Nathan woke up to complete silence. No radio static filled the room. No cats mewed outside, and no monsters growled in the distance. The indicator light on the radio cast no glow. He tweaked the antennae and turned the volume up and down, but it was dead.

The black fog had penetrated the castle overnight. It rolled under the door and through the windows, lazily eating away at the floor. The mist climbed the walls, erasing the hash marks Nathan used to keep track of the days.

Nathan hugged the radio and closed his eyes. He tried to remember the smell of his father's aftershave and the texture of his stubble when he'd kiss him goodnight. These things were important to him, even now.

He clutched the radio, pretending to hold on to his father and sang the words to "Wild Horses" until his voice was lost in the mist.

Secrets of the Forbidden Kata

Keith finished the last of his morning stretches, undressed, and sat naked and crosslegged on the floor of his Harlem loft. He focused on his breathing, bringing it into a slow, even rhythm, which was becoming increasingly difficult by the week. Next, he visualized the highest center of energy in his body, the crown chakra. It glowed with violet radiance in his mind and he concentrated on feeling its pulse.

Continuing the exercise, Keith followed the line of chakras down his body. The space between his eyes burned a deeper shade of purple. His chest ignited in a swirl of emerald fire. This continued, chromatic wheels of light bursting to life one by one down his spine, until he reached the final chakra, the root as it was called, which appeared like a whirlpool of radiant blood in his mind.

He opened his eyes. The meditation was complete, but he felt no different. His body still ached. His lungs still wheezed. His withering limbs still trembled.

One of his doctors had told him that meditation was a crock of shit. Keith disagreed. Too many people swore by it for that to be the case. The problem was him. He could never fully empty his mind, no matter how much he tried. Tethered as he was by threads of anxiety and pain, Nirvana was firmly out of his reach.

A curse slipped past his lips as he slammed the heel of his palm against the bamboo floor. Self-pity overtook him, but only for a few moments. He did his best not to let negativity linger. Sick thoughts led to a sick mind. A sick mind led to an even sicker body. He mumbled one of his mantras, an affirmation of the glory of life, and forced himself off the floor.

Putting the failure of his mediation out of his mind, Keith went about the rest of his morning routine. Thirty minutes of soft tai-chi followed his chakra meditation. Next came breakfast, which consisted of oatmeal with fruit and a pile of vitamins and herbal supplements, washed down with a glass of almond milk. He ate this at the kitchen table, far away from his phone or computer. The only distraction he allowed himself during meals was music, usually Charles Parker or Dizzy Gillespie. Jazz relaxed him, which he believed helped with digestion and the absorption of nutrients.

The rest of Keith's morning retinue consisted of a warm bath to relax his muscles followed by a cold shower to stimulate blood flow, an hour of piano to maintain hand strength and dexterity, and a visit from his masseuse who came by three times a week.

Like breakfast, Keith's afternoon meal was the same each day. An egg-white omelet with mixed greens and a protein shake. After lunch, he spent a few hours scouring medical journals, fitness magazines, and transhumanist forums for anything that offered even a remote chance at battling his distal myopathy. Most days his research proved fruitless, but occasionally he'd find a new diet, a new drug, or a new therapy. Most of it was bullshit, and the rest were stopgaps—tattered sandbags set up against the relentless tide of atrophy and pain.

Finding nothing new in the *New England Journal of Medicine, Black Belt* magazine, or the *Theosophist,* Keith headed over to the corner he'd set up as a home gym. There was still a rack of dumbbells against one wall, though it wasn't safe for him to lift free weights anymore. His grip was too unstable. Instead, he focused on an array of resistance bands, TRX equipment, a stair climber, and a few punching bags.

The walls were decorated with framed kung-fu comics from the 1970s and autographed photographs of martial arts figures he admired, everyone from Bruce Lee and Chuck Norris to Count Dante and The RZA.

Amid these figures, all of whom he regarded as titans, there was a picture of him at his prime, before this despicable disease began devouring his strength. He liked to tell himself that he kept the photo as a source of inspiration—something to remind him of past accomplishments and what he was capable of. In rare moments of self-honesty, he admitted the real reason for the picture of his strong and healthy self: it was there as a means of self-flagellation—a punishment for getting sick, for succumbing to the weakness of his genes.

Remember what it felt like to be strong and fast?

Look at what you were and what you've become.

You're nothing but a haunted house . . . nothing but walking ruins.

While Keith preferred jazz for his meals, he listened to rap when he worked out—acts like Wu-Tang Clan or Tech Nine. The beat, the energy, the anger—it was music for going to war. It put him in a state of mind where he could fight through the weakness and the pain.

Keith warmed up by hitting the heavy bag. His punches were slow and powerless, which he couldn't help, so he focused on timing and form. He pivoted on the ball of his foot, swinging his negligible weight into each strike. His fists followed the beat of the music, striking the target in a half-rime rhythm.

Halfway through the song, Keith's wrist jammed. Pain radiated up his arm. He fell to his knees, tears welling in his eyes.

Keith didn't wear wraps during bag work anymore. He figured his strikes were too weak to warrant the need for them. Evidently his dying muscles were too weak to hold up to even that negligible force now.

The voice rapping over the music boasted about absolute power. Keith wanted to smash the speakers for mocking him. He wanted to find the man rapping so he could murder him and devour his strength, like a vampire or a wendigo.

He pushed himself up, leaning on the weight rack for support. Enraged at his infirmity, Keith grabbed the smallest dumbbell, intending to fling it across the room. The weight was too heavy and it fell from his grasp, barely missing his foot.

Sobbing in frustration, he stumbled and knocked down a framed copy of *Harlem Samurai #1*. His legs gave out and he slid down the wall, landing on the floor next to the broken frame. It was important to let himself cry, or so his therapist told him, so he did. He sat on amidst the broken glass, weeping and mourning the decay of his body.

Keith had been a late bloomer, physically speaking. He'd been a cerebral and bookish child, pushed by his father to study hard and make something of himself. His dad was a genuine tough guy, well-muscled and well scarred. He'd done a stint at Rikers for assault and made his living as muscle for hire. A single father, he took work where he could. Sometimes that meant he was a bouncer at Paris Blues or another nearby club; other times he'd come home spattered in blood, his knuckles raw, and a hollow look in his eyes.

Not wanting his son to grow up to be like him, Keith's father kept him away from the neighborhood kids and pushed him hard academically. At thirteen he'd won several educational grants and earned entry to the Trinity School in the Upper East Side. Graduating salutatorian at Trinity earned a full ride to Yale, where he founded a tech start-up that he sold after college for eight figures. It wasn't until then that Keith discovered his passion for fitness and martial arts. A few short years later the sickness came and took it all away.

Sometimes he wished he'd never started working out. Coping with the disease would be easier if he hadn't learned to love his body and find comfort in his own skin. Losing his strength wouldn't be so tragic if he'd never found it in the first place.

The snarling face of Julius Jones, the titular Harlem Samurai, looked up at Keith from within the shattered frame. His hands were raised in a tiger stance, his muscles as tense as steel cables. A crimson glow outlined his body—a physical manifestation of spiritual power.

Julius Jones was the perfect balance of body, mind and soul. He walked the curved line of yin and yang with the cool and grace. It was a silly thing to aspire to. Grown men should know better than to try emulating comic-book heroes, but Keith couldn't help it. Julius Jones was everything he wanted to be.

Keith wiped his tears with his shirt, then dusted the broken glass off the comic and picked it up. He flipped through the pages, admiring the line work and smirking at the bad dialogue. The story didn't make much sense, and the writer seemed to find any and all manner of Asian esoterica to be interchangeable. Kung-fu mixed freely with Karate. Elements of Taoism, Shintoism, and Bushido, weaved together as part of the narrative tapestry.

Harlem Samurai was regarded with scrutiny by modern audiences because of those transgressions. Keith, however, found a measure of charm in it all. He didn't see it as exploitative or appropriative, but uniquely cosmopolitan. It was ahead of its time, putting a black man in a heroic role, smashing cultural barriers, and even heralding the rise of mixed martial arts.

Keith stopped on a page full of advertisements. Grainy photographs and cartoonish line art tried to entice readers into buying novelties and scams. Bold font above a busty cartoon vixen arm in arm with of a scrawny, bucktoothed poindexter promised the secrets to make any woman fall in love with you. An illustration of a man with a disgusted expression offered onion-flavored gum with which to trick your friends and family.

One ad stood out among the others. A shirtless man with rippling muscles stood in a fighting stance Keith had never seen. The poor contrast of the photo made his eyes look like black holes. Keith could almost feel the impossible gravity of his gaze from the newsprint.

Secrets of the Forbidden Kata. The words were written in a generic sort of pseudo-oriental font above the photo. The advertisement went on to make wild claims.

Defeat any foe.

Heal any wound.

Draw strength from beyond.

Keith ran his fingertip across the last phrase.

The padded envelope looked old. Deep creases marred the manila-colored paper and tufts of padding erupted from a ripped corner. The return address was printed in smudged and faded ink. Only the top line was legible. It read *HUNDUN, INC.*

Keith tried to tear the package open, but the packaging was too thick and his body was too weak. He reluctantly retrieved a pair of scissors and cut the envelope open. Inside was a thin booklet, really just a dozen pieces of yellowing paper folded and stapled down the middle. *The Forbidden Kata*—those were the words printed on the front page in ghostly, mimeograph blue.

There wasn't a copyright page inside the booklet, nor was there an author credit. The first page had only three sentences, roughly centered and double-spaced from one another. They were the same lines from the advertisement.

Defeat any foe.

Heal any wound.

Draw strength from beyond.

The following page read *Form 1* and went straight into diagrams of the positions and movements of the titular Forbidden Kata. Keith skimmed through the booklet, familiarizing himself with the various strikes and blocks. It started normal enough, similar to dozens of martial arts manuals he'd come across. The punches and kicks were reminiscent of Goju-Ryu, while the defensive movements seemed to be a mix of Shaolin Kung-fu and Muay Thai.

It was the beginning of *Form 2,* which started on page 8, that gave Keith reason to pause. The anatomy was off on this next set of movements. Wrists turned at impossible angles. Fingers bent the wrong way into inverse tiger-claws. Biting attacks were introduced with an image of a warrior with his jaw hyperextended, like that of a snake.

Keith's phone rang and he placed *The Forbidden Kata* down. It was his father. He called to check up on him every day. He had treated him like a child ever since the onset of his sickness. For all Keith's accomplishments in business, technology, and martial arts, all his father saw was a helpless cripple.

The phone call went the same each day. The same questions were repeated and re-phrased, like some bizarre ritual. *How are you? But how are you really? Is the pain manageable? Are your meds helping? Do you need my help?*

Do you need my help? That was always the core theme of the call. His father wanted to be needed as much as Keith didn't want to need him.

As hard as his dad had worked, and as much as he had sacrificed to ensure Keith's success, his independence and good fortune had saddened him. It wasn't that his dad wished him ill, he was just lost without that sense of being needed. During those good years when Keith was as strong as he was wealthy, his father sank deeper into depression. It wasn't until he got sick that he snapped out of it.

Keith generally tried to humor his father as best he could manage. He didn't want anyone's help or pity, but he owed the man the chance to indulge his paternal nature. Today he had no patience for it. He rushed through the song and dance of their conversation, offering single words in answer and finally ending the call with a lie about his accountant calling on the other line.

With his father dealt with, Keith opened the booklet again and studied the first few movements of *The Forbidden Kata.* He stood and mimicked the illustrations to the best of his ability.

Keith spread his legs and squatted into a horse stance. His legs ached and trembled from the stress of it. The mantra from the booklet echoed in his mind, strengthening his will as he performed the strikes and parries from the diagrams.

Sweeping, overhead block. *Defeat any foe.*

Forward palm strike. *Heal any wound.*

Downward block. *Draw strength from beyond.*

Cross block. *Defeat any foe.*

Downward elbow strike. *Heal any wound.*

Front kick transition to forward stance. *Draw strength from beyond.*

The world faded around Keith as he approached the black hole of Nirvana for the first time in his life. The gravity of the growing emptiness in his mind arrested his ceaseless pain and anxiety. All that existed were the movements and the echoing mantra. Soon, those too faded into oblivion.

Ceaseless buzzing called Keith back from the void. Mostly asleep, it took him several seconds to realize it was his phone making the noise. He reached around on his nightstand until he felt it vibrating beneath his fingertips.

"Hello," he mumbled, eyes still closed.

"Sweet Jesus, Keith! Are you okay?" His father was on the line, his voice rich with panic. "I've been calling you for nearly an hour!"

Nearly an hour? That couldn't be right. Keith shook the grogginess from his head and checked the time on his phone, letting his father's voice fade into a nagging whisper.

2:07 P.M. How could that be? Even if he'd forgotten to set his alarm or if he'd slept through it, there was no way he wouldn't have woken up hours before. The latest he'd gotten up in years was 8 in the morning, and even that was a rarity.

"Is it really two in the afternoon, Dad?"

"Yes! I was about to take a cab over and make sure you weren't dead!"

"Well, I'm not," Keith said, not bothering to filter the annoyance from his tone. "In fact, I feel . . ."

Keith moved his neck back and forth. There was no pain. He sat up in bed, feeling none of the familiar strain in his abdomen. His movements were not hampered by stiffness or fatigue as he stretched his left arm over his head.

". . . I feel fantastic."

"Fantastic? You slept through the whole morning and afternoon, Keith. Something must be wrong."

Was something wrong? He didn't remember getting undressed or going to bed. He didn't remember what he'd had for dinner. Everything after practicing the first form of *The Forbidden Kata* was a blank.

Keith stood up, letting his blanket fall to the floor. He walked over to the mirror and stared at his naked form. Lines of definition were clear all across his body. His triceps were still atrophied, but they had shape again. His pecs no longer sagged and the loose skin around his chest and shoulders had tightened up.

There was a firmness to his stance. His legs didn't tremble and his knees didn't threaten to buckle beneath his meager weight. He placed a hand on his thigh and traced the contours of his quadricep.

"Dad, I have to go. I'll call you later." He hung up before his father could protest.

Keith flexed his shoulders and biceps. They contracted with a measure of strength he'd not felt in a long time. How he'd yearned for that simple pleasure—the sensation of power in his limbs.

He threw on a pair of shorts and headed straight for his home gym. His glance bounced from one piece of equipment to the next until settling on the heavy bag. Raising his hands into a boxing stance, he jabbed at the bag. A childish grin crossed his face as his left fist struck out like a cobra rather than a slug. He jabbed again and again, then followed with his right hand. The punch landed with a solid thud, and there was no pain, despite the pop he'd felt in his wrist several days ago.

Like a distracted child, his attention shifted from the bag to the weights. He grabbed a ten-pound dumbbell from the rack and curled it. The movement was difficult, and his muscles burned by the fifth rep, but he'd done it. He felt like Hercules.

Keith chose to forego his daily routine. He didn't check his stocks or play the piano. He canceled his massage and felt no guilt for sleeping through his morning meditation. The rest of his afternoon was spent lifting weights and hitting the heavy bag while rap songs blared over his speakers.

Hours passed before his stamina was spent. Conceding to exhaustion, he stripped his clothes and strode naked past the massive windows of the loft. Twilight shadows and autumn-colored light from the setting sun fell over his body.

After a quick shower, Keith put on a Miles Davis album and made dinner for himself. He tried to sing along but found the lyrics missing from his mind. He could remember a word here and a phrase there, but most of the lyrics escaped him. Chalking his lapse in memory up to mental fatigue, he hummed and grooved as he chopped carrots and trimmed the fat from the chicken.

He hadn't realized how hungry he was until the scent of simmering sesame oil rose from his wok. A feeling of voracious hunger erupted in his stomach as he sniffed at the stir-fried chicken and vegetables.

Keith ate twice his normal serving at dinner. Years of illness and poor constitution had caused his stomach to shrink, and it hurt to eat so much at once. Regardless of how full his belly was, the rest of his body yearned for sustenance. His muscle fibers were hungry for protein and his blood wanted iron.

Unable to eat anymore without the risk of throwing up, Keith chose to distract himself from the deeper hunger that had descended upon him. He opened *The Forbidden Kata* again and mirrored the movements from the first section until his mind went black and the world vanished.

Keith's recovery had plateaued weeks ago. He was stronger, more energetic, and healthier than he'd been in years. His appetite was voracious. No tremors ran through his body.

That being said, he still struggled to bench ninety pounds. His energy faded quickly, leaving him to train in short bursts with long rests between each exercise. His strikes were fast in comparison to how they'd been before, but they still lacked power and explosiveness.

The Forbidden Kata was opened to the second section. Keith studied the diagrams, trying to make sense of the impossible anatomy of the figures. Line art warriors snapped their distended jaws and arched their fingers backward, defying the limitations of human joints.

It made no sense. The movements demanded by this second part of the kata couldn't be performed. But what if these impossible strikes and blocks . . . these grapples and counters that no man was capable of . . . what if they were the path to salvation from his disease?

He thought back to his childhood, studying his ass off, eschewing friends, sports, and games. His father had told him that there was a cost to everything, and that was the cost of escaping the ghetto.

His college days suffered from a distinct lack of sex and drugs. He never bothered with parties or even so much with friends. Loneliness had been the price demanded for him to maintain his grades and develop the software company that would make him rich.

The physique and the martial skills he'd developed in the years before he took ill had come at a cost of time, sweat, and discipline. Like school and business, the body demanded much. Strength and skill can only be cultivated through careful sacrifice.

In short, Keith mused, everything has a cost. That's how his father had always phrased it.

Closing his eyes, Keith gripped his right index finger with his left hand. Instead of trying to empty his mind as he'd done for years of failed meditations, he focused on the very nature of emptiness—the great nothing he had glimpsed while performing the first section of *The Forbidden Kata.*

His breath, rapid and shallow from the thought of what he was considering, slowed and evened out. The erratic beating of his heart regulated as his anxieties were stripped into the void.

With barely a conscious thought, Keith wrenched his finger back until it snapped. The pain tore him from the blankness of his mind. He howled an incomprehensible expletive and fell to one knee. Tears flooded his eyes and rolled down his cheeks.

Keith closed his eyes and evoked the hungry emptiness in his mind again. The agony dissipated up his arm, past his chest and throat, and into the base of his skull where it evaporated.

He snapped the middle finger next, then the ring. The trauma of each break interrupted his meditative state, but his suffering was only momentary. The kernel of nothingness in his brain possessed a gravity that siphoned away the pain nearly as quickly as his nerves birthed it. By the time it was his pinky's turn, Keith didn't feel a thing.

Keith sat at his piano, wearing a sheet like a cloak. With closed eyes, he toyed with the keys but couldn't remember how to play. His fingers bounced from one black key to the next as single notes echoed through the loft, then vanished into silence. He wondered where sound went when it gave into quiet? Did it dissolve and dilute until it was imperceptible? Did it die? Was it swallowed by the nothing?

The whir of the elevator distracted him from his train of thought. The old lift clinked and clattered as it rose. Sinister impressions—nebulous thoughts teeming with dread—formed in Keith's mind. He imagined terrible un-things clamoring at the emptiness he'd discovered in his meditations—formless monsters pounding at the gates of existence.

"Keith!" someone called out. The voice was followed by the sound of the elevator grate clanging open.

He turned on the piano bench, willing his heavy eyelids to open. The sunlight streaming through the windows blurred his vision and forced him to squint, but he could see the fuzzy image of a man striding with purpose into his home.

"You need to answer your phone!" he hollered in an almost familiar voice. "I thought you were dead, boy!"

Keith cast an angry glance at the intruder. His muscles tensed and he sized him up, trying to determine if the man posed a threat. He was broad-shouldered, not too tall, but sturdily built.

"What the hell do you think you're doing here?"

The man stopped dead in his tracks. Shocked indignation washed across his face.

"Oh no, boy! I know you value your independence and your privacy, but you do not get to speak to me like that!"

"Get out of my home before I call the police." Keith swung his legs over the piano bench. The sheet fell from him as he stood, revealing his naked body.

The man brought his hand up to his face, shielding his eyes from Keith's private parts, but looking at the rest of him with awe.

"Keith . . . your body . . ." Tears cascaded down his face as he smiled from ear to ear. "You look . . . like you again."

A feeling of unease set over Keith as he watched this stranger shifting through emotions like a lunatic. He didn't know what the intruder wanted. He didn't know why he'd broken into his loft or how he knew his name, but he wanted him out.

"Forget the cops. Get out now or I'll show you out myself."

Keith balled his hands into fists to drive home the implication of violence. He unclenched his fists and arched his fingers back. A small gasp escaped the man's throat, and Keith looked down at his hands. His fingers were bent back the wrong way, so the nails of each were touching the back of his hand. He wiggled them back and forth, his range of motion nearly 360 degrees.

"Boy . . . oh God . . . what happened to your hands?"

He thought back to the night before—to when he willfully broke his fingers. They should have still hurt. They should have been swollen and ruined, but they weren't. He didn't feel even the phantom of pain in any of his digits.

"Get out," Keith mumbled, admiring the preternatural dexterity of his fingers.

"Keith, what in heaven is going on here?" the man said, his question broken up between sobs.

"Get out!" Keith's voice was a growl.

The man backed toward the elevator and slammed the gate behind him. He mashed a button over and over, his eyes pinned on Keith until the elevator descended below his line of sight.

With the intruder gone, Keith put on a pot of tea, hoping it would calm his nerves. As the water boiled he approached the cabinet over the refrigerator where he kept his tea packets. Something caught his eye. The face of the intruder he had just kicked out of his home stared at him from a photograph magnetically held to the fridge.

He snatched the picture and studied it. It was the stranger, no doubt about it, standing next to him on graduation day. Their arms were slung across each other's shoulders and both wore giant grins. Keith turned the picture around to find it inscribed with blue ink.

I always knew you would make me proud. I don't say it enough, but I love you.—Dad

That wasn't possible. This wasn't his father. His father was . . . his father was . . .

He couldn't remember him. Not his face or his voice. Not a single argument or warm memory. Not a life lesson or a tender moment.

Keith dropped the photo to the ground.

Everything has a cost . . .

The words reverberated in his skull. Someone had told him that once, but he couldn't remember who.

Keith spent the next two weeks perfecting the second section of *The Forbidden Kata.* He could now perform each impossible strike and every anatomy-defying parry. The kata had not only healed him; it was also evolving him. It was making him stronger and faster than he'd ever been. It allowed him to move and bend in ways that other men could not.

This new journey of healing and becoming was painful, but so was any manner of growth. Toddlers wail in pain as teeth push up through their gums. Young hearts break so they can learn to love more deeply.

People lose faith in gods and -isms so they may find resolve within themselves.

To be fair, Keith's growth was a bit more visceral than all that. After he'd broken his fingers and mastered the inverse grapples demanded by the kata, he'd taken a hammer to his jaw, shattering the synovial joints so that his bite might extend to preternatural extremes. The many self-inflicted breaks in his arms and legs had healed bizarrely, leaving the bones in his limbs to function similarly to the spine of a serpent.

Bruce Lee had talked about the power of formlessness. *Be water, my friend.* That was a famous line of his, but even water had limitations. It could be blocked off or frozen. It could be polluted or evaporated. But to be vacuous? There is no attack or defense against that.

"Be nothing, my friend," Keith muttered to himself.

Keith sat at the table, his breakfast laid out before him in clear plastic containers. He didn't play jazz with his meals anymore. The music did nothing for him, and he couldn't remember a single line or melody.

His appetite had grown both in range and quantity over the past weeks. No longer could he start his day with fruits, oats, and bottled supplements. He craved whole foods—whole organisms—blood and bone and chitin.

He snatched a white feeder mouse from a plastic cage on the table. He tilted his head back and hyperextended his jaw. The mouse squirmed and squeaked in Keith's grip as he dangled it over his open mouth.

Keith released its tail, and the tiny rodent fell into his maw. Its squirming and scratching in his mouth didn't bother him. He found no unpleasantness in the texture of its fur or the crunch of its bones, though he was vaguely aware that such a meal would have disgusted him not long ago.

He washed the mouse down with a sip of green tea and opened *The Forbidden Kata* to a dog-eared page. The diagrams on the page laid out the third and final form of the kata. This section was not a solo exercise. It introduced the need for an opponent.

One line figure warrior delivered fierce, mutilating attacks to the other. The first few pictures demonstrated the breaking of arms. This was followed by a series of pressure-point attacks, meant to cause the failure of specific organs. The final illustration depicted a victorious warrior lunging at his victim, his mouth hinged open like a bear-trap.

Keith reached into a second plastic cage and scooped up a handful of crickets. He licked them up from his hand, giving little thought to the juxtaposition of crunch and viscosity as he chewed. Instead, he focused on the diagrams in the booklet.

Keith had planned on acting out the last piece of the kata. He'd strolled around Harlem at all hours of the night for the past week, waiting for some crackhead or gangbanger to try and rob him. Maybe New York had become too civilized, or maybe the gangsters and thugs gave him a wide berth because they could sense the hungry emptiness within him—his closeness to Nirvana.

The buzzing of his phone brought Keith out of his reverie. He looked at the screen to see that it read *Dad.*

"Hello."

"Hey, it's Dad." Keith didn't recognize the man's voice. "Please don't hang up. I want to be there for you, no matter what it is you're going through."

Keith stayed silent for a moment. He traced the final diagram in *The Forbidden Kata* with one finger as he listened to the stranger on the other line break into a quiet sob.

This man was blind to Keith's becoming . . . blind to his ascension. He wouldn't run.

"Sure. How about you come over?"

"Keith?"

A voice brought Keith out of his meditation. He hadn't meant to fall into a trance while waiting for his father to arrive. The emptiness of Nirvana, that temporary lack of being, had simply descended upon him. It happened more and more these days.

It was night, but darkness never truly fell over New York City. Countless lights from an army of buildings kept it at bay. The best one could ask for was a sort of cinematic darkness. That gray-washed night from a horror movie or a crime flick where everything is still largely visible.

The cage door to the elevator rattled open. Keith didn't call out or beckon his opponent to enter. He rose from the floor and stepped into the deeper shadows of his unlit loft.

"Keith? You okay, son?"

Keith watched from hiding as the man stepped off the elevator. Despite the dim lighting, he could see his opponent in fine detail. His beard was more gray than black, and his face bore the lines of age as well as the scars of battle.

The man's gait was slightly uneven, showing that his age was catching up to him, but he was broad and solid with hands the size of bear paws. There was an expression of concern on his face, but a hollow meanness resided in his eyes. It was a subtle emptiness that one less attuned to the great nothing might miss, the kind of abyssal gaze of one who is no stranger to taking lives. Yes, he would be a worthy opponent.

"Keith! Come on, man, you're scaring me!"

The man fumbled with his phone, turning on the flashlight to guide him through the dark loft. Keith retreated before the light could reveal him. Silent and invisible, he flanked his opponent.

Keith had become so close to Nirvana . . . so attuned to nothingness that the somethingness of this man announced itself like a lightning storm. From more than an arm's length away he could feel the heat radiating from him. The pounding of the man's heart reverberated in Keith's ears. He could smell the anxiety in the chemicals of his sweat.

Keith's lashed out with his left hand. The air snapped from the whipping motion of his serpentine arm. His knuckles connected like the knotted end of a scourge, drawing blood.

The man cursed and stumbled back into a boxer's stance. Keith stepped out of the shadows, pressing his attack. He struck out with his first two fingers, aiming for a pressure point below the ribs. His opponent dropped his elbow, blocking the attack.

"What the hell, Keith? Are you out of your damn mind?"

Keith ignored the man's words and focused on the mantra of *The Forbidden Kata.*

Defeat any foe.

He swung his leg high and brought his heel down into the

stranger's shoulder. The man groaned in pain and his stance weakened, but he managed to keep his footing.

"I don't want to do this, son," the man said, shuffling back, but maintaining his stance. There were tears in his eyes, but that look of meanness had intensified.

Keith pressed forward with a spinning back fist. His opponent blocked the attack, but Keith's arm coiled around his wrist like a whip. The man pulled his arm back with quickness and strength that took Keith by surprise and knocked him off his feet.

Staggering to get up, Keith didn't see the kick coming at his ribs. He fell onto his stomach, gasping for breath.

"Stay down, boy." The man's voice quivered as he spoke. "Take a breath and tell me what this is about."

Heal any wound.

Keith pushed himself up from the floor and was met with another kick to the side. The pain was fleeting. It barely had a chance to flash across his synapses before it was sucked into the gravity of Nirvana.

The man lifted his foot to stomp on Keith's back. Keith anticipated the attack and grabbed him by his other leg. With incredible strength and speed Keith whipped his arm back, knocking his opponent onto his back.

Keith scrambled on top of the stranger, pinning his shoulders with his knees. The man gasped for breath. Keith leaned over him and inhaled deeply, sucking in the emotions radiating from his opponent's mind. It was a wild blend of contradictions—pride and resentment, love and anger, and several flavors of fear, all bound together by a profound sense of confusion.

"Why?"

Keith responded by punching the man in the face. Blood exploded from his broken nose. He coughed and moaned.

"I love you, son." His opponent's words were slurred and muddled, but understandable. For a moment Keith thought he could recognize the man's features. His hunger slackened and blurry childhood memories surfaced.

The two of them nursing a hurt cat back to health. Funnel cakes and hot dogs at Coney Island. Sledding at St. Nicholas Park. The memories came into focus like developing Polaroids in his mind.

With Keith distracted, the man wiggled his arms free and grabbed Keith by the hair. He pulled him down and headbutted him hard in the nose. Keith fell to the side, blinded by pain. His opponent scrambled away, yelling for Keith to stay down.

Draw strength from beyond.

Keith rose to his knees and closed his eyes.

He focused on the pure and beautiful nothingness that the Kata had shown him and allowed all sense of self to evaporate into that deepest darkness.

Without thought or will, Keith opened his eyes and unhinged his jaw until his cheeks split. The man's pleading cries were lost, siphoned into Keith's black hole core. His body followed, his dimensions stretching in a gruesome, cartoonish manner. Tissue ripped from bone and spilled blood formed a spiraling geyser into Keith's gullet. The man's shoulders caught on the tattered edges of Keith's mouth before they collapsed in on themselves, and then he was gone.

The sliver of nothingness that wore Keith's flesh stared dispassionately over the New York skyline. Alive, but not quite sentient, it gazed out the window. The million electric lights that kept the darkness at bay—the endless cacophony that vibrated through every molecule of air—it was all so alien.

The unthing watched people stroll down the street, their faces aglow from the light of their phones, while others huddled on stoops, puffing away at cigarettes. It felt no kinship to those people, nor did it realize how closely the dimensions of its flesh mirrored theirs. It had no sense of self.

Hunger was its only drive. The churning chaos and entropy aroused its appetite, and this new universe had so much to feast upon.

The un-thing opened Keith's mouth to inhuman proportions. Light distorted around the empty man's face as the growing singularity within him fed upon light and heat . . . upon space and time.

She Born of Naught

Never loved . . .

Love was a stranger until I met her. She—born of naught—summoned from the abyssal nothing. She—born of naught—given form by my thoughts, my needs, and prayers. She—born of naught—the whore of uncreation.

I tried to find love before her. There's somebody out there for everyone they say. The world is wide and deep and full. But I learned, after years of searching for meaning, that the world is not deep. No, it's not even shallow.

Yes, I ripped that last part off and probably butchered it. It's a second-hand insight from some first-rate fool—the musing of a dead intellectual who'd possessed enough hubris to try and make sense of existence and that which lies before and beyond it.

But that's unimportant. All that matters is her. At first, you wouldn't believe she was nothing given shape. The curves and the dark sheen of her body. The sexy purr that echoes from deep within her. That *Je ne sais quoi* that comes from the perfect balance of class and danger. The more you stare at her—and trust me, you can't help but stare—the more you realize just how perfect she is . . . and nothing is perfect.

She came about the way most things do—as a dream, then a musing, and finally rendered in physical form. I'm not sure how exactly, but her birth was slow. It always reminded me of that Johnny Cash song, the one where he builds his car one stolen piece at a time. That's not quite how she came together in my garage, but close enough. I didn't assemble her one piece at a time, but that's how she grew each day. And I didn't steal from Ford or Chevy to make her, but I stole from somewhere, even if I didn't mean to.

None of her parts came from Detroit, Wolfsburg, or Aichi. You can't order an injector pump for her at O'Reilly's or get a new odometer from AutoZone. Each pump, bolt, and tube inside her is unique and integrated. She's organic, as much as you or I—a creature of living steel with a black hole soul.

I watched her gestation for nine full moons. She was just a steel frame at first, but soon she was more. Springs and axles grew out of her metal bones as she sweated grease and oil. Tubes, belts, and cables grew like hair. Glass formed in the mirrors and windows like those crystal science kits you buy for little kids.

I fell in love with her before she was even whole. I think I was in love with her when she was just a thought, to be honest. I'd like to think it was my love that brought her to the world, that I channeled her from the void beyond existence. I'd like to think that she came because she loves me back.

And she does love me, even if others can't see it. I'm her world, and she is my oblivion. Everything else is roadkill.

Never sure . . .

I was never sure about anything until I was sure about her. I couldn't stick with a job. Couldn't stick with a chick. Couldn't stick with a god. Nothing ever made sense to me, and it took finding her to realize that was okay. Nothing made sense, and that's all that needed to. In her I found my religion.

So I cut my ties with everything and everyone. I don't need a woman because she is my woman. I don't need a job, because she is my job. I don't need a home, because she is my home.

Never whole . . .

You never realize how alone you are—how incomplete—until you aren't. It's wild what love can show you. Wilder still, what it can do for you. I don't eat anymore, because her love sustains me. I don't sleep because I find peace in her embrace.

It works both ways, of course. My love fuels her. She doesn't run off something as crude as gasoline. She runs off of me—my passion, my pain, my blood, my life.

There's this cliché that couples in love complete each other, that they become one, but in our case it's true. We've grown into one another, quite literally: my animal veins melding with her rubber arteries; her steel cables piercing my flesh and intertwining with the gristle beneath. My heart pumps in rhythm with her fuel injector. Every mile on her odometer adds another wrinkle to my face—another gray to my hair.

Never question . . .

Life never made sense before. I second-guessed everything. Nothing was beyond scrutiny—no taboo, no dogma, no sacred wisdom. I had the answer all along of course . . . only nothing was beyond scrutiny.

Her I never questioned. Not when she was just an image in my mind. Not when she grew from naught into a two-ton machine. Not when she whispered murderous fantasies from her speakers.

I never flinched when we ran those people down beneath the full moon, reducing them to nothing. I never asked why we left them broken on the asphalt. I never asked how many more, not after the first, nor any of the seven that followed.

Never alive . . .

None of their lives mattered, because life is an illusion. What is life? A haphazard series of chemical reactions. What's the difference between any of us and a dead seagull caught in the plastic rings from a six-pack? A bit of metabolism and some firing neurons? We're all just breathing, pissing hunks of meat. We insist on placing ourselves at the center of the cosmos, but our very beings, our souls if you will, are just chemical side effects, as insignificant as the heat and foam that comes from mixing vinegar with baking soda.

We're just as fleeting, too. One moment we're killing and fucking and singing, then you blink and we're heaps of compost beneath tarnished brass markers. Nothing is forever.

Never alone . . .

Together we race down bleak highways and abandoned roads. Her tires rip up blacktop and leave tracks of pre-cosmic emptiness in their wake. The illumination from streetlights and stars gets siphoned in through the lenses of her headlights. Her intake manifold steals the breath of any living thing we pass, leaving their lungs empty and collapsed. Mile by mile, we bring more nothing into this world.

Never dead . . .

We've butchered eight people under the moonlight—a smear in the road for each month, from January to August. I never asked how many more, because I knew it in my heart. There were nine to destroy, and I am the last of their number.

I'll have no mourners and there will be no funeral. My final ride won't be in a hearse at the head of some mournful procession. No, it will be a drag race against time and space. The glass on the speedometer will crack as we pin the needle to the right. My skin will tear and my bones will shatter as we careen through the veil between this place and the infinite. Our bodies will crumple and fold, her steel and glass merging more intimately with my flesh upon impact. My blood will spill and flow through her ruined form. We will be one, not just with each other but with that which came before all this and that which waits at the other end.

Never Regret . . .

Everything Smells Like Smoke Again

December 12

He's dead. Eric's worried because I didn't cry. I overheard him talking to the boys, telling them that I'm keeping a stiff upper lip. That's not it, though. Truthfully, this has been a long time coming, and he doesn't deserve my tears. That well ran dry long ago, and mostly because of him.

Do I feel a tad abnormal about my callousness? It's fucked up, I suppose, but not as much as Eric must think. He can't really comprehend what it was like for me, growing up the daughter of addicts. His childhood wasn't perfect, but it was normal: vacations, family game nights, never finding suicide notes and empty pill bottles.

Eric and I are from different worlds. My in-laws, the people he grew up with, are wonderful and I love them, but their stability has always left me feeling out of place. The way they have their shit together—it feels alien and untrustworthy.

Still, after fifteen years of holidays with them, anxiety swells inside me as I wait for things to go sideways at every get-together. I look at Eric's dad and wonder how many beers he's had and if this will be the one that pushes him over the line from buzzed to monstrous. I wait for my mother-in-law to take some off-the-cuff comment the wrong way and send Christmas dinner whizzing past my head. It never happens. I know it will never happen. Still, that fear persists.

It's the same with Eric himself. My husband is a caring and hard-working man. He's not a drinker or a party guy or a skirt-chaser. Although he has proved his worth over fifteen years of marriage, I get a knot in my stomach if he's late from work. I feel sick when he catches the occasional buzz. Jealousy and insecurity overcome my heart if he mentions some female colleague too many times. Not once has the man ever given me cause to doubt him, but when the floor falls out from under you for eighteen years straight you learn to tread lightly.

It's over now. Dad's dead. To be fair, he'd had one foot in the grave since Mom passed. After her death he quit partying and abandoned street narcotics, more fully embracing his pedestrian, solitary addictions—cigarettes, pain pills, and nostalgia mostly. I can think of maybe two times in the decade-plus since Mom died that he'd left his depressing little subsidized apartment for anything other than a trip to the dollar store or the packie.

I suppose I could have been a better daughter. Yes, I could have reached out and been a shoulder to cry on. The kids were young, though, and Eric and I were building our own life—a healthy life for the family I had chosen, rather than the one that fate had burdened me with. My father wasn't going to ruin that with his depression and addictions. Enough of my life had been compromised for him. I wouldn't allow him to take what I'd built for myself.

When he started getting sick last year, really sick as opposed to his normal state of perpetual unhealth, Eric suggested he come to live with us. I shot the idea down straightaway. Sure, I dreaded the thought of being around him, but that wasn't it. There were also the kids to consider. I didn't want them to see him sitting there day after day, popping pills and smoking butts, waiting for the reaper.

In addition to his habits and addictions there was also just . . . him. His backward, victim mentality and that acidic anger born of insecurity. How could I let his noxious *woe-is-me* worldview infect their minds? To Dad, nothing was ever his fault. He was destitute because he had "been dealt a losing hand," not because he burned every dollar he could have saved. His poor health was part of that same unlucky draw, and certainly had nothing to do with the abuse he'd put his body through. Even when Mom died, he blamed everything from God to fate to poor health insurance; but never the shitty life decisions the two of them made. I couldn't let my kids grow up around that, thinking it was *normal.*

Is there a level of guilt for letting him wallow in the purgatory he'd built around himself? I suppose. We all make our own beds.

December 13

I couldn't sleep last night. After the kids had gone to bed and Eric turned in for the night, I lay awake thinking about my father's lifeless face, framed by the funerary upholstery of his casket.

There is a level of surrealness at any funeral, staring down at a corpse that looks like an amateur wax-museum replica of a loved one. The subtleties of their complexion are off just enough to make you doubt the legitimacy of the body. That one-size-fits-all expression of peace. The whole thing conjures thoughts of body snatchers and doppelgängers.

It was with such ideas in my head that I smelled smoke drift into my bedroom. Not the smoke from a stove left on or an electrical fire in the walls, but the distinct smell of burning tobacco.

I didn't smoke and neither did Eric. We never had. I wondered if one of the kids might be dumb enough to take up such a filthy habit, and in the house at that. My nose crinkled as I rose from bed to investigate.

Our room was next to the boys'. I poked my head in to check on them and sniffed at the air. I could still smell the smoke, but not any stronger than I had from my own bed. Both Kyle and Georgie lay fast asleep, the funeral having been emotionally exhausting for them as well.

I turned and followed the smell down the hall, across the checkerboard tiles of our kitchen. It was dark and still. Neither the stove nor the oven were alight. Visible in the darkness, a trail of pale smoke snaked across the threshold, beckoning me into the living room.

Moonlight from the December sky poured through the open curtains, lending an otherworldly glow to the smoke, which terminated a few feet above the couch. Marla, our dog, growled low and glared at the wispy cloud. Her tail was tucked between her legs, and hackles stood up like a porcupine's quills.

I searched between the cushions, looking for a burning ember of . . . something. Nothing was there. I placed my hands over the outlets, feeling for heat. More nothing.

A glowing dot of orange formed in the air—an angry little pixie—then faded away. A fresh puff of smoke followed the disappearance of the glow. Ashes from the burning nothing floated to the hardwood floor.

Not believing what I was seeing, I knelt down and pressed my finger into the gray soot. It was warm to the touch and left a charcoal smear across my fingertip.

Eric called from the other room, concerned that I had wandered from bed. I looked up from the floor to find that the smoke had vanished and no angry, burning dot floated above me. Still, my finger was stained with ash. Confused and afraid, I pressed my finger to my tongue. The bitter taste confirmed the ash as real.

December 18

I wished I were sleepwalking, experiencing some somnambulant night terror, but everyone could smell the smoke now. Eric grilled the boys, sure it was them secretly lighting up in the house or carrying the smell in on their clothes.

It wasn't Kyle or Georgie, of course. Eric doesn't listen when I tell him that, and I can't quite be truthful—that each night I'm awoken by the smell of phantom cigarettes. What kind of nuthouse would they lock me up in if I told him how it mocks me through the night—the floating ember, burning to life then vanishing, followed by the puff of smoke exhaled from an invisible man.

Yesterday I cleaned the house while Eric and the boys went shopping. I sprayed the couch and the curtains with Febreze. Ignoring the cold, I opened the living room windows, and let the crisp winter air fight the acrid odor. It was then I noticed the stains on the wall. Yellow smears of tobacco, like the ones in the house I grew up in.

Scrubbing didn't help much. Neither did the Febreze. Nothing really gets smoke out, except for time.

December 21

Things were getting stranger. Things were getting worse. I hadn't slept in days. Last night I was determined to ignore the smell. At ten o'clock I snuck a few Tylenol PM capsules and rested my head. This is my new bedtime ritual, though it didn't keep me asleep in this particular circumstance.

Just after midnight a sound came from the living room and drew me from slumber—audial accompaniment for the smell of tobacco. Laugh tracks and pleasant, inoffensive music called out.

My eyes were heavy from the pills as I shuffled into the hall and through the kitchen. A blue glow, shifting in intensity, poured across the threshold. The ghosts of tar and nicotine were afire in the cold radiance.

Crossing into the living room, I could see the now-familiar burning dot floating above the couch. It pulsed in and out of existence, clouds of cancer billowing from the nothingness in between the moments of fiery glow.

The TV was on. This was a new phenomenon. A young Ron Howard looked up at Don Knotts, taking poor advice with earnest. Everyone laughed. Everyone except for me.

I clicked off the TV and went back to bed.

December 28

For the past week the TV wouldn't stay off at night, and the smoke had become ever-present. I couldn't sleep anymore, not without chemical assistance, and the recommended dosage wasn't cutting it.

Eric and I got in a fight. He thinks I have a problem—that I'm abusing the Tylenol PM. Listen to how stupid that statement sounds. It's an over-the-counter painkiller, not OxyContin. Also, I would fucking know if I had a problem. I grew up with addiction. I watched it every day of my childhood. What the fuck does he know about it? He watched an after-school special once? Or maybe a piece on Dr. Phil?

So I overslept and missed a few days of work. Who cares? It's not like I'm the breadwinner. I only work so we can have play money.

The actual reason he's pissed, if I were to guess, is because of Christmas morning. He and the kids couldn't wake me and had to go about the morning ritual sans Mommy.

I get it. He had a perfect fucking family, and Christmas was magical. Well, the kids are almost teenagers. They don't need Mommy to get up and watch them open their presents. If I want to sleep in a little on a day off, then who the hell is Eric to judge?

He says I have a problem, and that I should talk to someone about losing my dad. I do have a problem, but it's not the death of my loser father. It's finding him in my house, breathing his poisonous tobacco, dragon smoke all over my life.

December 30

Everyone's avoiding the living room. They don't consciously realize he's there, haunting our house, but they all feel it on some level. The TV only plays old black-and-white shows and movies. Every channel is monopolized by the monochromatic dead. Kyle and Georgie don't even bother with it.

Marla won't step in there. She's abandoned her dog bed and sleeps on the cold tile beneath the kitchen table. Even passing through the living room on our way out for walks makes her fur stand on end. She growls and yips in the direction of the couch, at that taunting, invisible specter.

Eric keeps complaining about drafts and insulation. He goes on and on about getting new windows, not realizing that the chill is emanating from my father's rotten ghost.

January 2

New Year's was a shit show. It started off well enough. We stayed in the kitchen, playing board games and listening to music. We ate cheese and crackers and drank Pepsi and champagne. There was even an unspoken agreement to pretend that the living room didn't exist. I was perfectly happy with that.

Around midnight Eric decided he wanted to watch the ball drop on the big TV. Georgie and Kyle seconded him. I nervously assented and we adjourned to the living room.

It was cold and reeked of smoke. Kyle's nose crinkled in disgust, and everyone's mood dropped three notches after crossing the threshold.

Eric turned on the TV. It went straight to a *Twilight Zone* rerun, the one where the last guy on earth loses his glasses and can't read all the books. Dad's favorite.

Eric fought with the remote and the cable box for two minutes before finally bringing up the New Year's countdown. When the camera moved away from the gathered crowd and came to focus on Ryan Seacrest, in lieu of the late Dick Clark, the signal wavered, sending ripples of static down the screen.

I turned to look at the couch. As I expected, an angry puff of smoke manifested itself in the air. My dead father was throwing a temper tantrum because he wanted the New Year's host he was used to.

Eric grumbled about the cable company and the reception, but my eyes were focused on the pulsing ember that floated in mid-air. On the TV, everyone in Times Square counted down from ten, as did my boys, but all that was background noise behind the labored moans of my paternal ghost.

Eric joined in with the counting, abandoning his grumbles about the wavy lines obscuring the broadcast.

Five. Four.

The smoke in the air took on familiar features. My father's miserable, ethereal face stared through me and at the television. He looked the same as he had in life, greedy for misery and pissed at the world.

Three. Two.

The line of smoke that formed his mouth twisted into a hateful smirk. A second before midnight the image collapsed into a formless cloud and the lights cut out. Sparks erupted from the power strip, the fixtures, and the sockets.

Georgie let out a cuss word that we ignored, then all was silence. After a few moments Eric chimed in with a sarcastic "Happy new year?"

I disregarded my husband's satire. My back was turned to my family. I stared intently at the couch, waiting for the orange dot of my father's cigarette to appear. When it did, I lost my mind.

"Get the hell out!" I screamed. "Get the hell out of my house!"

I can only imagine that Eric and the boys stared at me with slack-jawed horror. A hand touched my shoulder, presumably Eric's. I shrugged it off and continued my verbal assault:

"You can't have this! You're dead and this is mine! My house! My family!"

The phantom cigarette vanished and a puff of white smoke hit me in the face. I collapsed to the floor screaming, not words but raw audial emotion. I kicked and thrashed on the ground until Eric restrained and calmed me.

He got me into bed, then took the kids aside. He probably gave them some feel-good psychobabble about how their mom wasn't crazy, just emotionally strained.

Soon after that, he came to bed. We didn't speak. He just held me as I cried. The smell of smoke wafted in, but I ignored it and gave myself to my husband's embrace and to sleep.

January 7

They're gone. Eric. Kyle and Georgie. Marla. Gone.

Eric kept begging me to get help, especially after New Year's. I refused. What help was there to be had? Maybe if he meant an exorcist . . . But he wanted me to see a damn shrink, as if talking about my feelings would send the ghost in our living room packing.

It was becoming unbearable. The smoke, the blue flickering light of the TV, the bullshit happy façade of classic television.

I upgraded from Tylenol PM to Ambien. When Eric found out, he lost it. He threatened to leave me and take the kids. I knew he was bullshitting at that point, trying to scare me, but then my fucking father ruined everything. Just as he'd always done.

I know I put the cover on the pills. I know I put them away, but somehow they spilled. Poor Marla gobbled them all up. She died painlessly, but that didn't make things easier for any of us.

Eric didn't believe me when I said my father dumped out the pills and killed our dog. He didn't believe that the dead bastard wanted to take everything from me.

We screamed and fought. Eric made terrible, unfair accusations. He said I was just like my parents, letting the boys find me passed out with pills strewn across the floor. He cried and hit the walls, blaming me for Marla's death.

I fought back. I hit and screamed and told him it wasn't my fault, but he wouldn't listen. All the while my father sat there on my couch, puffing away, watching Wally and Beaver as my life crumbled around me.

That was yesterday. I called Eric today, but he wouldn't answer no matter how many times I tried. At first I was cordial. I tried to apologize and pretend everything was normal. Each time his voicemail picked up I grew angrier until my messages were seething with venom and my voice was hoarse from screaming.

January 25

I've stopped avoiding the living room, and I can barely smell the smoke over the gasoline. Andy Griffith is playing on TV. I forgot how much I used to like it. Classic television is really one of the only good memories I shared with Dad, so I might as well make the best of it.

It seems Eric and the boys aren't coming back. Eric says he can't let me near our sons until I get some help, but what help is there? This is just the hand I've been dealt.

I light up a cigarette and sit down next to dear old Dad. The gasoline soaks through my jeans. The carcinogenic mist burns my lungs, but pain is a familiar place. Falling back into its embrace almost feels good. It's like waking up from a dream of normalcy.

I tell my father that I love and forgive him. He places a cold hand on my knee. We both lay our cigarettes down on the couch and wait for the fire to take us home.

Waspqueen Sestina

A nest of wasps rests within my attic
The disembodied face of a goddess
Malice hums deep behind her open mouth
And angry soldiers pour out from her eyes
A thousand souls rest in her sacred mind
A thousand more I'd give her to be mine

I offer her lovers who would be mine
Bound and displayed for her in my attic
When her children feast it eases my mind
Lovers pained screams are prayers to my goddess
Venomous tears weep from my lady's eyes
An approving purr echoes from her mouth

In hours away, I dream of her mouth
And her cruel touch stripping this flesh of mine
Through my daily toil glaze covers my eyes
No glint of life this far from my attic
Smiles from women, each a false goddess
Can't replace the absent buzz in my mind

Homecoming brings the peace of the hive mind
Thanks, love, and praise are all sung from my mouth
I fall to my knees, below my goddess
I offer my soul and all that is mine
In this holy place, my temple attic
Here where her presence has opened my eyes

Her children crawl across my face and eyes
She penetrates my flesh, my soul, and mind
Wedding bed whispers sound through the attic
I place my lips on her paper-like Mouth
Winged venom kisses—her tongues licking mine—
Leave me bloated with lust for my goddess

Entropy wears away at my goddess
Paper flesh turns brittle around her eyes
But her gray complexion replaces mine
Her voice is silent, all but in my mind
And a thousand-wasp buzz leaps from my mouth
Never again will I leave this attic

Now it is mine, the role of the goddess
I wait in the attic with wasps for eyes
For one to bewitch with my mind and mouth

The Green Man of Freetown

"I don't care what they charged him with. He's a murderer. He killed my little girl! He killed my grandson!" The scathing accusations of his father-in-law are just static mumbles to Charlie Jacobs. They barely exist, same as the iron shackles around his ankles and wrists.

"He's a murderer, and you shouldn't ever let him out!"

Charlie is in another place and another time. Wholesome smells like storm-born ozone and wildflowers replace the rancid piss, sweat, and disease that permeates even into the rooms outside of general population.

"Thank you, Mr. Reilly," someone from the parole board says, politely informing the grieving old man that he's said enough. He doesn't argue but begins to weep.

Charlie gazes down at the cement floor. It is hidden beneath memories of bare, muddy earth. His name is called and he looks up. Even when he tries to be in the here and now, the cramped dimensions of the hearing room are lost to sylvan walls of maples and oaks.

"Do you have anything to say to the parole board, Mr. Jacobs?"

Scripted words, bullshit platitudes that his lawyer wrote, roll off Charlie's tongue. The tears that run down his face are genuine, however. They fall into the blood and mud at his feet. He spews more insincerities. Lies about the grace of God and incidental confessions of humility. A trail of gore, diluted by the torrential rain, leads off into the darkness between the trees. Something moves in those heavy shadows—a monster, or a ghost.

The prison chaplain is the next to speak. He testifies about Charlie's character, his dedication to Bible study, and his record of good behavior.

Charlie squints, trying to make out the creature hidden behind the veil of shadow and rainfall. Something stumbles out from the darkness. It's his wife, Amber, but broken and ruined. Her face is painted with mud, blood, and bruises, her blond hair streaked with crimson.

"If granted parole, Mr. Jacobs, do you have a plan for reintegrating into society?"

His son cries out for him from beyond the tree line. A hand with scaled, waxen skin reaches out from the shadows and grabs Amber by the hair. "This isn't how it happened," she says in a monotone voice at odds with her expression of abject terror.

"I do, sir," Charlie says aloud. "I have a plan."

A green highway sign declares that Freetown State Park is two exits away. This stretch of road should be familiar to Charlie, but it isn't. In the light of day, beneath a cloudless, powder-blue sky, it looks benign. Fresh blacktop and crisp white lines stretch on to the horizon. There's no roadkill smeared across the lanes. Not even so much as the blown-out corpse of a tire on the side of the road.

When he last took this drive it had been dark as the devil's soul. Charcoal clouds had obscured the moon and cried black rain tears over the asphalt. He looks in the rearview and ponders how much older he looks now. The last six years took a toll on him. His eyes are vacant, framed by crow's feet. His beard is more white than blond, the same as his hair. Scars he earned on the inside mar his face.

Another four miles pass and Charlie buzzes by exit 38. Some pop song he's never heard, something that came out while he was behind bars, plays on the radio, but he doesn't hear it. He's humming "The Sweater Song," out of tune and out of time with the number coming from the speakers. It was what they had listened to last time. They sang it loud and discordant, with joyous abandon. An anthem of resistance against the darkness and the storm.

Charlie flinches as the highway merges with a small bridge. Below the bridge and to either side, the forest stretches out for miles. The paint on the guardrails is inconsistent. Faded mint with spots of orange rust gives way to John Deere green, then back to mint. Tears obscure his vision as he drives across. In the time it takes him to blink them away, he's over the bridge, and farther down the highway than the three of them had ever made it.

Charlie's car is parked several miles back. It took almost an hour of hiking along trails, and then another through the untamed forest to find his way to this clearing. He looks up at the highway overpass that bridges the canyon. The sinking sensation of freefall makes him nauseous as he looks up at the steel framework.

Shaking off sickness and vertigo, Charlie turns his attention to the ground. The soil is dry and thirsty. Rich colors fill up the landscape—dark brown earth, jade foliage, and flowers of the deepest scarlet and azure.

Despite the familiar bridge above, he second-guesses if he's found the right place. He finds proof in the hard-packed earth, however. Jagged stumps of broken saplings. Half-buried shards of safety glass. Bits of broken plastic, all translucent, tail light red.

A tarnished hood ornament—a rust and chrome ram's head juts out of the dirt, like a sphinx lost to the desert sands. Charlie crouches down and rubs the ram's horns, the same way Ash would before every car ride.

"Have you seen my boy?" Charlie asks the hood ornament. It does not respond.

"He's here somewhere. I need to find him."

The chrome idol rests stoically, and Charlie sighs. He prayed the ram would break its silence. He needs an ally.

The forest was full of devils, despite the illusion of serenity it presently wore. Charlie had researched the place in depth during his trial and his stay in prison. Stories abounded in regard to Freetown. Ghosts of angry natives and murdered settlers wandered between the trees. Sirens called men and women to suicide. Witches lived in caves and hollows.

Charlie falls to his knees before the rusted chrome totem. He begs it for guidance. "I know you saw what happened," he breathes. "Whatever stole my son, just tell me where it took him."

His only answer is the call of birds and the buzz of insects. Charlie falls onto his back and screams at the clear, taunting sky. His fist bangs against the hard earth and comes up bloody. He looks at his hand, then the ground. Broken glass surrounds an outcropping of golden, funnel-shaped mushrooms.

Charlie picks one and examines it. It gives off a sweet, subtle smell like apricot. Like his wife's perfume. He stands and notices more patches of the same mushrooms. They form a sparse trail into the tree line. The world turns dark and wet in the blink of an eye, and the trail of mushrooms is replaced with a stream of watered-down blood, then everything is bright and dry again.

The gaze of the ram's head is set in the direction of the golden fungi, and Charlie knows which way he has to go. He thanks the hood ornament aloud, bites into the mushroom in his hand, and follows the others into the trees.

The mushroom doesn't taste like it smells. Not like apricots, nor like his wife. It has a subtle, peppery flavor, along with a hint of copper from his own blood drizzled over it. Charlie wonders if he should be eating it, or if it will make the other mushrooms angry. Will they shuffle around, leading him away from the truth?

He shrugs off the absurd thought and continues along the mushroom trail for miles. He grimaces at every tree root or rock which interrupts the path. Did Amber's skull smash against these protrusions as she was dragged? Was Ash's flesh lacerated by unflinching stone and uncaring wood?

"Don't leave us," Amber mumbles, and Charlie isn't sure if her words are being whispered in his ear or in his memory. Up ahead the golden trail of fungus stops.

Charlie half expects to see his wife waiting at the end, even though she is years dead. Instead, he catches familiar bits of geography. He's never been this far in the Freetown woods, but he recognizes certain landmarks from courtroom pictures. The fieldstone foundation of a long-abandoned cabin. A rusted bootlegger's still half-buried in the dirt. The dead husk of a tree with an inverted cross carved in the bark.

"This is where they found you," Charlie mumbles, as he drops to his knees and runs his fingers along a rust-colored stain on the foundation. The dim light filtering through the lush canopy above vanishes. The bird songs and insect buzzing of summer give way to the patter of raindrops, and Charlie feels the rain running down his cheeks. It's warmer than it should be, but he gives it no thought.

On the ground before him lies Amber. Mud and rain mix with the blood in her shredded belly. Brackish water pools out of her open mouth, like a broken, morbid fountain. The blue of her eyes, normally so startling in their richness, seem dull juxtaposed against the crimson of burst blood vessels.

Yards away, a song plays in the trees. It's "The Sweater Song," but slow and uneven in pitch, like a warped record played at half-speed. Charlie stares into the tree line and sees a figure in coarse, earth-tone robes. Beside the robed figure is a little boy in Ash's clothes. His back is turned to Charlie and he stands deathly still.

The thing in the robes places a hand on Ash's shoulder, but it is no human appendage. The fingers are a rich green and covered in overlapping scales. No, not scales, Charlie thinks. It's even further removed from man than that. More like the bracts of an artichoke. Its face is hidden by storm and by the shadows of its hood, but golden whiskers, like stalks of barley, poke through the shadows. Charlie can't see its eyes, but he knows it stares at him, challenging him.

A gurgling sound comes from Amber's corpse. A bubble forms in the water in her mouth. It pops and releases a word into the air.

"This . . ."

Another bubble forms and pops.

"Isn't . . ."

Charlie looks back into the tree line. The robed figure is gone, and so is Ash. The warped music still plays in the forest ahead.

Pop.

"How . . ."

Charlie jumps to his feet, his heart in his throat.

Pop.

"It . . ."

He doesn't give his wife another glance, nor the opportunity to finish saying her piece. The light of the real, present-day world nearly blinds him as the darkness retreats into his mind and soul. Charlie can't see the robed monster through the flora, but branches whip and leaves tremble in its wake. He follows into the woods and his mind fractures.

He is simultaneously in two different places and two different times. Unrelenting sheets of water assault his windshield as he drives through the ghosts of night and storm, all the while he gives chase through the daylight summertime forest of the present. He and his family sing along with Rivers Cuomo on the radio, while a mockery of the same music echoes through the trees. The smell of beer, cigarettes, and vanilla air freshener fills his senses in one reality, while the scents of pine and dead leaves dominate the other. He's aware of both. Experiencing both moments as one.

The grade of the earth steepens ahead of him, and Charlie rushes recklessly downward. In another place and time, he presses down heavier on a gas pedal. Amber tells him to slow down. Her words carry from the past into the present, but he heeds them in neither. A moment later his foot catches on a tree root and his tires lose traction on the bridge.

Charlie tumbles down the hill, collecting bruises and lacerations. The thirsty soil sups upon his spilled blood. The Ram crashes through the guardrail. An airbag explodes out from the steering column and breaks Charlie's nose as the vehicle careens into the canyon below.

He rolls to a stop at the bottom of the hill in the summertime forest. Nothing feels broken, but he's lost his wind and can't stand. In the noontide storm, he is met with an explosion of glass and omnipresent pain. The radio is still playing, indifferent to Amber's pained moaning. But Ash . . . Ash is too quiet.

Unable to stand, or even breathe, Charlie sees the monster clad in burlap robes. It's crouched over his son, holding him down with dendritic appendages. Slurping and ripping sounds echo off the trees, not lost beneath a warped, droning song decrying that the singer has come undone.

Charlie cuts the engine and the song dies. He calls to his son in the backseat while pushing away the deflating airbag, but Ash doesn't respond. He doesn't even whimper or cry. Looking behind him, he sees the back window next to Ash smashed, and the boy's face is a scarlet mask.

Breath returns to his lungs, and Charlie screams for the monster to get away from his boy. It looks up at Charlie, giving the man a clear view of his son. The child's features are shredded and torn beneath a crimson wash. His beautiful little boy is barely recognizable.

"I need to go get help," Charlie mutters, struggling to open the driver's-side door. Amber begs him, between labored breaths, not to leave them. Her voice holds something greater than desperation. The severity of her tone frightens him to his bones.

The monster throws back its coarse tan hood. What lies beneath is more flora than fauna—a mockery of Charlie's own face, sculpted from hops and nettles, with a beard of golden barley. Blood drips down its chin and covers its lush, green hands.

Charlie drags them both out of the wreckage. Amber screams in pain as he clumsily pulls her from the passenger-side door and lays her in the mud. Ash is quiet and still.

"You killed my family!" Charlie screams at his floral doppelgänger. "This isn't how it happened," the thing replies, in a slurred voice. Even from yards away, Charlie can smell the scent of blood and fermentation on its breath. His thoughts get fuzzy and a subtle vertigo sets in.

The mud gives way under Charlie's feet as he scrambles up the incline of the canyon. The steep walls shrug him off, indifferent to his desperation. His buzz is gone, but his motor skills are a wreck, whether from trauma or drink he isn't sure.

He screams for help as blood loss and exhaustion knock him to the ground. Cradled by the wet earth and blanketed by the storm, he reluctantly drifts into unconsciousness.

"This isn't how it happened," Charlie mumbles into the mud of six years past and at the monster before him in the here and now.

"Oh, but it is, Charlie," the Green Man replies.

"No! You dragged them away and murdered them!" Tears are running down his cheeks as he cries out the accusation.

"You killed them, Charlie, and coyotes dragged them away while you slept it off."

Charlie mumbles "no," over and over again, shaking his head as if the gesture will make the word true. Coldness washes over his body and he finds himself alone, a bottle pressed to his lips. He sits at the bottom of a hill, in a patch of golden mushrooms with his back to an ash tree. A face stares at him from the label on his bottle—a Celtic Green Man with a grim expression.

Through the trees he hears Amber and Ash, both begging him not to leave. He swigs down the rest of his beer, smashes the bottle against the ground, then leans back and lets the cold buzz overtake him.

"I'll never leave you again."

With a terrible calm, he grips the neck of the broken bottle and plunges its jagged edge into his own throat. He falls over, next to the shattered glass. From the beer's paper label the Green Man watches Charlie die, its severe gaze softening as his blood sates the soil.

Monsters Have No Place in the World That Is to Come

In the last days of the war, Goebbels had told our people that we, the werewolves of the Hitler Youth, would keep fighting for them. He bragged about our elite training, how well we were outfitted, and how we would never stop. We were to be the vengeance of the Führer.

After Hitler's death and the German surrender, the Allies told their people that we, the Nazi Werewolf terrorists, would keep fighting. They warned of how treacherous we were—how savage and ruthless. We were the terrible ghosts of the Reich.

When the Soviets rounded up and executed German youth, they said it was because we, the Werewolves, had to be exterminated or we would never stop fighting. They warned how dangerous it was to help us . . . how dangerous it was to know us. We became the specters of defeat.

We were all those things, of course. Heroes. Monsters. Ghosts. But we were also children—children who lacked the training and the supplies that everyone seemed to think we had. There was little food and less ammunition. We had no leadership. We had no country. Only our hatred and our pride kept us going.

We carried out a number of attacks, but none of them were remarkable. It is no great feat to break into a collaborator's home and murder him in his sleep. There is little glory in cutting the throats of traitorous women or their Soviet lovers. There is no strategic genius in stringing piano wire between trees to decapitate occupying soldiers on motorcycle patrol. Nothing we did mattered beyond temporarily sating our thirst for vengeance and stoking the fires of our mythology. Unfortunately, that fire was all we had to keep us warm.

As I said, we were children—children cast alone into the dark wilderness. Everything had been taken from us. Our fathers had been chewed up by machine-gun fire and tank treads. Our homes lay in ruins atop our dead mothers. Our leader—our God—had taken his own life, his dying command an impossible task. Things being as they were, we took solace where we could and there is a species of bleak satisfaction that comes from being the bogeyman.

For over a year we assassinated collaborators and ambushed occupiers. Month after month we sabotaged vehicles, disrupted supply lines, and instilled fear. Nothing changed. Nothing got better. Our efforts were moot.

Our numbers dwindled quickly. Heinrich, the youngest of us, took ill and died in a cave we had camped in last winter. Felix, our leader, deserted us, leaving a note that simply read, *I'm sorry.* Richard and Hans, twin brothers from Austria, had been captured after a botched ambush on a Soviet SMERSH detachment in the spring. By June of '46 I was the only one left.

My ammunition was almost depleted, as well as my food. The enemy was getting stronger. More and more of our people cursed the Reich and all it stood for. They pretended that they had not rallied beneath the spectacle of torchlight and the magic of our Führer's voice. To the west, they fell in front of the altars of greed and God. In the east, they bowed their heads to the Red Tyrant.

I needed to take decisive action. I needed to do something that mattered. But Hitler was gone. Our fathers were gone. Even my brothers in arms were gone. With no one to lead me and a dark future lying ahead, I turned my hopes to the past.

I had learned of the runes in our Hitler Youth training. I was taught their meanings and told of their power. I carved the futhark into the bones of the animals I hunted. Under the dying light of the Solstice sun, I chewed upon a leaf of Stinking Nightshade and cast those bones, painted and empowered with my own sacred blood, upon the soil of my homeland.

The runes spoke of power, symbolized by Thurisaz—the thorn. They spoke of death and rebirth. The Odal rune invoked the holy connection to this land of my birth.

As I studied the runes, cast upon the earth, the Nightshade took effect. My heart raced and my body shivered. Voices called out to me—hundreds of spirits, all shouting over one another. Black clouds merged in the sky. They coalesced into the form of a massive wolf overtaking the horizon. The beast's gaping maw, filled with teeth like long swords, bit into the sun and the world went black.

Fever overtook my body and I fell trembling to my side. The earth trembled with me, the ground cracking as if the whole world were being crushed in the coils of a titanic serpent. As I lay there, not knowing if the light of the world had been extinguished or if I had been stricken blind and mad by the toxic leaves, the words of one spirit rose above all the others—a husky, feminine voice calling for me to seek out a grave at the end of the world.

I thought her words were meant to consign me to oblivion. I thought I would die there, a relic of a boy, surrounded by discarded symbols from a bygone time. I did not die that night, however. The grave she spoke of was not my own—the end of the world was not a metaphor for my death.

When the Nightshade wore off, the world returned to a state of rationality, or as rational as I had ever known it to be. I sat and pondered the meanings of the runes I had cast and considered the words that had been spoken into my mind. I thought of Gibraltar. The ancients had believed it to be the end of the world. The Americas came to mind, as did the Far East. I had cast the Odal rune, however—the symbol for home and hearth. Whatever I sought, it had to be close.

The answer came upon me like a lightning strike. Berlin. My world had ended in Berlin, and there was only one grave there that mattered to me.

My heart sank as I entered the city. My vision went as red as the enemy flags fluttering over the place of my birth.

Everyone I walked past stared at the ground, all fire and life extinguished from their eyes. Some would glance at me, fear and shame written across their faces. It was as if they knew what I was—a wolf among the sheep.

I couldn't go to the grave in the light of day. No one went there. It was a forbidden place—haunted and feared. I waited for nightfall, biding my time in a pub. As I nursed a beer and watched the sad, broken Berliners drink themselves into a slow death, it occurred to me how little time I'd spent with the average German. My life had been youth camps and war—training to kill, then killing.

I listened to a fat old man crack quiet jokes about Jews while sharing drinks with American soldiers. I watched women flirt with drunks and degenerates. These were not the people from the propaganda I had been raised with. Berlin was not a city of blond beasts and Teutonic knights. I saw nothing superior in these people—nothing worth the sacrifice of my youth.

Night came with a sense of relief. The stink of the pub and the putrid aura of the people within it was overbearing. The full moon and the cool night air were a balm for my soul.

I made my way to the ruins of the Führersbunker. Twisted, rusted rebar jutted out through broken concrete. The remnants of the building had collapsed. The ruins had sunk crooked into the earth, one corner of the building facing toward the sky.

This was where Hitler died. This was the grave at the end of the world.

I ventured into the ruins of the world's end. I trod upon the same earth that the Führer walked, but I was not overcome with solemn emotions. I found myself angry. Angry that he had sacrificed my childhood to these unremarkable people. Angry that he had sent my father to die in some frozen Russian hellhole. Angry that he killed himself and tasked me with cleaning up the mess.

In a scorched crater, framed by a sliver of moonlight, I came across a bramble of thorned vines woven through the skeletal jaws of a dog, or maybe a wolf. I knelt before the canine death's-head, which sat like a gravemarker, and stared into its empty eyes.

You don't belong here, Alger. The feminine voice was the same that I'd heard when casting the runes. *Monsters have no place in the world that is to come.*

"You think I'm a monster?" I asked.

I am she who births tragedy. I am the mother of monsters. There was no judgment in her voice, only love. *I know my own children.*

I gazed across the ruins of Führersbunker. In the distance I could see the banners of invaders fluttering over Berlin. My mind conjured images of the soulless wretches at the bar. She was right. I was not of this time or place. I considered that perhaps I was a monster after all. There was no doubt I had been born of tragedy.

Spill your blood and come home.

Moonlight kissed the back of my hand as I pressed my palm against the thorny brambles and the jagged teeth of the canine skull. I raised my hand to the moonlight and watched the blood flow down my arm. Fat crimson drops fell onto the blackened soil.

I doubled over as muscles and cartilage tore from the bones beneath my skin. Joints cracked and contorted. My nails thickened and grew into predatory claws. My teeth loosened from my gums, and rows of porcelain daggers grew to force them out.

I could feel my face caving in, then expanding. My jaw popped out of place, the skin around it tearing then knitting itself back together. Flesh sloughed off me like skin from a boiled rabbit, revealing silver and golden fur beneath.

The process was painful—excruciating—but I was well acquainted with pain. Once it was over, I felt better than I ever had. Gone were the aches and pains of years of fighting and sleeping on hard ground. A hundred new and wonderful smells flooded my sense. I could hear the insects in the dirt—the mice running through tall grass. I was one with the earth, in a way I had never dreamed. This was a true merging of blood and soil, not some cheap slogan.

I looked back over the city one last time. The place meant nothing to me and neither did the flags raised above it. I didn't care about Soviets or Americans. I didn't care about Jews or Germans. I didn't care about Hitler or Stalin or any of the other men who aspired to be wolves. I was the real thing—something they would never understand.

Come home, the mother of monsters urged. I howled my assent and ran into the woods, leaving mankind to their petty machinations.

Thurisaz

(in the negative aspect)

They came first—the gods of the thorn
Howling titans of the abyss
Entropy bound and chaos sworn

From their demise was all life born
In our blood, we still hear their hiss
They came first—the gods of the thorn

The source of all in us forlorn
And of our own venomous kiss
Entropy bound and chaos sworn

They live in the scars we adorn
And in our wicked, wartime bliss
They came first—the gods of the thorn

We call upon their names with scorn
While our own nature, we dismiss
Entropy bound and chaos sworn

Sons of Saturn, we eat our born
Violence apotheosis
Entropy bound and chaos sworn
They came first—the gods of the thorn

The Rye-Mother

David pressed his fingertip into the jagged edge of the school bus' torn vinyl upholstery. There was a sharpness to it, but the thin material gave way and folded over before it could cut into his skin. He wished the upholstery was made of tougher stuff—something that might lacerate his fingertip and cloud his mind with physical pain.

Other children laughed and hooted in their Halloween costumes. In the context of the day, their pageantry was normal. The wizard robes, clown wigs, face paint, and superhero capes had become temporarily commonplace, leaving David to look like a madman in his wool sweater and khaki pants.

Only one other child, a Muslim boy named Bahir, stood out in mundanity amongst the ostentatious masses. Their religious beliefs—or, more accurately, the religious beliefs of their parents—forbade either boy from celebrating pagan rites such as Halloween. This had made them temporary allies, or at least bus buddies for the ride home.

"So how come you aren't dressed up?" Bahir asked, trying to spark a conversation with David, who had a reputation of being quiet and antisocial.

"My parents are Jehovah's Witnesses," David remarked, tonelessly. "We don't do anything fun."

"Oh," Bahir responded. "We're Muslims."

David didn't respond but rather stared out the window at the passing houses decorated in cotton webs and crawling with plastic spiders. He admired the jack-o'-lantern grins that stared at him from porches, the sinister and the silly alike. Tomorrow they would be smashed, most of them anyway, their day having come and gone. There was a kind of beauty in that, or at least a poetry, David mused.

He wondered how much candy, and what kinds, were hidden behind the doors of these houses. It was his belief, aided by the mutterings of other kids, that the houses decorated the best gave out the best candy—stuff like Snickers, Twix, or Reese's cups. The houses that didn't decorate, he had heard, were more prone to handing out whatever was cheap at the drugstore.

David would have jumped at the opportunity for any of it. Sweets, like Halloween itself, were not welcome in his parents' home. Instead, they might allow him a box of raisins tonight as a concession for being locked away from the magic outside of their home.

The bus turned a corner, leaving the neighborhood right around the school behind and heading on to Route 2. The residential homes yielded to stretches of forest and the occasional concrete oasis of a gas station or fast food joint. David looked out the window with a steadfast gaze, not at the passing commercial mundanities but through them and toward something that lay beyond—something he could feel in his soul.

"My mother lets my sister and me each pick out two chocolate bars from the store," Bahir added, after a long pause. "I guess she feels bad about us missing out, so that's her way of compromising."

"The candy would be nice," David responded, eyes still pinned to something beyond his field of vision.

The candy would indeed be nice, but David's concern was deeper than sugar, or even costumes. David's interest in Halloween was deeply spiritual and esoteric, though he did not have the words to express it as such. No, to him it was simply magical.

The bus wound past a tiny strip of stores featuring a liquor store and a bait shop, and on to some side road. A half-mile down, a farm came into view through David's window. Gingham Farms was the name, but it wasn't a real farm as they have out in the Midwest. No, it was a tourist farm. Rather than cows and grain silos, Gingham Farms was a glorified pumpkin patch with hayrides and a "haunted" corn maze.

The corn maze.

Something strange beckoned David from within it. He'd felt it every year growing up, but only on Halloween. He never understood why until a few months back when he'd read a book on holidays last Christmas in the school library and learned the true nature of Halloween. On this last day of October, the veil between this world and the other is at its thinnest, and spirits, fairies, and all manner of other creatures may travel from fairy hollows. David felt with every fiber of his being that the corn maze held such a hollow.

That book had led him to another, and this one had taught him about changelings—fairy babies swapped out with mortal young. The young fairies left in the human world would be out of place, perhaps seeming sickly, insane, or simply out of place. For David's entire life he had felt out of place, if not insane, and while he wasn't sickly per se, an allergy to iron-rich foods did complicate his health.

"Yes, the candy and the costumes would be nice," David repeated, "but the corn maze is what I'd really like to do."

"I wish I could get dressed up," Bahir replied. "I think I'd be something scary, like Jason or Jigsaw. What would you be?"

"I'd be myself," David stated flatly, his hand pressed up against the window.

"Who's ready for Taco Tuesday?" David's father asked, with an exaggerated excitement and a preternaturally white grin.

His mother raised her hand and jumped up and down in the kitchen, feigning the same enthusiasm. Or perhaps it was real. David couldn't ever be sure about such things. He had a hard time reading other people and even greater difficulty relating to them. His psychologist had called it narcissistic personality disorder, not to his face, but in loud whispers to his parents. There were other issues the doctor had brought up, but this was the most troubling, or so David had overheard.

The doctor had wanted to put him on meds—little magic pills that would subjugate his nature like a whipped mutt. Luckily his parents wouldn't have any of that and chose instead to depend on the power of prayer. David did not wish to change and was thankful that God had not heeded his parents' wishes.

David wondered how often they reconsidered putting him on

drugs. It was clear they didn't understand him, and sometimes it seemed they had to try extra hard to like him—much harder, he suspected, than other parents had to try to like their own children. At least they gave it a shot. The kids at school, even most of his teachers, didn't bother. In some ways he preferred their honesty, but it did occasionally feel nice to see people delve to amazing depths of self-deceit just to try and make you feel wanted. Sometimes a nice lie was preferable to the truth. But not tonight. Tonight he needed something genuine—something his parents could not offer.

Brooke, David's baby sister, looked up at him from her high chair. She was too young for tacos, but her tiny fists shook with the contagious excitement of their parents. Looking into her dull brown eyes, David wondered if that was to be her lot in life—absorbing the emotions and passions of others, like human tofu. He supposed, in an introverted way that belied his age, that all people were something like tofu. Why should he expect Brooke to be any different?

There had been, of course, the hope that she would be different—an odd duck like himself. It would be nice not to feel so alone. Even if the eleven-year age gap between himself and his sister would remain unbridgeable, a shared strangeness would make the world much more bearable for David. It seemed that wasn't in the cards.

There was strangeness out there tonight, however—an ethereal weirdness leaching out from the hidden fairy hollows and into the drab world of man. It turned children into monsters and myths and implored rational adults to fear the dark. That was, after all, why jack-o'-lanterns glowed in front of all the houses, save his own—to scare off the dark spirits adults claimed not to believe in.

Father urged David to take a seat across from Brooke. He did, then began assembling a taco from the ingredients spread across several bowls and trays. In lieu of beef, there was chicken. The family rarely ate red meat, what with David's problems with iron. This particular medical issue had always bothered the young man, up until last winter when he learned that fairy folk and other magical creatures were also harmed by iron. Now it felt like something of a badge of honor.

Mother placed a plate of squashed avocado in front of Brooke, while Father assembled tacos for her and himself. David waited patiently, knowing he dared not take a bit before his father led them in saying grace. A few moments later, once all the plates were made up, his father began their mealtime prayer.

"Thank you father for this feast . . ."

With closed eyes and folded hands, David pretended to listen. Instead, his mind was on the haunted corn maze and the fairy hollow he knew must be there. He wondered what manner of strange things walked within the rows of corn.

Father's voice cut out, and David followed the cue to say "amen" before opening his eyes. The family began eating and a few moments passed before David worked up the nerve express his desires for the night.

"Maybe after tacos, we could drive over to Gingham Farms and check out the corn maze?" David used his most practiced "normal" tone as he posed the question.

His father raised one eyebrow, disapproval written on his face. Mother glanced back and forth between the two of them, waiting on her husband to arbitrate.

"Come on now, champ. You know we don't do Halloween."

Champ. David hated that nickname. He'd never been champion of anything, and it felt condescending. Despite this, he wore a fake, casual smile.

"It's not really a Halloween thing," David countered. "More of like a fall thing. They keep it open past Halloween."

"Then we can go after Halloween," Father said with a smile. David cursed within his mind. He'd misspoken and now the argument was lost. Anything else he said would fall on deaf ears. David took a bite of his chicken taco and gazed down at his plate.

Shouts and laughter penetrated David's window through the glass and the bars. His parents had installed the bars after he tried to run away last year, and they served as a reminder that he dwelt in a prison, rather than a home.

Instead of focusing on the last bit of homework on his desk, some mind-numbing geography assignment, David looked down at the street from his bedroom window. Through the bars he could see a group of teenagers with costumes consisting of nothing more than black hoodies and plastic masks walking with bulging pillowcases. They passed a gaggle of younger children, all decked out in proper costumes, trailed by smiling grownups. A black lab with a pair of bat wings strapped to its back trotted along aside them, occasionally sniffing the ground for fallen candy.

David smiled, but it wasn't a happy smile. He envied those people out there, but he also pitied them. For all the fun they were having, it didn't seem any of them truly understood the specialness of the night. Candy and costumes were all well and good, but Halloween was about that breach between the worlds and the magic that poured in.

Then again, maybe they did get it, he thought, somewhere deep within. Why else would they brave the cold night, scouring the town for candy that could be bought at half-price tomorrow? David pondered that perhaps there were things that could be understood by the soul, even if they never registered in the mind. He hoped that was the case, for their sake. While he found trouble relating to most people, he generally wanted the best for them.

He closed his shade, distracted by and jealous of the passersby, and looked down at the map of Europe on his desk. The assignment was to label each outlined area with the proper country. It seemed a thankless task to David. His father had mentioned that countries in Eastern Europe change names and borders like clothes. What was the point of learning where Serbia was if it was going to merge with Bulgaria in five years? It was all so artificial.

A better use of his time, of all their time, would be to learn about the constants of geography. What locations had been regarded as sacred throughout history? What parts of the ocean were connected to other worlds, like the Bermuda Triangle? Where were the fairy hollows in the British Isles? Those were questions worth answering, not what flag flies over some arbitrary chunk of land.

David closed his eyes and let his pen hover over the map. He imagined himself as Volund, King of the Fairies, flying high above Europe on wings forged of iron, rather than the butterfly look of a Disney movie. He was looking for a way home—a fairy hollow that would lead him to Otherworld.

A magnetic force drew David's pen to the paper, startling him from his daydream. The tip of his pen had pierced the map, just east of the French/German border. David pulled the pen away. Burning within the pinhole poked through his homework was an intense, amber light, as if someone were holding an LED against the underside of the paper. Confused, David flipped the map over and saw no strange light—nothing but the tiny hole.

With a bit of hesitation, he turned the paper around once more and held it straight in front of him. The needle of light pierced through the German landscape with brilliant intensity. David stood up from his desk and moved the map around. No matter which way he turned, or how high or low he held it, the light continued pouring forth.

With a trembling hand, David pressed a finger against the needle of amber light. It was warm. It felt pleasant. He pressed harder, forcing the pinhole to expand beneath his touch. Pale orange illumination poured out from the tear in the map.

The hole was large enough to see through now. David brought the map close to his face and peered into the hole. On the other side he could see his bedroom, or more accurately a place that looked something like his bedroom. The windows and the door were in the same places, but the walls were rough, hewn from natural stone rather than smooth, painted drywall. His floor was a patchwork of dirt and tree roots. The cool blues and greens of his real-world bedroom gave way to bright, earthy tones in the world that lay on the other side of the hole in the paper.

To David, the world on the other side of the paper seemed more real than that which he had known all his life. It was like opening his eyes from a dream for the first time. When he pulled the map away from his face and looked around his room—his real-world room—everything felt dull and washed out by comparison.

He picked up his pen again and jabbed a second hole through the page, roughly two inches from the first. David forced the plastic body of the pen through to make the hole wide enough for viewing, then pulled it back, but no otherworldly light poured out. Even with his eye pressed against this new tear in the map, only his washed-out, mortal world room lay on the other side.

Placing the map back on his desk, David considered this conundrum. One hole, the one just barely past the French border in Germany, shone with amber light and revealed a surface of grainy, golden oak beneath it. From the other, which had been bored through the cellulose likeness of some Eastern European nation David had not identified, gave off no illumination, and beyond it lay only the vinyl laminate of his IKEA desk.

David closed his eyes again and instinct guide his hand, rather than poking an arbitrary hole. He could feel the magic pulling at the ballpoint tip of his pen. It stabbed into the paper, and David felt that the pen was more in control than him.

When he opened his eyes, his pen had pierced through somewhere in the southern UK. Lines of orange-yellow light crept out of the pinprick in his homework and up along the shaft of the pen. A wild smile crossed David's lips and he used the pen to carve an eyehole, working out from that tiny, glowing tear. Just as with the first hole, when David looked through this one, the world was a dayglo negative of this one.

"What are you doing there, champ?" Father's voice called from behind.

David turned around with a guilty look, his glance darting back and forth between his father and the glowing paper. His father's expression betrayed no acknowledgment of the fairy fire burning from the holes in the paper.

"Um . . . just being weird."

His father smiled and tapped his wrist. "Well, be weird tomorrow. It's almost bedtime."

"Sure thing, Dad."

The door closed and his father was gone. David glared at his bedroom door, then at the bars on his window. He pressed the map to his face and found that both magical rips lined up perfectly with his eyes. He scanned the room through the magical filter of the map, and his gaze fell onto the window of this fairy world version of his bedroom. While its size and shape were similar, no iron bars blocked his path while he peered through the hollows on the map.

David smiled. He placed the paper face down on his desk and reached past his "word a day" calendar for a box of crayons. A green face of angular features began to take shape around the two eyeholes.

The sound of wind battering the paper mask David had fashioned from the map was deafening in his ears. The sidewalks were empty around him, and the will-o'-the-wisps glowed where there should have been LED streetlights.

He pushed the makeshift mask up above his head, and the knot to the shoelace holding it to his head caught in his hair. Without the aid of the fairy hollows within his now mangled homework, David could see that he was not alone on the street at all but surrounded by trick-or-treaters and mischievous teens. Left only to his own senses, the world looked dull and monochrome, save for the bits of Halloween magic—a fiery carpet of brittle, dead leaves, bits of rainbow candy strewn across the ground, the wavering illumination from jack-o'-lantern flames. The veil between worlds truly was thin, and wonders could be gleaned by those with eyes to see.

David was not sure what he hoped to find on this night, but he knew where to look. The corn maze at Gingham Farm.

Gingham Farm was a bit of a walk—not that David minded, but he thought it might be sensible to procure some food for the road. He ignored the more pedestrian houses, those bare of decorations, save for those where people waited on porches or stoops with buckets of candy. He was eager to find the fairy hollow at Gingham Farm, so he only knocked on the doors of houses with the most elaborate decorations. What he'd heard was true: the people who went all out did give away the best candy. He'd even scored a full-size Snickers from a house where the fog billowed out from the front door and obscured red glowing eyes beyond the threshold.

After a handful of houses, five candy bars, and an hour's walk, David could see Gingham Farm ahead and to his right. The cornstalks glowed a faint silver beneath the moonlight, though to credit their soft radiance to this world, even to the sky, seemed too terrestrial. Surely the light they gave off was drawn from the magical portal deep within the corn maze.

David crossed the street and stepped onto the grounds of the farm, his paper mask sitting on his head. Even through the soles of his shoes, he could feel the power leaching through the soil, beckoning him to Otherworld. He was not the only one who heard the call, but he reckoned he was the only one to recognize it as such.

A line of people—teenagers, families, and twenty-something couples—stood in line outside the maze waiting to pay for the chance to get lost in the twisting rows of cornstalks. David had no money. He also had no intention of paying to get into the maze, nor of waiting in line. As he had done at home to slip past his barred windows, the boy pulled his homespun magic mask back over his face.

Through the view afforded by the eyeholes, no one stood between him and the entrance to the maze. With slow, deliberate steps he approached the mouth of the labyrinth. From feet away he could feel heat from the cornstalks, which through his fairy vision mask appeared to glow with golden light rather than silver.

A whisper—words too soft to comprehend—echoed amongst the rows of corn. To other children the sound might have been foreboding, but David found it comforting. There was something familiar about the soft voice. It drew him in and made him feel safe. Feeling more sure about his next steps than he had been about anything else in his short life, David entered the maze.

An orange glow, far more intense than the general amber glow of the mask's vision, burned a trail in the ground. David likened it to a river of magma glowing just beneath the surface. He followed it from the entrance of the labyrinth and down every branch that it snaked.

Wind coursed through the twists and turns of the corn maze. It pushed him back, and David thought of the magnetic repulsion that occurs when two forces of the same polarity come together. Was this further proof that he belonged there, in Otherworld? Was his spirit made of the same stuff?

The cracking racket of wind battering the paper mask filled David's ears. He dared not lift it from his face, though. He didn't want to risk losing the glowing trail marked out on the ground for him, nor did he wish to be suddenly caught in a crowd of terrestrial souls who could only sense the magic of this place on the most basic level. It was better, he supposed, to suffer the cacophony and press on, so that is what he did.

The magma glow of the ground twisted right and left, left and right, meandering through paths cut between the luminescent grain. With each step the wind pushed harder against David, and the magic of the hollow compelled him more fully to move forward.

David turned right at an intersection and came to a dead end. The trail of magic below the soil continued, beyond the wall of cornstalks. Reaching out, he parted the corn with both hands and stepped forward.

It was nearly blinding within the row of corn. The spectral luminescence of each stalk was magnified by the light given off by its neighbors. Vertigo and nausea overtook the boy and he feared that the overabundance of chocolate and sugar in his belly might escape through his mouth.

Stumbling through the cornstalks, his eyes shut tight against the blinding light and his ears deafened by the angry wind, David reached for his mask. It was too bright and the magic was too much for him. He needed to tear off the mask and shut it out. Before he could manage this, his feet came out from under him and he tumbled into a circular clearing.

David opened his eyes. The glow here was less intense than it had been within the row of corn, and his vertigo subsided. Still, the soil burned with the same consistent orange as the trail through the maze had been. The wind still battered him with wicked fury, but here it whipped forward in a circuit around the clearing, kicking up a whirlwind of soil, rocks, and debris. The cracking sound of the paper mask being battered by the weather grew nearly unbearable.

Stranger than the cyclone in the clearing, or the fairy glow of the earth, was the woman—or rather the creature—who stood at its center. It was female; David could tell this from the sagging, midnight breasts that hung down to her waist, and the thick patch of gray hair between her legs, but she was not human. Her face was a mask of exaggerated features. An elongated nose hooked down over lips that stretched too far across. Calloused ears, riddled with coarse gray bristles reached up into fine, pointed tips. A mane of hair, mostly white but mixed with occasional streaks of glowing amber, stretched from her head down to the soil.

"Eldon?" she asked, her lips peeling back to reveal teeth like broken glass.

Eldon. That was right, he thought. Eldon was his name, not David. Eldon had always been his name.

"Why to the hollow has my child roamed?" the creature asked, in a musical voice, incongruent with her nightmare visage. He was amazed that her words carried above the raging wind.

The voice brought back a flood of memories. Songs sung to him in infancy. Songs in a beautiful language he had forgotten existed. And then memories of terrible quiet. Not the complete silence reserved for the dead or the deaf but the muted sounds that a drowning man hears when cast from the world of light above and into the frigid darkness of the world below.

"Mother?" David—no, Eldon—asked.

A clawed hand with knuckles like splintered obsidian reached out. David, who now remembered he was Eldon, took the hand of his forgotten mother. She pulled him to his feet and dusted him off.

"To come here was solecism," the dark fairy scolded. "What good does this pilgrimage either of us do?"

The boy looked into the monster's dayglo eyes and found in them a love and a passion he'd never seen in those of the woman who masqueraded as his mother in the world of man.

"It called me," he replied. "You called me."

Leathery fingertips caressed his cheek, and sadness overcame the cartoon features of the woman-thing.

"I want to come home," David, who was really Eldon, added.

"Too unripe you are, my little love," Mother—the real mother—

added, with a sad undertone to the natural harmony of her voice.

Tears formed in the eyes of the boy named both Eldon and David. They dripped down his face and soaked into the paper of his mask.

"Please," he implored. "I hate this place and these people. I can't stand the washed-out colors of their world and the washed-out magic of their souls."

The overly wide lips of the mother-thing formed a downward arch, which brought the corners of her mouth down to either side of her chin. Shimmering, metallic tears carved wet lines down her face. Her hand, atop of his, trembled.

"Oh, my dear Eldon," she said with melancholy written across her face, "complete is the trade. By blood and word it is bound. There is no coming home, not until you are grown."

The wind grew stronger around them. Sticks and pebbles bombarded them both, but neither seemed to notice or care.

"No one understands me here," he pleaded. "I'm so tired of being alone."

"The trade has been made," the creature reiterated, a sadness hanging over her words. "Rules are rules are rules. I say it thrice."

"To hell with the rules!" screamed the boy.

He rushed toward her, or rather he attempted to. The cyclonic winds pushed against him, knocking him off balance. He lost his footing and tumbled to the soil. Loose dirt and detritus swirled around her—his real mother—as he looked up pleading from behind his mask.

"Spirits of chaos, that is man. Phantoms to them are rules and law. Tangible are they to us. Bound to our oaths are the fey, Eldon."

Corn husks broke away from stalks as the wind's intensity increased. Angry gusts drummed out a timpani roll against David's mask and in his ears. The fairy woman's hair whipped about, a thousand tattered ribbons in a helter-skelter Colorguard display.

"Please!" David cried out, tears soaking into the paper of his mask.

"Slaves we are to our word, but you mustn't be alone. Other bargains there are to be made." Her voice was quiet but clear despite the cacophony of the gale.

"What bargains?"

Before she could answer, the cruel wind ripped the mask from David's face. The magma glow of the soil vanished, as did the amber radiance of the world at large. Cornstalks stood still and dark, barely reflecting the glow of the silver moon above. No gale-force winds kicked up the dirt or stirred the rows of corn.

In front of David stood a shabby scarecrow. Washed-out straw served as its hair and stretched down to the brown soil. A gnarled piece of wood, maybe a bit of tree root, stuck out of the middle of its dirty, burlap face like a long, crooked nose. The stick reached down over a lunatic smile painted from one ear to the other.

A signpost was hammered into the ground before the dismal scarecrow. Scrawled across the wooden placard in black spray paint was the word *Rye-Mother.*

David or Eldon, or whatever the hell his name was, scanned the clearing for his mask. He needed it. He needed to know what manner of bargain they might strike, but the mask was lost in rows of corn. The mask was lost, just as he was in this gray, mortal world.

The boy stood and reached out to touch the scarecrow. Her face was coarse beneath his fingertips and there was no trace of life in her burlap flesh. No magic shined in the black button eyes he gazed into.

"Please . . . tell me . . ."

She did not.

David lay in his bed, staring at the ceiling. His parents, or the human things his real mother had given him to, berated him for sneaking out. Their words were lost on him. *Do you know how dangerous, blah, blah, blah . . . What were you thinking . . . bullshit, bullshit, bullshit.*

Why had she given him up, he wondered. Why had she swapped him with some mundane, human animal? What kind of bargain had been made?

David thought of posing that last question to Mother and Father but thought better of it. They might not even realize a bargain had been struck. Such was often the way with fairies.

"David, you look at me right now!" his father demanded. David turned toward the voice, a blank expression on his face.

"How could you do this again, after last year?" Father demanded. "What do you have to say for yourself?"

Finding that no words came to mind which wouldn't upset his supposed parents, David chose to stay quiet.

"Answer your father!" his mother, who was not his real mother, exclaimed. David, or Eldon as he now thought of himself, shifted his eyes to her. She stood behind his father, balancing little baby Brooke—his alleged sister—on her hip. The tiny child gazed stupidly at David with brown, bovine eyes. She clearly belonged here in this tepid reality, just as she belonged with these lukewarm people. David hated her for that.

His parents began scolding him further, but he had already tuned them out again. Instead, he kept his gaze focused on poor, stupid baby Brooke whom he would never have anything in common with, and that is when the Rye-Mother's words came back to his mind.

She was right. He didn't have to be alone, he thought as he gazed at Brooke's soulless expression. Other bargains could be made.

Elvis and Isolde

Isolde sat naked on one side of her bed, curls of hair trailing down her back like cascading flame. Elvis was beside her, his rain-soaked clothes discarded on the floor. Isolde tapped his forearm, just below the tourniquet. A blue vein pulsed beneath his pale skin. She smiled and looked up at him with eyes the color of glaciers.

"You have good veins for this." Her voice was creaky and raspy, yet possessed a strange charm. "I'm telling you, baby, you've never had a high like this."

Elvis shook his head, but he knew there was no point in arguing with her. There had never been a shortage of beautiful women in his life, but none had ever enraptured him like Isolde. Everything about her was irresistible, from her wild mane, streaked with the colors of autumn, to the slight brogue that slipped through when she was angry or excited. All it took was one tilt of her head and he would do anything she asked.

"You're old man's gonna put me in the ground if he finds out we're shacked up and shooting dope."

"Don't you worry about my father. He's a pussycat."

"Is that why they call him the Celtic Tiger?"

Isolde kissed Elvis, barely brushing his lips with her own, then leaned back and jabbed the needle into his arm. A feeling of warmth coursed through his veins. It was a strange sensation but not bad by any means.

"My turn."

Elvis tightened the band of surgical tubing around Isolde's arm. She pumped her fist and showed him which vein to use. He scrunched his face and apologized as he pricked her.

"Sorry, little lady," Isolde said, mimicking the deep timbre of his voice and the charm of his drawl. "God, if the rest of the world knew what a cute little square you really are."

Elvis placed his forefinger to his lips and raised an eyebrow. He held the expression for a few seconds before they both broke into laughter.

Isolde climbed onto Elvis's lap. She grabbed his thick black hair and pressed his face into her chest. He kissed her naked flesh, teasing with his lips and teeth, as he grabbed her ass and pulled her hard against him.

The high of the drugs and the sex washed over Elvis like the warm rays of dawn. Isolde rolled onto her side, once they were done, and rested her head on his chest. The thought occurred to him that life might never get better than this moment. He held her close and shut his eyes as the opioid haze and the patter of rain lulled him to sleep.

Dreaded wakefulness crept over Ulvis. The soft touch of his queen . . . the campfire scent of her hair and the warmth of her breath . . . it all evaporated like mist beneath the sun. He tried to pull her close, but she wasn't there. She hadn't been for a long while now.

Ulvis opened his eyes and stared at the bruised sky, black and purple with sickly ochre clouds. He missed the days when there were—well, when there were days. The world once spun and night gave way to morning, but now it was broken and still.

Twin moons illuminated bands of stony debris that arched from one horizon to the next. The rings were made from shattered land masses and mountains that had crumbled and floated away after the world had been cleaved. Ulvis hated the rings. There was a certain manner of beauty to them, yes, but they reminded him of death and failure.

A comet flashed across the dark heavens, and Ulvis felt a twinge of envy. If only he could fly away from this mortuary world to some other place or some other time. If only he could burn across the sky.

The lyrics to an old folk song popped into his head—something about a falling star lighting up the purple sky. That was one version of it, at least. It was an ancient tune, from a time lost to memory.

Ulvis's back and ribs ached from another night on the hard ground, but he didn't want to get up. No, he wanted the earth to give way beneath him—for it to suck him down into its maw of crumbling stone and grind him to pulp.

The ground did not oblige him, which he knew in his heart was for the best. He still had one final sacred task to complete . . . one duty to fulfill. That was why he was alive and everyone else was dead.

Ulvis rolled up his sleeve and examined his arm. Yellow veins stretched from his right hand and halfway up to his bicep. Soon the infection would reach his heart, and then his brain. There wasn't much time left to do what must be done.

He packed his gear and headed home to save his queen and kill the man who poisoned the world.

"Who's that?" asked Hodge. "The gal waiting for you back home?"

Aaron stared at his notebook, proud of the way his pencil marks were coming together to form the closest approximation of a woman he'd seen in months. He wasn't a great artist by any means (he'd always been more of a singer), but he'd spent his downtime in the trenches honing his skill. His landscapes of barbed wire and artillery craters were grim and lifeless, riddled with perspective issues, but his pinup girls were coming along nicely. It helped, he supposed, that he was handsome enough to know his way around the female form.

"Naw, that ain't Aaron's girl," Esposito piped in. "They don't make girls that pretty in Tennessee."

"You sound pretty sure of that for a guy who never left Chicago before the war," Aaron retorted.

The three men snickered, each holding onto the brief moment of levity as if it were gold.

"So is that your girl?"

Aaron took a moment to admire the woman on the page. Her face had a delicate, elfen quality to it. Her eyes were kind, yet overbrimming with secret knowledge. Long curls of hair fell over her chest, keeping the drawing from straying too far into indecency. She looked just as she did in his dreams.

"I think she is," Aaron replied.

"You think she is? What the hell does—"

Esposito's words were cut short as a mortar round exploded further down the trench. The ground shook and Aaron was half convinced that it might just open up and swallow them all. Before he could fully visualize that terrible thought, his attention turned toward the crumbling wall of the trench and the sandbags tumbling down at him. They clobbered him, knocking him to the ground. His head connected with the wooden edge of a makeshift bunk and the world twisted and turned before him.

More sandbags tumbled down on Aaron, crushing his chest and stealing his breath. He looked to his friends for help, but Hodge was lost to him, hidden somewhere in the cloud of dust and earth that the mortar blast had kicked up. Aaron could see Esposito, but the man was in the dirt, twitching and bleeding from a shrapnel wound in his neck.

Cold exhaustion set over Aaron, even as mortar rounds shook the earth below him and thundered like the rage of chained titans. Tears leaked out of his closed eyes and he shook his head, desperate to fight off the unconsciousness about to beset him. He feared he would never wake up if he passed out now. The young soldier was not strong enough to fight off the encroaching sleep, however. He mumbled to himself as he drifted away, a paraphrased bit of Poe about loathing little slices of death.

Uneasiness gnawed at Elvis's unconscious mind, urging him to wake. He fought through the heroin haze of his brain, struggling to find the strength and the will to open his eyes. The warmth of his high was fading and something cold pressed upon him.

Elvis unclenched his jaw and moved his tongue around, willing saliva into his dry mouth. He opened his eyes to find Isolde still resting her head on his chest. Her fiery hair was soft against his skin, but her flesh was cold and her muscles stiff. No breath came from her nose or lips.

"Isolde?"

He pushed the hair from her face, revealing blue lips and ashen skin.

"No, no, no . . ."

Elvis shook her, but she didn't stir. He sat up and her body rolled off of his, her limbs set in place and her posture frozen. He pried one eye open. It stared back jaundiced and lifeless.

"Baby, wake up!" Tears rolled down his eyes, and any remnants of his high evaporated. "Please, please wake up!"

He picked up the phone and began to dial 911 but stopped after two numbers. He looked down at her face, her incredible beauty marred by the ugliness of death. She was gone. What good would it do to be here when they found her? He'd lose everything. Every rag in the world would run the story.

And then there was Isolde's father. If he found out that Elvis had been shooting dope with his daughter when she died, he would not be far behind her. He hung up the phone and he stroked his dead lover's hair.

"I told you we shouldn't have messed with that stuff. Why? Why didn't I put my foot down?"

Bang!

Elvis jumped, then looked around for the source of the noise. After a few seconds, the banging began again. Someone was pounding at the door to Isolde's apartment.

"Isolde, open up!" The voice was deep and smooth with the hint of a German accent.

Elvis scrambled for his clothes, muttering curses under his breath. He tripped and fell as he fumbled into his boxer shorts.

"You all right, Princess? Party a bit too hard, perhaps?" His words were accentuated with a cruel laugh.

"Goddamn it," Elvis muttered, slithering into his tight jeans. Dampness—a tactile reminder of strolling down rainy streets with Isolde the night before—made the pants harder to put on. They clung to his thighs and resisted his attempts to pull them up.

"Have it your way. I'm done knocking."

A loud bang echoed through the loft apartment and the door shuddered in its frame. Elvis pulled his jeans up over his hips but didn't bother with the zipper or button. He snatched up his leather jacket in one hand and a single shoe in the other.

The door flew open with a loud crack. A tall and gangly man stood in the doorway, his overcoat a bit too short around the wrists and his slacks too high over his ankles. Thin wisps of hair, black, gray, and orange like burning embers and ash, framed his scarred face. There was something of a serpentine quality to his hunched posture as he crouched through the doorway.

Elvis knew the man. He worked for Isolde's father and went by the nickname Lye. Word on the street was that his specialty was arson and insurance fraud. He was also Isolde's drug hookup and had supplied the dope that killed her.

Lye locked his gaze onto Elvis, then shifted to Isolde's corpse and back again. He smirked, wide and cruel.

"Things went south, eh, pretty boy? The perils of rock 'n' roll decadence, I suppose?"

Lye drew a revolver from beneath his blazer and stared at it with admiration. His eyes traced the gleaming barrel and the contours of the chamber as one might study a naked lover.

"I was hoping the dope would have nixed the both of you. Would have been cleaner that way."

Elvis stood frozen for a moment, unable to process this betrayal. "You . . . you poisoned us?"

A laugh like the crackling of kindling echoed from Lye's throat as he leveled the pistol at Elvis's chest. The barrel of the gun seemed to glare at Elvis, like an obsidian-eyed cyclops. He stared back, angry and defiant, and flung his shoe at the gunman, hitting him in the forehead with the hard-soled heel. Lye fired, but the blow caused his shot to go wide. Plaster dust exploded from the wall just to Elvis's right.

Elvis turned and ran from the gunman. Shielding his face and arms with his jacket, he dove through one of the loft's massive picture windows. He tried to stay calm as he crashed toward the grimy Hollywood street two stories below. He prayed that his body would know what to do when he hit the ground—that all the time working with stuntmen and Karate masters had paid off.

He rolled with the impact, minimizing the damage from the fall. It hurt like hell when he hit the ground, but nothing felt broken. He struggled to his feet and took off running.

A pistol's report eclipsed the nighttime sounds of the city. Elvis ran across the street and dove behind a parked car. He crawled on his hands and knees, rushing between cover from vehicles and palm trees until he was able to scramble around a corner and take off at a full sprint.

Elvis kept running, putting distance between himself and the gunman at Isolde's apartment, but fear and adrenaline were quick-burning fuels. Within minutes his breath grew ragged and vertigo set in. He stumbled into an alley and leaned against the brick façade of an apartment building.

Tears welled in his eyes as his back slid down the graffiti-covered wall. Images of Isolde's rigid corpse strobed in his mind. Her dead lips glistened in his imagination, a darker shade of blue than her eyes—lips that he would never kiss again. He sobbed, knowing he had failed her . . . knowing he had helped her die.

The great carnelian walls around Drombeg had crumbled. Once they had kept out the wild ones from the eastern wastes and the vagabond armies from the fallen kingdom of Glicoas. Now they were but heaps of dull red stone and Ulvis climbed over them with little effort.

It had been years since he'd set eyes on the city of his birth. He stood atop a heap of carnelian debris and looked upon the city. Founded on spilled blood and stolen gold, Aillacht had grown into a city unlike any ever known—a shining light of civility and reason in a dark and violent world. He looked at the ash-covered streets, the abandoned guard-posts, the ruins of palatial homes and toppled, powerless idols. Far off, rising high above the razed villas and abandoned temples, all the way up into the cancer-yellow clouds, stood the Palace of Lynx.

"How did it come to this?" he asked aloud, even though he knew the answer. It was Lye. Lye the jester. Lye the warlock. Lye the king killer.

Ulvis, the last of his order, had been exiled by the fiendish sorcerer who poisoned Princess Iseult's heart and usurped her father's throne.

That serpent-tongued betrayer had him beaten and dragged in chains beyond the wastes, to the ruins of a city by the sea that had been forgotten before the first of the Lynx clan founded Aillacht. Surely Lye had thought he would perish in that empty and ancient metropolis, but Ulvis would not take death's hand until he fulfilled his duty to protect the rightful queen.

He slid down the ruins of the great carnelian wall and landed in the ash-caked street. He scanned the ruins of homes, hoping to find men or women but knowing there were only monsters. Yellow eyes glittered in the darkness behind shattered windows. Hateful gibberings and tortured howls filled the night.

An emaciated ghoul stalked through sickly weeds that had once been a garden of unrivaled beauty. The monster was a mockery of man—a walking corpse with bloodshot, jaundiced eyes sunken into dark sockets. Filthy, ragged clothes from its former life hung from its wiry limbs and clung to open sores on its chest.

The ghoul crouched behind thin stocks of knotwood, scrounging through ashen soil for any vermin it might eat. The monster scooped up a handful of soot from the ground. Ulvis cringed as ash and saliva dribbled between its grinding teeth.

He pushed out his bottom lip and blew an unruly black curl from his forehead. Taking a deep breath to steady his hand, he raised his revolver. The iron sights of his pistol floated in a tight circle at the center of the monster's face.

The gun let out a massive report that echoed off of ruins and abandoned alleyways. Instead of exploding in a rain of blood and gore, the ghoul's head crumbled like sand in the wind. Ulvis could hear its hidden brethren fleeing from the gunfire. Ghouls were vicious in close quarters, especially in numbers, but they spooked easily. Still, they'd be back, and soon. As cowardly as they were, their memories were too short to be scared for long.

Ulvis approached the ghoul's corpse. His eyes traced the ugly contours of its body. Its arms and legs were spindly, but there was a lean, wiry muscle to them. Scars adorned its swollen knuckles, painting the picture of a man who'd labored hard before Lye's magic had corrupted him.

It wasn't any of this, nor even the creature's collapsed skull, that made Ulvis's stomach flip, however. It was the network of yellow veins running like a spiderweb beneath its skin and merging over its heart.

Ulvis looked down at the infection spreading through his arteries. It was only a matter of time until those lines of disease weaved themselves into his heart—only a matter of time until he was just like the dead thing on the ground.

"Sergeant? Sergeant, I need you to stay awake. All right, soldier?"

The woman's voice was creaky and hoarse, but not unpleasant. Her tone was warm, with just an edge of authority. A slight accent added a comforting charm to her voice. Still, he couldn't help but feel a smidge angry for her waking him—for pulling him from the absurdity of his nightmare and into the stark terror and pain of real life.

The stench of death and infection almost blocked out the acrid smell of smoke wafting in from the Western Front. The faint sound of machine-gun fire kept a constant, chaotic rhythm. An all too brief state of unconsciousness had dulled his pain, but now his head throbbed and his ribs ached.

"You have a concussion. I need you to stay awake."

"What about my friends?" Aaron asked, his eyes still shut. "Hodge and Esposito? Did they make it out okay?"

"I'm sorry, but I don't know. What I do know is that you need to open your eyes."

Aaron did so, reluctantly, and was awestruck by the woman's face. There before him was the woman from his drawings—that perfect image of beauty that had haunted his imagination for as long as he'd been thinking about girls. The resemblance was uncanny, from the elfin features of her face to her pale blue eyes and fiery braids. The dirt on her face and the bloodstains on her clothes did nothing to detract from her beauty.

Aaron's eyelids sagged beneath the weight of his exhaustion. He knew he was supposed to stay awake, but if he died now, with this gorgeous nurse as his final vision . . . well, the European Theatre certainly presented worse ways to go.

"Stay with me, Sergeant," the nurse urged.

"I've dreamed about you," Aaron slurred. The nurse smiled and placed her hand on his.

"Tell me about yourself, Sergeant. What's your name?"

"Folks mostly call me Aaron. That's my middle name."

"Keep those eyes open, Aaron. Tell me where you're from."

Aaron gave the nurse a crooked smile, despite his pain and exhaustion. The nurse smirked and cast her gaze down. Aaron was pleased to know that he still had a way with women, even when laid out on a filthy cot just outside the trenches of war.

"Memphis, by way of Tupelo. What about you, doll?"

"I'm from Drombeg."

The place sounded familiar to Aaron, but he didn't quite place it. Somewhere in Ireland, he guessed. She looked Irish and certainly sounded it.

"And what's you're name, miss?"

"The other girls call me Izzy."

"A pleasure to meet you, Miss Izzy. Wish it were under better circumstances."

She smiled again, more with her eyes than her lips. It was a tired smile, strained from the terrors of war, but it was sincere—a small spot of sunshine in the darkness.

Aaron adjusted his position in the cot and pain coursed through his body. He winced but held back the curse that threatened to spring from his lips. His mama hadn't raised him to speak profanity in front of a lady.

"Any chance I can get something for this pain?" Aaron said, nodding toward a morphine drip by one of the other cots.

Izzy glared at the morphine bag. Aaron could read a sense of conflict in her strained expression. Her eyes were daggers, yet her lips trembled with desire.

"You don't want that stuff, soldier." Her voice creaked. "It's a comfort for the dying. But if you aren't dying? Well, it will certainly get you started."

Elvis wondered the side roads south of Santa Monica Boulevard, his mind reeling from Isolde's death and the idea that Lye was out there hunting him. Red-eyed and crying, he shivered in the night air, dressed only in damp jeans and a leather jacket.

The streets were dark and quiet, at least by Hollywood standards. The moon ducked behind titanic clouds, hiding its face in shame for what it had witnessed this evening, but it could not hold back its light, which lent a yellow pallor to the night.

Why would Lye poison them? What did the gangster stand to gain by their deaths? Was it a Machiavellian move to climb up the rungs of the gangland ladder? Was it jealousy? Pure sadism?

Lye's motives didn't matter, Elvis reckoned. Isolde was dead. He'd never hold her again. Never hear her laugh or feel her breath on his lips.

He was dead as well. It didn't matter that he was still walking around, heart pumping and mind racing. Whatever violent end awaited him, whether doled out by Lye or from Isolde's father, would only be a formality.

Even if he could put Lye in the ground and somehow escape the wrath of Isolde's father, his life was over. There would be no more movies and no more records. There was no coming back from something like this, and honestly, he didn't want to. What was the point of all the money and the fame if he couldn't share it with her?

An orange Impala lurched onto the street, up by the corner of Havenhurst. The driver was going too fast and drunkenly swerved across the asphalt. The car's headlights momentarily blinded Elvis and he shielded his face with one arm.

A fleeting suicidal urge flashed through his brain. He imagined throwing himself into the car's path—sacrificing himself upon its chrome bumper and beneath its whitewall tires. He could almost feel his pelvis shattering, to the delight of all those it had offended, and imagined the labored pain of drawing breath with broken ribs.

"I deserve it."

Suddenly the car jumped the curb and careened right toward him. All thoughts of suicide vanished. Elvis turned and ran.

The headlights eclipsed him, painting a long and spindly shadow of him onto a building on the next block. The car's exhaust grew louder with each second. He could feel the heat radiating from its engine.

Elvis reached the edge of an alleyway and dived in. The Impala sped by, splashing him with puddled rainwater, and made a reckless U-turn. He condemned himself as a coward for not standing his ground against the oncoming car. Isolde was dead, and if he'd had any class he would have joined her.

The car drove up to the narrow mouth of the alley. Smoke and heat radiated from beneath the hood, carrying with them a burning stench. The driver revved the engine.

Elvis looked down at the rippling puddle. The face staring back at him from the water's surface looked nothing like the one on his album covers or movie posters. His reflection showed a haggard, broken man with glassy eyes incapable of hiding their sorrow or cowardice.

No, it was worse than that. Elvis was gazing at the face of a ghoul—a heartless thing that had no business drawing breath.

He wasn't going to spend his final moments like that—a groveling monster in a filthy alley. Elvis pushed himself up and glared through the darkened windshield. He couldn't see the driver, but he knew who it was. His fists clenched, ready to avenge his lover or join her at God's table.

The Palace of Lynx towered over the scorched landscape. Its white fieldstone, mottled with spots of black and grey, stood in stark contrast to the blackened earth. Crooked lines of spongy, ochre fungus grew in the cracks of the stone façade and spread out across the soil, like streaks of fossilized lightning.

The countless windows were dark, save for the two enormous oblong dormers that looked like eyes above either side of the open portcullis at the center of the palace. Cyclones of moonlight eddied across the sky, drawn into those two giant panes.

Ulvis navigated around deep cracks in the earth. The fissures weren't so bad here. Each was narrow enough for him to step over. This wasn't so in the farther reaches of the world. In his return from exile, Ulvis had seen canyons form and swallow colossal towers of glass and steel. He'd walked along newly formed cliffs where coastal villages had collapsed into the depths of the hungry sea and where ghosts sang melancholy hymns.

While the fissures were less severe in Drombeg, there was no doubt that this was their epicenter. Each vein of cracked earth, just like the yellow moss, led back to the Palace of Lynx.

Ulvis stepped through the open portcullis and took refuge in the shadows of the long corridor beyond. Noises echoed from the darkness beyond the corridor. It wasn't the sound of desperate ghouls scrounging for vermin, nor the squeak and pitter-patter of rats. It sounded like creaking metal and the clicking of steel against stone. Ulvis wondered what manner of abomination awaited him in the great hall.

Whatever the source of that noise was, Ulvis had no desire to confront it. He was tired of fighting and just plain tired. He wanted to stop right there. How easy it would be, he thought, just to slide down this wall and accept the cold comfort of approaching doom.

"Not yet," Ulvis whispered, thinking of Lye's scarred face and his burning ember eyes. "But soon."

Ulvis ran his hand against the wall until he found a torch set in a sconce. He retrieved the metal lighter from his pocket, a relic given to him by Princess Iseult, and flicked the wheel that conjured fire from nothing. He placed the flame to the head of the torch, which ignited with a sulfurous flash.

Ulvis marched to the end of the corridor, his torch in one hand, his pistol in the other. The rhythmic clicking and creaking ahead of him grew louder with each step. He came to the corridor's end and the torchlight cast a wavering light into the great hall beyond.

A sentry stopped its patrol and turned toward Ulvis. Its armor was scorched and tarnished. Soot and ash obscured the seal of the House of Lynx embossed upon the chest plate. A great helm, blackened and battle-worn, hid the face of the warrior beneath.

Ulvis leveled his gun on the sentry but didn't fire. He'd not seen a living man or woman since the world was cleaved, only ghouls. He was not ready to extinguish the rare miracle of life unless it was necessary, especially the life of a man he may have served alongside.

"Is that you, Red?" Ulvis asked, hoping this was a man he knew—a man he could reason with.

The sentry remained stoic and still.

"Lamar?"

A long screech echoed off the walls as the sentry drew its sword from a rusty scabbard.

"Whoever you are, Sir Knight, I implore you to stand down in the name of the rightful Queen and the House of Lynx."

The sentry did not concede. It strode toward Ulvis, its sword poised to cut him down. Ulvis fired a warning shot. When the knight continued forward, he aimed his gun at a gap in the metal plates. The slug cut through a layer of chainmail, but the sentry continued forward, unperturbed by the gunshot.

Shaken, Ulvis fired again, but this time his shot landed center mass. It barely dented the sentry's breastplate and did not slow his advance.

Ulvis didn't retreat but instead rushed to meet the knight. He parried a downward strike with his torch, then shoved the muzzle of his pistol up beneath the sentry's helmet and fired. No gore exploded from the helm, nor did his adversary yield. The muzzle flash had banished the shadows behind the helmet's visor, just long enough for Ulvis to realize there was no flesh behind the steel.

The phantom sentry pushed Ulvis back, then swung again with his blade. Ulvis parried. This time the wood gave way and the flaming torch head fell. It burned on the ground, casting shifting shadows across the walls.

There was no reasoning with the thing coming at him. There was no destroying it either, not with any weapon of man. It was a piece of the void, dressed in the armor of a dead man.

Ulvis had a deep knowledge of these abominations—these unthings. Iseult had whispered the poisonous secrets of oblivion into his ear, just as Lye had shared them with her. There was a cost to those secrets—the sickness inching through his body, threatening to devour his mind—but there was also power within them.

Ulvis dropped the stump of his torch and continued backing away as the sentry sought him out. He opened the chamber of his revolver, dumped the bullets to the ground, then slammed it back into place.

Focusing on the empty chamber, Ulvis muttered a curse that few living beings had ever heard. A tiny vacuum formed within the gun—a bead of non-existence, sucking at the air and the dust. It pulled at anything it could and Ulvis could feel it tearing away layers of his soul.

He pulled the trigger, firing his hex into the sentry. The armor twisted and warped around that blackhole slug. The sound was horrific, like an animal screeching for the release of death, but it was brief. In less than a single breath, the sentry was gone. It was as if it had never been there.

Ulvis could still feel the emptiness that had possessed the armor, however. It was still present, reaching out, searching and yearning for a new vessel.

A sharp sting radiated across Aaron's cheek, stirring him back to consciousness. He groaned, more at the various traumas in the rest of his body than at the pain of the slap.

"Aaron, I need you to wake up." Izzy was shaking him, panic in her eyes.

The grim song of war played close by. Suffering moans and shouted orders pierced the silence between gunshots and explosions. The ground trembled and clouds of dirt and smoke rolled into the tent.

"What's going on?" His words were slurred from dry mouth and exhaustion.

Nurses exchanged anxious glances and soldiers sat up in their cots. Some clutched at crosses or rosaries. Others fumbled for sidearms that weren't there.

"They're coming," she said, urging him out of his cot. "He's coming."

"Who?"

Izzy ignored the question and helped Aaron to find his balance. She threw his arm over her shoulder and pulled him along. The pain in his ribs exploded and he hissed through gritted teeth.

"Who's coming, Izzy?"

Dark yellow gas wafted in through the tent's flap, as if in answer to his question. Nurses and soldiers shouted panicked vulgarities and prayers at the sight of the toxic mist. The men who could stand clambered out of their cots and retreated from the entrance. Most of the nurses followed suit, but a few stayed at the bedsides of the more grievously wounded.

"Lye . . ."

A horrible scream, the worst sound Aaron had ever heard, filled the night. The mustard gas billowing in through the tent flap took on an amber hue. Aaron stared at the strange glow of the gas as Izzy pulled him away. A pillar of flame appeared in the entrance, catching fire to the tent.

Aaron thought for a moment that the gas had ignited, but that wasn't it. The column of fire did not consume the mist. The flame screeched and danced a grim pirouette, twirling and flailing before collapsing against a cot. Only then did Aaron realize it was a human being he was looking at—an immolated man suffering a gruesome death before his eyes.

He wanted to turn away but found himself enthralled with the horror playing out before him. He could make out details behind the flame. A lipless mouth stretched out in an endless cry. The buttons on his jacket, melting into slag. Charred fabric melding with molten flesh.

Izzy tugged at Aaron again. He tore his eyes away from the burning soldier and allowed Izzy to lead him to the far end of the tent. Someone had cut a slit in the fabric and soldiers and nurses were rushing through the impromptu exit. Izzy stepped through the slit, but Aaron paused.

"What are you doing?" she asked.

Aaron scanned the inside of the tent. The mustard gas rolled across the ground and over the cots of the bedridden. The fire was spreading across the fabric of the tent and the cot where the immolated man lay dead had turned into a bonfire.

"We can't just leave these people."

She looked at him, pleading with her eyes. "Aaron . . ."

Izzy's words were cut off by a thunderous woosh. A stream of fire, like a dragon's breath, shot through the tent's entrance. The flame arced from left to right, catching sheets and mattresses along with the soldiers confined to them.

"We can't help them, Aaron. No one can."

A man dressed in the field gray of the German army followed in behind the flame. His helmet was scuffed and battle-worn, and he held a long metal nozzle in his scarred hands. The light from his flamethrower reflected off the black lenses of his gas mask and Aaron found something disturbingly familiar in that lifeless gaze.

"We have to go!" Izzy screamed, tugging on his arm.

Aaron watched helplessly as the German set fire to the wounded and the nurses attending them. Their dying screams reminded him of the screech of twisting steel.

Izzy pulled him back, through the slit in the tent and away from the yellow poison that billowed toward them. They stood in the cold night air and Aaron watched as the roof of the tent gave way to rising flames. He wasn't aware he was crying until Izzy wiped the tears from his cheeks.

"I know, baby, it's horrible, but we can't let him get us. Not again."

Elvis turned around, his lips curled into a sneer and his hands balled into fists. The Impala sat at the edge of the narrow alleyway, its headlamps upon him like prison yard searchlights.

"Lye!" he screamed. "Come fight me like a man, you son of a bitch!"

The high beams turned on, blinding Elvis and forcing him to cover his eyes. For a moment he could feel an intense heat wash over him as if it were streams of flame bearing down on him, rather than Chevrolet headlights. Maybe he was getting sick—catching a fever from the rain, the dope, and the stress.

The engine revved and the car inched forward. It was an idle threat. The Impala couldn't fit down the alley. Lye would have to get out and come for him.

"Come on!"

The car backed up and stopped. The driver's-side door opened and the smell of cigarettes and burning hair filled the alley. A gangly man stepped into the glow of the headlights. His silhouette was familiar and vaguely inhuman—his limbs too long, his posture too fluid.

"Why?" Elvis demanded. "She was smart and sweet and beautiful."

"Why?" The word dragged on Lye's tongue, mimicking deep consideration. "I am the husband of sorrow and the father of death. You may as well ask why forests burn or why stars collapse."

Elvis shook his head back and forth. His fists trembled and tears ran from his eyes.

"We never did you no harm!"

"You're looking for sense where there is none, Elvis . . . or Ulvis . . . or whatever she called you here."

Images of a broken world bathed in the light of twin moons flashed before Elvis's eyes. The thunder of artillery and the shattering of mountains sounded in his ears. Disease burned in his veins, and he gasped for breath through aching ribs.

"It's a bit much when it all syncs up, eh boy?" Lye smirked.

Elvis fell to one knee, his mind overwhelmed and his nerves on fire with phantom pain. He could hear Lye approaching, one slow taunting step at a time, just as he could hear machine-gun fire and the creaking of twisting steel in parallel worlds.

Lye stopped in front of Elvis and pressed the muzzle of his pistol against the top of his skull.

"There is no hope, in this world or any other. I will burn that witch's heart to ash wherever she hides."

Streams of light twisted down the corridor which led to the throne room. Ulvis could feel his will and health being sucked away, along with siphoned radiance. His skin glistened with fevered sweat and his muscles ached with fatigue.

Lye waited in the heart of the palace seated upon the throne of Drombeg. The scorched crown of the deposed king sat crooked on his head. Princess Iseult stood behind him.

Veins, yellow with infection, shone beneath her paper-thin flesh. They branched across her body, like the strangling roots of a weed, and merged with the veins of moss growing out from her feet. Ulvis could see her charred heart beating in her open chest, siphoning bands of swirling light, stolen from the twin moons.

Ulvis stepped into the throne room, pistol in hand. Lye stood and raised his marotte, a relic from his days as a jester, like a ridiculous cudgel. The carven face of the costume scepter was a grotesque likeness of his own visage.

"Time to kill another king."

Ulvis blinked, confused by the regicidal sorcerer's comments. Lye had murdered Iseult's father, but Ulvis was no king. Somehow, someway, a kernel of truth seemed to resonate from Lye's words. That was his way, of course . . . to merge truth and fiction into monstrous deceptions.

Ulvis held his pistol out toward Lye, but his eyes were locked on his beloved. To see her body ravaged by black magic, to be met by her vacant expression and her hollow eyes, to gaze upon her exposed and poisoned heart—it was more haunting than the cloven earth and the never-ending night.

"Iseult . . ." Ulvis's voice quivered.

Lye circled Ulvis, mocking his concern. Ulvis ignored him and called out to her once more.

"Iseult, my love . . ."

The princess tilted her head in Ulvis's direction. It was a mechanical movement, lacking will, like a plant stretching toward the sun. There was no sign of love or concern in her eyes, not even a twinge of recognition.

"There's nothing left in there, boy." Lye's voice was as cold as it was smooth. "Iseult has left the building."

Lye was a master of deception, but unbearable truths were a delicacy to him. Iseult's mind was empty and her body reduced to a burning conduit between that which is and that which never was.

Ulvis stared at the charred organ beating in her open chest—a black lamprey suckling at the dying light of their world. There was no saving her life, Ulvis realized that now, but perhaps he could save her heart. First, however, he would have to deal with Lye.

The mad sorcerer circled Ulvis, tracing runes in the air with his marotte and leaving scorch marks in the empty space. He uttered sounds and words that had never been heard or dreamed, giving voice to Ginnungagap—the abyss that exists before and outside of time.

Ulvis thought of the hex he'd used to dispatch the golem—that terrible spell in the language of naught—the same language that Lye currently spoke. He wanted to use that magic again. He wanted to summon a sliver of the great nothing—a tiny singularity—and watch as Lye was pulled into its orbit and crushed beneath its gravity. The idea was so powerful that he could almost feel a bit of his soul stripping away just from the desire to invoke that bit of black magic.

But Ulvis needed his soul . . . Iseult needed his soul . . . far more than he needed revenge. Ulvis dropped the antique weapon to the floor and turned to his lover.

Lye ceased his incantation. He shouted taunts and boasts, insults, and challenges. Ulvis ignored them all. Lye was nothing and Iseult was everything.

He stepped into the path of the siphoned bands of light. They burned him and drained his strength, but he moved forward until his arms were around Iseult's vacant form.

"Pick up your gun and fight, Ulvis!" Lye screamed, his voice like the roar of a forest fire. "You can't save her!"

Iseult's fire-blackened heart drew out Ulvis's warmth and his life. More importantly, it fed on his love, and if anything was abundant enough to sate her spirit's hunger—if anything was strong enough to heal her charred heart—it was his love for her. Ulvis opened his arms and gave himself to the void in her chest.

Izzy led Aaron through a labyrinth of canvas tents. A rolling wall of mustard gas—a tireless, incorporeal behemoth—followed them through makeshift alleyways where dead and dying men lay in the dirt. Aaron pulled away from Izzy's grasp and knelt beside a deceased MP, taking the man's sidearm for himself.

Aaron looked back and toward the toxic cloud and he could see the glow of a German flamethrower through the yellow haze. The crackle of burning canvas and smoldering flesh populated the space between miserable wails and thunderous gunfire.

"Go. I'm too banged up . . . too slow. No sense in us both getting killed."

"I'm not going anywhere without you," Izzy responded, taking Aaron's free hand in her own.

The cloud flashed with amber radiance and the German's figure showed black like a phantasmagoria against the hazy backdrop. Aaron fired at the enemy soldier, but the round passed through him like a fly through a shadow.

"You need to leave! Get on!" Aaron shouted, backing away from the oncoming mustard gas and the nightmare soldier striding through it. He had dreamed of this woman for as long as he could remember. He'd drawn her a hundred times and kissed her in a thousand fantasies. The thought of her suffering a miserable death was unbearable.

"Run!" Arron implored, readying the weapon he took from the dead MP. "I'll buy you some time."

"No." Izzy's tone was resolute.

The German stepped out from the cloud of mustard gas. A small but hungry flame clung to the tip of his flamethrower.

Aaron fired again. The round hit the German's gas mask, shattering one of the lenses. The enemy soldier discarded the mask, revealing a wicked smile and an acid-scarred face. His hair was thick and orange, streaked black and gray with soot and ash.

Aaron recognized the German, just as he recognized Izzy. The man had plagued his sleep for years, hunting him from one dream to the next. Sometimes he was a gangster; other times he was a god. No matter what guise he took, he smelled like kerosene and ash and always flashed that wide, hateful grin.

"Lye . . ."

Aaron stood dumbfounded and Izzy snatched the gun from his grasp. She spun the cylinder to an empty chamber and uttered impossible syllables. The summoned dot of nothingness inside the gun's chamber began to suck at the gas and the flame—at the air and the moonlight, and all the ambient sorrow of war.

Yellow spiderwebs glowed on the back of her neck as she pulled the trigger. A tiny sliver of non-existence rocketed toward Lye, leaving a streak of primordial darkness in its wake.

Aaron, for some reason he wasn't quite sure, expected the German to collapse in on himself—to implode into a bloody mess, then vanish. Instead, Lye snatched the kernel of oblivion from the air and held it aloft like a marble.

"Little witch, I have courted the Nil across the nine realms and beyond." His voice was deep and smooth, with just a hint of a German accent. "Did you think you could end me with a mere splinter of the void? A cantrip of my own design?"

Lye flicked the dark pellet into Izzy's chest. She fell to her knees, gasping and clutching at her smock.

Aaron lunged forward, ignoring the pain in his head and his ribs. He clenched his fist and swung at Lye with everything he had. His fist landed hard on the German's chin, but the effort left Aaron gasping in pain.

Lye wiped the blood from his lip and let out a short laugh before pistol-whipping Aaron with the end of his flame thrower. The young soldier fell to the earth, several teeth broken and his cheek seared.

"I told you, boy," Lye said, aiming his flamethrower at Aaron's prone form, "I will burn her heart to ash, in this world and all others."

Aaron curled into a ball and waited for the impending agony of his fiery death. He heard the flamethrower's whoosh and felt heat, but the fire never touched him. The flames swerved away from him, forming a fiery vortex terminating in Izzy's blackened chest.

"But I only have to beat you in one," Izzy said, her gaze as hot as Lye's flames.

"Nothing can stop me, Iseult."

"I know, Lye."

The black hole in her chest sucked at the heat and the flame, but still it spread across her, igniting her clothes and hair. Her skin blistered and bubbled, yet she stood calm and reached into the void in her chest. From that cavity she pulled a shining thread, almost too thin to see.

"You may not have warned me of the cost, but you taught me how to pluck dreams from naught."

Lye screamed and cursed in every language he knew, giving his weapon all the fuel he could. Izzy did not stagger or flinch and her thread did not burn. She shoved the barrel of his weapon aside and threw herself upon him. His uniform ignited and his hair went up in a flash.

"A perfect love that nothing can kill," she said, wrapping the thread around Lye's neck. "A pauper's riches, and a dead man's baritone."

The shimmering thread crawled to Lye's face and sutured his lips. It curled around his body like a serpent, binding his arms and constricting. He struggled and moaned but could not break free.

"The sins of a saint and the doubt of a zealot . . . with these things I bind you."

Lye fell to the earth burning and bound. Izzy stumbled away, leaving him to be consumed by the mustard-colored clouds that rolled in around them.

The vacuous hole in her chest had now extinguished the flames that had engulfed her, but her body was charred and ruined. She fell, smoking, into Aaron's arms. He cried as he stroked her brittle flesh, recalling every sweet dream he'd ever had of her.

"I should have saved you." He wept. "I should have been stronger. I'm sorry . . . I'm so so sorry."

Izzy hushed him and stroked his face with blistered fingertips.

"I dragged you into all this. I always do. It was never your job to save me." Her words were a creaking whisper. "But you did."

Aaron cradled Izzy, amidst the burning tents and poisonous gas. She took his hand in hers and stared into his eyes.

"You are my heart, in this world and all others."

Vermis Paranoos

Did you know that your gut flora—the microscopic bacteria in your intestines—can control your mind? They have appetites all their own. Some like sugar; others like meat. Whatever their poison, they throw temper tantrums when they don't get their way and they chemically alter your mood. They make you crave what they crave and bully your emotions into irritability until you give in or they die off.

Gut flora are not the only little beasties that crawl inside other lifeforms to hijack them. There are plenty of others, and most are far more nefarious. Tiny bacteria can invoke paranoia and hallucinations in a host, forcing it to react to things that aren't there. Parasitic worms overtake the brains and pulse within the eyestalks of unsuspecting snails. Invasive fungi infect tarantulas and replace them cell by cell.

Most animals are mercifully ignorant of their parasitic possession. Even humans are mostly unaware of the gut flora driving them to disastrous eating habits. Sadly, I can't say the same. I'm painfully cognizant of the parasites overtaking my muscle and bone.

Out of all the aforementioned examples, I suppose the fungal spider parasites are the closest thing to the tiny monsters in my body. Like the parasitic fungus, they attack my flesh rather than my mind. With incredible patience they are overtaking my body, cell by cell, in a slow and agonizing process.

It started as a rash, or so I thought. Within days of the first signs of irritation on my right thigh, the skin turned black and necrotized. Terrified, I went to the hospital, but the doctor claimed that she could see no blemish. She said there was nothing wrong with me and sent me on my way.

My first thought was that the doctor was mad, or perhaps she took an instinctive dislike to me and wanted me to die (this is often the case, even with my own family members). The second and third doctors said the same thing, however. Even though the necrosis spread down to my knee and up to my hip, each of them claimed they saw nothing wrong with me.

They should have been less obvious with their subterfuge. It didn't take long for me to connect the dots. The doctors—the entire medical industry, in fact—were in cahoots. They had infected me with some sort of parasite, and they had done so on purpose, just to see what would happen. I was nothing but a lab rat to them.

It was no surprise. Did you know that most sickness in the U.S. is caused intentionally by the medical industry? And not for money either. It's done out of malice. America's Medical Industrial Complex, as we understand it today, is based on the work of Soviet bio-weapon science and used to implement revenge on the people of the United States for the fall of Communism and the murder of Che Guevara.

That's neither here nor there. The point is, I wasn't going to get help from hospitals or doctors. I was on my own.

As I said, the infection was spreading, albeit slowly. The necrotized area was mercifully numb, the nerves killed off and transmuted into the growing tissue of my parasite. This was a fortunate turn of events, as it allowed me to cut away the compromised flesh without the distraction of pain.

The black mass of my thigh gave easily to my blade. I had expected it to crack and flake, like burnt toast. Instead, it was a smooth cut, the tissue wet and spongy. Maybe it is a fungus, like the one that takes over tarantulas. Whatever it is, the flies seem to like it. They swarm the dark filets as they drop to the floor, eating and nesting.

Come to think of it, my rash started when the flies first showed up. Could they be the carriers? Is that how the CDC transmits the parasites?

I didn't think I would bleed so much when cutting away the foreign tissue. I figured I wouldn't have bled at all. Clearly, I was wrong, judging by the amount of blood pouring down my leg. I guess my circulatory system is still my own—kind of like ancient Roman sewers buried beneath the diseased modern city that overtook that once-proud capital.

Speaking of Rome, did you know that the concept of Jesus Christ was a mind virus? He was created as a psi-op by the Romans to replace the desire for a warrior messiah with a figure totemic of false and disastrous axioms. The experiment got out of control, as we all know of course, and Rome itself fell to the spiritual disease it created and weaponized.

I wonder if that will happen to the madmen in the Medical Industrial Complex? Will whatever parasite they infected me with grow beyond their control? Will I transmit it back to them? I can certainly try.

I've carved away most of the dark tissue, but I'm so tired now. The blood loss is getting to me. I'm tempted to tie a tourniquet on my leg and close my eyes for a few minutes. Normally I wouldn't call the jackbooted paramedics at 911 for help. I feel like I should, though.

I'll let them patch me up. I'll let them walk through the swarms of flies around my discarded flesh—let them breathe in the spores from the tissue I cut away—let them come in contact with my infected blood—let them take this parasite back home to roost.

And that is my choice—a decision born from my desire for revenge. It's not the will of the parasite. I'd know if it was the parasite. My mind is sharp as ever.

Great-Uncle Bendix

June 24, 1987

We made it to our new home, for better or worse. I found myself missing New York as soon as we crossed the George Washington Bridge, but Mary refuses to bring up a child in Manhattan. She insists on a slower pace for our lives and a more wholesome place to raise our family. She wants a fresh start as well. I guess we both do.

Maine wouldn't have been my first choice for a change of scenery or lifestyle. I think I'd have preferred Vermont or somewhere in the Carolinas, but I've been sitting on my great-uncle's big old house outside of Lewiston for ages. There's no mortgage to worry about and no one wants to pay what it's worth, so what the hell. Seems foolish not to take advantage of that. Sure, it needs a lot of work, but if we hate it maybe we can fix it up and sell it in a year or two.

We left late last night to avoid the New York traffic and arrived just before sunrise this morning. The silhouette of Great-Uncle Bendix's house on the hill was like a cutout of black construction paper against the navy blue pre-dawn sky. Our poor four-cylinder Cavalier struggled up the steep dirt road. I'm amazed we didn't pop a tire on any of the rocks or shards of broken bottles jutting out among the weeds that had reclaimed the private road leading to the house.

Near the hilltop, our headlights revealed a rusted cast-iron fence around the property. The shadows around the fence and the sagging gate shifted and retreated in response to our approaching high beams. They seemed to be alive, at least to my sleep-deprived brain. Mary made a comment about it spooking her, and I teased her; but truth be told, the darkness and quiet of rural Maine freaked me out as well.

I parked the car and approached the gate, leaving the headlights on so I could see what I was doing, but also because I missed the comforting and ever-present radiance of Manhattan. The beam of the headlights revealed the grounds beyond the gate—a landscape of broken pavers, overgrown weeds, and bleached-out Miller cans. Unsurprisingly, it would seem that the local kids liked to come party at the spooky old house on the hill.

The lock on the gate was broken and probably had been for years, but I still had trouble getting it open. The rusted hinges squealed in resistance and the sagging spires dug into the earth. Mary called out from the passenger seat asking if I needed help. I huffed and waved her back. After a few minutes of cursing and sweating, I managed to swing both sides of the gate open enough to squeeze the car through.

"I could have helped," Mary smirked as I got back in the car. "I'm pregnant, not crippled."

We pulled through the open gates and the first hints of sunlight were just edging above the horizon. Seeing the house illuminated by the headlights, I could tell that it was as run-down as I'd expected—peeling paint, a few broken windows, and whatnot—but it was huge. The few pictures I had seen did not do justice to its immensity.

"Can you believe the size of this house, Jon? Why on earth does nobody want this place?"

We'd already had this discussion a few times, the way married folks tend to repeat the same conversations. I answered her anyway, acting as if this were the first time.

"My great-uncle was a black sheep. He made a fortune as a bootlegger during Prohibition and ran one of the first outlaw biker gangs in the country. My grandfather cut all ties with him, I guess, but Bendix still left him the house."

To my knowledge, my grandfather never lived or even vacationed at the house in Maine, and neither did my father. Maybe they didn't want anything to do with the dirty money. Maybe they were afraid of trouble from Bendix's biker pals. Who knows?

I inherited the place from my old man ten years ago, and by that point it had become this kind of forgotten, invisible asset. Until today I'd never set eyes on it, save for a few grainy black-and-white pictures. It was more impressive in real life and more foreboding. I suppose fifty years of disrepair will lend a sense of dread to most any home.

I brought the car to a stop right before the front door, letting the headlights shine a path across the broken pavers, up the stairs, and to the door. Curling paint and detritus cast tiny shadows on the ground, and my own form, mirrored in gloom, stretched up to the doorway like some grossly elongated shade.

Ignoring the monstrous penumbra of myself, I approached the door and selected a key with an oversized hexagonal head. The deadbolt spun with a satisfying click. When I placed my hand on the patinated doorknob it was cold to the touch, despite the late June warmth. Dozens of cycles of freeze and thaw had warped the frame out of square, so a bit of physical persuasion was necessary to swing it inward. A cool, musty breeze escaped the house as the door opened, as if the house had been holding its breath until a new owner showed up.

I reached my hand into the dark entryway and felt around the edge for a light switch. I'd had the power set up for us before we left New York, but I was still surprised that the lights went on.

"It's beautiful," Mary commented, ushering me into the house ahead of her. "There's so much we can do with this, Jon."

I scanned the area—the inch of dust covering everything, the ratty furniture with faded upholstery, the pentagram and penis graffiti left by drunk teenagers—and I found myself wondering if we were looking at the same house.

That's one of the reasons I love her, though. She sees the good in most things. She's the type of woman who loses a wallet with a hundred dollars in cash and thinks *well, maybe someone less fortunate will find it.* I shouldn't be surprised that even after leaving our apartment in the greatest city on earth she could see the potential here at 1313 Mockingbird Lane.

I wish I could be like that: kind, positive, and forgiving. I try to find the best in things, the way she does, but damn, is it hard!

In the foyer, I came across a framed photograph of Great-Uncle Bendix and his biker pals. I'm not going to lie, the picture sent shivers down my spine. The arch of his eyebrows . . . his sharp nose and jawline . . .

"Holy shit, Jon," Mary said, finishing off my own thoughts. "He looks just like you!"

Under the old school tattoos, the greased-back hair, and the handlebar mustache there was indeed a striking resemblance. It was a bit unsettling.

On the wall, framed beside the photograph, was a biker vest, the kind with the three patches on the back. An embroidered image of an ebony stallion in mid-gallop adorned the middle, and the words "The Black Horsemen" framed the image.

"I'm surprised no kids stole his vest," Mary said, running her fingers through the heavy coat of dust on the glass.

"I think that gang is still active," I told her. "The local kids probably know better than to steal some biker legend's vest."

There is more house to explore, but Mary and I are exhausted from the drive. We looked around just long enough to find the master bedroom. Bendix's bed is still there, a massive piece of furniture framed in a canopy of torn and stained silk, but we decided to stick with our blow-up mattress for the time being. Fewer bugs and rat shit that way.

It's awfully cold in the house, especially given that it's the end of June, but I think these old places are insulated like that. They stay cold for most of the summer and warm for the beginning of winter. That's what someone told me anyway.

There is a fireplace in the bedroom. If the covers prove too little comfort for Mary, I'll drive into town tomorrow and pick up a bundle of wood. If nothing else, a fire and some wine will be romantic . . . well, maybe not the wine. I suppose that wouldn't be very good for the baby.

June 25, 1987

Sleep was not kind to me last night. Terrible nightmares—gruesome vignettes of miscarriage and death—kept me tossing and turning. I don't have the heart or desire to write about those dreams in this journal, other than to say that they left me unrested. I'll chalk them up to the stress of the move and the fast food from the rest stop.

Thankfully the nightmares are already beginning to fade in the light of day, and so is the creepiness of our new home. I've explored the first and second floors at length and it seems the bones of the place are solid. No rot. No termites. We'll need to rewire the whole place and do a lot of cosmetic work, but Mary was right about it having a lot of potential.

There's even a massive garage behind the house. The hill going down to it is quite steep and I can't imagine driving down there in the middle of the winter. Even walking down the path on a summer day I found myself afraid that I might break my neck.

I suppose this is where Great-Uncle Bendix and his biker buddies must have worked on their motorcycles and made their moonshine. It smells like gasoline and death, and I'm guessing there's the corpse of some tiny creature rotting in the walls. Otherwise, it seems as if I just need to scare away the spiders and raccoons and give it a good sweep.

Sadly, there were no vintage Harleys or Triumphs in the garage, but there were quite a few other treasures packed away in there: an old still covered in a dirty, canvas tarp; some gorgeous antique wrench sets; even Bendix's journal and ledgers. It seems he was the type of guy who liked to get his hands dirty, literally as well as figuratively, and he did most of his thinking around his bikes and booze.

I flipped through a few of the notebooks. The ledgers were mostly lists of income, dates of shipments, and records of debt. It's a safe bet that these are the ledgers for his various criminal enterprises, but the details are left ambiguous. There's nothing in there so damning as sections labeled "Protection Money" or "Loan Shark Interest."

His journal is surprisingly detailed and almost eloquent. I only gave it a cursory skimming, but he talks at length about the horrors he experienced in the first world war as well as his trouble adjusting to life back in the civilian world. I'll give it a better read when I have more time.

For now, I need to get into town and pick up some firewood and groceries. The house is still quite chilly inside and I don't want Mary or the baby getting sick. Can unborn babies catch colds from their mothers? Best not to take the chance.

June 28, 1987

Mary is snoring away. I spent some time watching her sleep, the firelight illuminating her soft skin and amber hair. God, she is beautiful. Sometimes I can hardly believe she's my wife—that she chose me over every other man in the world. It's crazy to think that we've made a person together—that our child is growing within her. I keep trying to imagine what he or she will look like. Will it have her hair and my eyes? Will it have her lips and my chin?

Will it have anything of me?

Of course it will. I need to clear those toxic thoughts from my head.

Let's change gears, shall we?

It's still cold in the house, even with the fireplace burning in our bedroom and the June warmth outside. I'm having trouble sleeping. I read a bit more of Bendix's journal in an attempt to court slumber, but it had quite the opposite effect. I couldn't stop reading.

I feel bad for my great-uncle after reading his most intimate thoughts. I wonder if my grandfather had any idea what kind of horrors his older brother had seen in the trenches of Europe, or how those years spent in the constant presence of suffering, fear, and death had affected him. Had he given any thought to how a man is expected to come back to the world of baseball games and interest rates and pretend it is anything other than a shabby layer of paint over the predatory nature of reality? That last bit was lifted from Bendix's journal. I'm a soft-bellied city boy and I can't take credit for such an insight on my own.

It's no wonder he went to a life of crime after returning stateside. I imagine some men just can't go back to an office or a forty-hour work week after years spent fighting for their lives while breathing in gunsmoke and death.

I skipped ahead a bit, past the war, and he doesn't go into much detail about the biker stuff. It does say that his gang was all ex-military—guys who, like him, couldn't pretend that everything was okay after coming home. Nothing is incriminating in there. I was kind of hoping for some wild stories about drunken brawls and gang wars, but it would seem he was too smart for that. Mostly it's details of road trips they made, hand-drawn maps to interesting places, and the occasional nude sketch of his sexual conquests. Great-Uncle Bendix evidently loved women as much as he did bikes and booze. I can't say I blame him.

Since the journal was keeping me awake instead of putting me to sleep, I decided to put it aside for the night and hope that doing some writing of my own might tire me out, and it did. Time to draw close to my wife and close my eyes. Lots more work to do tomorrow.

June 30, 1987

The nightmares keep coming. Last night was the worst so far, just one terrible fever dream bleeding into the next. Foxholes and corpses. Living shadows and maniac bikers. Grinning, stillborn monsters.

It's stress, I'm sure. The pressure of the move and the pregnancy, mixed with the Hammer Horror feel of this house—it's all getting to me.

And that's after I manage to fall asleep, which is no small task. What I'd give for the sweet lullaby of wailing sirens and rumbling subway cars. I wonder if there is a place in Maine where one might hire drug addict transvestites to gibber outside your window at night.

The new bed arrived this morning, so maybe a proper mattress will make it easier to fall asleep and rid me of my nightmares. I've demolished Great-Uncle Bendix's mite-riddled canopy bed and set the new one in its place.

It's incredibly comfortable, and Mary is in love with it. I was apprehensive about spending the money on it at first, but I'm glad we did. It would have been a pain in the ass to drag our old one from NYC to Maine. More importantly, if I'm being honest, I'd grown to hate it. I'd taken to sleeping on the couch in Manhattan because I couldn't touch the mattress without becoming nauseated at the thought of what had occurred there.

But that's in the past.

Speaking of the past, I dove back into Bendix's journal. It seems as if my great-uncle got something of a happy ending later in life, despite being ostracized. The past fifty pages have been about a young woman named Ashleigh who managed to steal the bastard's heart. She was quite a bit younger than him, which was normal for the time, and pretty damn hot from the sketches he drew of her.

Strangely, there are no photographs of her in the house—none that I've found, anyway. My grandfather and my father never mentioned her either. Granddad had cut ties with Bendix years before he met Ashleigh, so it's possible he didn't even know she existed.

The way Bendix talks about her—the softness of her skin, the timbre of her voice, the fullness of her lips—he seems absolutely in awe. I know the feeling. My love for Mary is the same. Perhaps Bendix and I are kindred spirits in that regard—a couple of hopeless romantics.

July 4, 1987

The oppressive silence of this place, broken only by the songs of insects, still creeps me out. The same with the deep, overwhelming darkness of the rural night. By the light of day, however, I'm beginning to like it here. The coffee maker doesn't offer the same pick-me-up as a morning jaunt to Caffe Reggio, but a mediocre cup of joe isn't a bad trade-off for a fresh start and smog-free air.

I opened up every window in the house today. I figured it might be good to let the house breathe. Maybe some of that warm summer air will make its way inside and curb the chill in the walls.

I left the garage door open, too. I can't go ripping the walls down to find the dead raccoon or whatever is stinking the place up, but maybe some sun and a fresh breeze will do it some good. Hopefully, nothing else finds its way in there. I hadn't even thought of something sauntering out of the forest and into the open garage. I'm not used to worrying about wild animals intruding on my domain. Nothing wilder than a rat at least.

Today Mary and I will take a ride into Lewiston, grab some lunch and see if we can catch a film. I'd love to stay in town to catch the 4th of July fireworks if Mary is up for it, though I'm a bit worried the noise might scare the baby. Is that an absurd thing to worry about? Perhaps.

Even if we don't stay for the fireworks it will be nice to have a day out. It's been a while since we've gone on anything close to a proper date, and I do like showing her off. As far as I'm concerned, she was the most beautiful woman in all New York. The yokels here in Maine will be absolutely drooling when they see her.

Sorry fellas, she's all mine.

July 5, 1987

I'll kill him. I swear to God I will kill put a knife through his heart if he shows up here. Harry Jackson. Harry goddamned two-faced Jackson.

We left New York because of that son of a bitch and he dares call my new home! And to tell Mary he loves her . . . to tell Mary he has a right to our child . . .

It's not his.

It can't be his.

It was only the one time, she swore.

God, it killed me when I found out. And then when she told me she was pregnant . . . I asked her if it was mine, and she said it was. I asked if she was sure—if it could be his. She said it didn't matter if the baby *could* be his because it *is* mine.

We cried and kissed and cried more. We fought and yelled and fucked. But in the end, I knew that the baby inside her had to belong to me. My wife was not carrying Harry Jackson's bastard child. Life just wasn't that cruel.

It turns out I'm not the only man in my line cuckolded as such. Great-Uncle Bendix's oh-so-perfect bride was prone to sleeping around as well. He talks about it at great length in his journal, and the pain held in those pages seems even greater than in his recollections of sleeping among dead comrades in foreign trenches. Her love had healed his troubled soul, but only so that her betrayal might shatter it completely. His words are those of a man utterly and completely devastated.

Reading through those entries, especially on the tail of my marital wounds reopening, was too much for me. I put the book down, and I don't know that I'll have the heart to go back to it. My own heartbreak is too much to bear. I don't think I can carry the burden of a dead man's sorrow as well.

Mary tried to calm me after the call. She took the phone off the hook and stroked my hair and reassured me that our child was actually our child . . . that it had to be mine.

I cried again, and so did she. We just wanted to put this behind us, but you can't cut off your own shadow, can you?

I held her in our new bed, unsullied by indiscretion and infidelity. Our baby kicked in her belly. I pressed my hand against her and tried to imagine its face. It didn't have my features, though. It had Mary's amber hair, and Harry Jackson's chestnut eyes . . . Mary's full, pouty lips and Harry's squared jaw.

July 6, 1987

We need to leave this place. I know why my grandfather never came here and why he told my father not to either. Any sympathy that journal made me feel for Bendix is no more. The man was a psychopath, and this place is alive with his evil. That's why no one ever wanted to buy this place. That's why it's always cold and why the shadows swell and shift.

I don't even know that I should commit all this to the page, it just seems too mad. Surely I'd be locked away if anyone found what I'm about to write. Still, I need to get it down for my sanity.

I awoke in our bedroom last night and, despite the well-stoked fireplace, my breath was visible in the air. Goosebumps ran up and down my bare arms. Tiny shadows danced around the room, in rhythm with the shifting flames.

In the distance I could hear something roaring in the night. It wasn't an animal but perhaps thunder, or the growl of a motorbike. Neither the noise nor the cold stirred Mary, however. She rested peacefully beneath the comforter.

Bendix's journal, which I had returned to the garage, sat open on an old bedside table that we'd kept. I found myself frightened to look upon the open pages, but I did.

Dear Jonathan,

It had my goddamn name! The entry was addressed to me!

I loved Ashleigh so much. I loved her with everything I had, but It wasn't my child that she carried. It was something inhuman—a bastard of hell—nay, not even hell. It was spawned from someplace darker and further removed from our understanding. And now It grows again, inside your wife.

My hands trembled and the text became an unreadable blur. My heart threatened to burst from my chest and the world began to spin.

"No," I said, over and over. I don't think there was anything else I could say. It was just too unreal.

I shook my head clear and forced my eyes to focus on the pages. I willed the ink to say something sane when I looked back at it, but it just got worse.

Go to my whiskey still in the garage. Open it and see the monster for yourself. See the truth of what grows inside your wife. See for yourself and you'll know that you must end her, just as I ended my beloved Ashleigh.

He killed her! This woman who was his everything. This beautiful creature who awed him so. He murdered her, and for what? A one-time mistake?

Angry and terrified I threw the journal into the fireplace. The flames devoured the old, dry paper, but Bendix's words were not gone. They still echoed in my mind.

It was madness, of course. His wife had not carried a monster but the seed of another man. Right?

I closed my eyes and tried to forget the whole thing. I held Mary close and placed my hand over her belly, but when the baby kicked all I could imagine was a monster with Harry goddamn Jackson's smile.

As insane as it was, I got dressed, grabbed a flashlight, and made my way out to the garage. Shadows shifted and danced along the treeline and around the fence of our property. I shined my flashlight back and forth, banishing the things I imagined waiting just beyond the glow of the beam. In the distance, I could hear the growl of motorcycles again. This time I was quite sure that's what they were, and I wondered if they were members of Bendix's old biker gang, called here by his ghost.

The garage door was still open, just as I'd left it days ago, but the smell of death and rot had not lessened. Panic gripped my heart as I began to doubt that the smell came from a rodent in the walls.

My flashlight flickered as I entered the garage. I shook it and cursed, and thank God it stayed on. The narrow beam led me past benches and toolboxes to the back of the garage. My heart felt like a hunk of lead as I removed the filthy canvas tarp from my great-uncle's still. A tarnished copper boiler sat beneath, connected to a pipe that coiled down into a wooden whiskey barrel.

The top to the boiler chamber had corroded and calcified, leaving a mottling of green and white over the tarnished copper. It was stuck on damn tight and I cut my fingertips forcing it, but it finally came off.

The smell that erupted from that thing—death, and rot, and putrid fermentation—hit me like a sucker punch to the gut. I coughed and gagged before covering my nose and mouth with my T-shirt. But the smell was nothing compared to what I found inside.

God, I can't believe it was real . . . I don't know that I can even write it down . . .

There, amongst the rotten mash of the still, was the deformed corpse of a stillborn child, so similar to what I'd seen in my nightmares. The poor thing, a little girl I think, had to have been sitting in that makeshift tomb for decades, but it was disturbingly well-preserved. Maybe the alcohol from the fermented wheat had pickled the corpse. Maybe it was something even darker than that.

I could see why Bendix could have thought it a demon. The child's head was misshapen, and it looked almost feral. The eyes, open and amazingly still intact, cast a yellow glow, like those of a cat in the dark, but its vertical pupils were blacker than the night sky. It was all in my head, I'm sure, but I could almost feel those eyes sucking the warmth and the life from me.

Regardless, it was still just a child, despite its ghastly appearance. Right?

God, Bendix, what did you do?

My stomach clenched and I retched until there was nothing left in my belly and then a bit more for good measure. When I looked up I saw something more disturbing than the moving shadows all around the house, or even the mummified baby in the still. My great-uncle's diary, the very same book I had just burned in our bedroom fireplace, sat blackened and smoldering on his workbench.

Reluctant as I was, I inched over to the book, casting my flashlight upon the open pages. One sentence was written there, in the familiar scrawl of my dead great-uncle.

The monster lives on in your wife.

I ran from the garage, clamoring up that steep earthen driveway and leaving Bendix's terrible secret in the dark. The sound of motorcycles drew nearer, though I saw no headlights in the distance. Were they outlaw bikers of today, riding blind through the nighttime woods, or was I hearing ghostly motorcycle gangsters—dead men who had once marauded alongside my dead ancestor?

Whatever is happening here, be it a genuine haunting or my mind coming unhinged by the desolation of this house and these woods, I don't intend to investigate it any deeper. Some mysteries are better left just that.

I need to pack a few things—just the basics. We can come back for anything else, or write it off as a loss. Tomorrow morning I'll wake Mary and take her away from this place. I'll go see the authorities and let them deal with the poor dead child in Bendix's garage. And when it's all taken care of I'll demolish this cursed house and bury the ghost of my great-uncle in its rubble.

July 7, 1987

I didn't bother going back to sleep. Even if I had managed to, it would have been a study in terror. No doubt I would have been greeted by dreams of dead children, ghostly bikers, and cheating wives.

Maybe I should have tried. Maybe if I had I wouldn't have heard the phone ring. Maybe I wouldn't have answered it.

But I did.

A chill ran through my body as I touched the handset. Even before I picked it up I could hear the static and feedback over the line—the interference that comes with a long-distance call from hell. I knew in my heart that it would be the gravelly, hollow voice of my dead great-uncle urging me to kill my wife. I was wrong, though; it wasn't Bendix on the line. It was much worse.

It was Harry Jackson on the other end and he was drunk . . . drunk and honest. He told me everything—all the secrets Mary had tried to hide. He told me how it all started between the two of them. All the nights they spent together while I worked late to pay for our Manhattan lifestyle. Their secret weekends and their whispered lover's lies.

Just the one time, eh, Mary?

Harry begged me to get a paternity test. He argued that we all owed it to ourselves to know the truth.

But I know the truth, right? Mary is carrying my baby, not his. It has to be my child.

Or maybe she isn't. Maybe it's not Harry's child either.

I never bothered packing our stuff to leave here, not even the basics. Instead, I went back to bed and held Mary tight. My hand rested on her stomach for sleepless hours as the thing inside her kicked. In my mind's eye I could see its deformed head and its alien features, so unlike my own. Those yellow cat's eyes burned in my imagination, the empty slits that bisected them blacker than any darkness I've ever known.

I don't think we'll leave after all. Not yet anyway. When Mary wakes I'll tell her that there are no more secrets in this family. Not for her, or myself, or even Great-Uncle Bendix. I'll take her to see the garage and show her what's inside the still. Maybe then . . . maybe we'll see what's inside her.

The Truth about Vampires

The purpose of these meetings is to determine if you are mentally fit to stand trial for the murder of Courtney Waugh. Do you understand?"

The suspect shifted his gaze rapidly from one part of Dr. Barnabas Vogel's office to another, his eyes never resting on any one detail for more than a second or two. In truth, the room was very plain, decorated only with diplomas, a free-standing coat rack holding a charcoal fedora and a matching overcoat, and a few personal keepsakes on the desk that took up its center. Despite the unremarkable nature of Dr. Vogel's office, the suspect seemed overwhelmed by it, as if he were a third-world farmer suddenly dropped off on the Vegas Strip.

"I, um, can you repeat the question?"

"Do you understand why you're here?"

"I, um, I like your suit. That whole look you have going on." His voice was weak and coarse, his tone almost hollow. "What do you call that?"

Dr. Vogel smoothed out the lapel of his tweed sportcoat, thinking to himself that his fashion sense might be called academic/jazz fusion. He kept this thought to himself, though. They weren't here to talk about him or his clothes.

"Please answer the question. Do you understand why you're here?" Dr. Vogel asked, this time more slowly.

"Because, um, because my lawyer says I'm crazy," the suspect said, looking down at his own fidgeting, shackled hands.

"We're here to judge if you are fit to stand trial, Mister . . ." The doctor let his sentence trail off, hoping the suspect would fill in the blank, but it didn't look as if that was going to happen. At least not without some nudging.

"Still not ready to give us a name, huh?"

"I don't have a name," the suspect said, looking at Dr. Vogel as if he were daft. "They took my name."

The suspect, who was identified in the paperwork only by his pre-trial number, reached out for the nameplate on the doctor's desk with his shackled hands and mimed a snatching motion. "Pluck," he said in a low deadpan. The syllable popped as he spoke, hitting Dr. Vogel with a burst of foul breath.

"I see," the psychiatrist said, taking down a note on the legal pad in front of him. "So you used to have a name, but someone stole it? Is that right?"

"That's, um, that's one way to think of it, but it's deeper than that, you know? If someone steals something from you, you still have it in the past, as if it was still yours at one point, but when they take something it's like you never had it to begin with. No memory. No lingering value from that thing having touched your life. You're just left with, um, like a hole in the shape of what they took. You're like the wastebasket scraps left over from a paper doll."

Dr. Vogel scribbled a note onto his legal pad, then looked back up to study the suspect. The poor bastard was emaciated, barely more than a skeleton. His cheeks were sunken, and black bags hung under his eyes. Vogel wondered how the guy had managed to murder anyone, considering how sickly and weak he looked.

Aside from the suspect's obviously poor health and his insanity, which Vogel had not yet concluded to be genuine or contrived, there was nothing remarkable about him. His ruddy brown eyes matched his short-cropped hair. He was clean-shaven and neither handsome nor ugly. No scars, tattoos, or other identifying marks marred his pale skin. He was a perfect everyman, gone wrong.

The suspect was squinting and wincing. A look of pain radiated throughout his face.

"Doc, can you, um, close the blinds?"

Dr. Vogel turned and drew the blinds, leaving them to talk in the dim, filtered daylight.

"So who did this to you? Who took your name?"

"Not just my name, doc. They took everything."

"Can you be a bit more specific?" Dr. Vogel asked.

The suspect leaned forward in his chair, fidgeted wildly with his fingers, and let out a hollow laugh that echoed with insane despair rather than humor. The sound made Dr. Barnabas Vogel's skin ripple with goosebumps.

"It's like I said. When they take something, it's like it was never there. So no, I can't tell you the details of what I, um, had in my life. Best I can do is kind of feel around the ragged edges of the void in my soul and guess at what's missing."

The suspect reached out and tapped the pewter edge of a picture frame that sat on Dr. Vogel's desk. From his position the suspect could not see the picture inside the frame, just the black cardboard backing and stand, framed by scrolling metallic edges.

"That a picture of your wife, doc? Maybe your kids too?"

"My wife and I." The doctor nodded and turned the photo around so the suspect could see the image within—he and his wife dancing at some jazz club in Chicago. He was always reluctant to give patients, especially criminal patients, any personal information. But pragmatism sometimes dictated that one must give something to get something.

"I think I had a family once. I don't remember them, though. No dates ring a bell in my mind as birthdays or anniversaries. There's no scent that reminds me of love or lust or brings longing to my heart. No faces for me to dream of and no spirits to mourn. But I can feel the agony of their absence, like the phantom pain they say amputees get."

Vogel tugged at his goatee and pondered this for a moment, his mind drifting to the neuroscience of such a thing, even though he knew the suspect's story to be a lie or a delusion. He imagined snippets of a person's consciousness suddenly missing, and the electrical signals in the brain hitting the brick wall of their absence. It was an interesting concept, and he was a man prone to contemplating such theoreticals.

"All right," Vogel said, having to stop himself from adding I can dig it. "And who did this to you? Was it the woman you killed? Courtney Waugh?"

"Courtney Waugh was no mere woman, and I can't say if she's the one who took everything from me," the suspect replied, his eyes studying Vogel's numerous diplomas on the wall. "She swore up and down that it wasn't, but it was someone like her anyway."

"Someone like her? What do you mean by that exactly?"

The suspect's gaze shifted over to Dr. Vogel, and their eyes locked. Once again, the nameless man looked at Vogel as if he were a dimwit rather than the holder of two doctorates. His expression seemed to say *Try and keep up, doc.*

"A vampire."

"A vampire?" the doctor asked, making sure that he heard correctly. "Like Count Dracula?"

"God, I wish it were something like that—a cut-and-dried monster, sated by something as simple as blood. The truth about vampires is far worse than all that."

Dr. Vogel jotted down a few more lines on his pad, hoping that this guy was the real deal and not some run-of-the-mill dirtbag looking for an insanity plea. If this nameless, unidentifiable murderer really turned out to believe he was hunting vampires, then treating him could make Vogel's career. There'd be book deals, news show interviews, maybe even a made-for-TV movie.

"And what is the truth about vampires?" Dr. Vogel asked, placing his pen down on his pad.

The suspect met Vogel's gaze, his distracted paranoia replaced with a disturbing intensity. "Are you sure you want to know that, Dr. Barnabas Vogel?" His finger tapped the doctor's nameplate, like the bouncing ball in a children's music video, as he spoke his name. "The truth has a price."

Vogel didn't like the way the suspect enunciated his name. It made him uneasy, but he did his best not to let it show.

"I do."

"Well, first off, like I said, they don't feed off blood. That's—best I can figure, that's a, um, a misunderstanding of symbolism mistranslated across time and cultures. What they really consume is anything of worth in a victim's life. Their health. Their loved ones. Their very identity. The things that really make up a life, you dig?"

The doctor wrote in his pad and urged the suspect to continue.

"And when they take those things from you, doc, it's like they were never yours. It's like the vampire always had them, instead of you. That woman you've been in love with for twenty years? She's been bedding the monster for two decades, and you've never met her. The idiosyncrasies of your speech that you picked up from your old man—turns of phrase that only you, and he, and maybe your granddad say—you've never heard or uttered them, but the vampire has. The years and years you've put into learning the piano never happened, and somewhere some evil thing is playing 'Satin Doll' while you stare dumbly at the ivories."

The suspect hunched over and pressed his palms against his forehead. Deep, wavering breaths escaped his lungs.

"It's okay," Dr. Vogel said. "Take your time."

It took a minute or so for the suspect to regain his composure. When he sat up, he was wiping tears from his haggard face. The flush brought to him from crying actually gave some life to his complexion. The doctor handed him a tissue, which he took with a mumbled thanks.

"For all the terrible power they have, though, vampires do have weaknesses. There are rules, as in the folklore and the movies, but different. They don't sleep in coffins, and you can't keep them at bay with a cross or a clove of garlic, but it's true that they can't hurt you unless you invite them in. Not like into your house, but into your mind and into your heart." The nameless man tapped his own forehead, then laid his hands over his chest. "But you don't care about the rules. You want to hear about the one I killed."

"That would be a good place to start," Vogel agreed.

The suspect blew his nose into the tissue that the doctor had given him to wipe his tears. He sniffled and shifted in his chair, trying to get comfortable. The shackles around his ankles rattled like the chains of a restless ghost.

"I guess it all started on my last birthday. I was standing on a folding chair, in the dingy, pay-by-the-week room I rented at the Bishop Hotel, which wasn't a hotel at all but a flophouse for addicts and losers. I'd just turned forty years old, and I had nothing at all to show for my life, you know? No skills. No passions. No one to love."

Tears were coming down his cheeks again as he told the story. He wiped them away with the snotty tissue balled up in one shackled hand.

"Air conditioners weren't allowed at the Bishop Hotel, since the manager didn't trust the screw-ups living there not to drop one out of a window and kill someone, so the room had a ceiling fan. That's what I used to string myself up from with a sad, makeshift noose I'd crafted from a piece of electrical cord. I fitted the budget slipknot around my neck and looked down at the roaches and rats that had come out of hiding to watch me die. That's when I had, um, what do they call it? A moment of clarity.

"As I looked down at the vermin around me and got ready to kick out the chair, I took a moment to reflect on my life and realized that I had no life. And I don't mean I'd fucked it up or threw it away. It wasn't as if I'd been orphaned or that my parents were dead or estranged. I simply never had parents, which of course is impossible. Same with friends and lovers. It wasn't that I'd driven them away with my shit lifestyle and lack of personality. They had never been there. Ever. Who goes through life never making a friend?

"And it went beyond relationships. I had no talents, no interests, and no passions. I couldn't recall a single happy memory, and the depressing history of my existence that I could remember was an incomplete thing. There were memories of loss, pain, and hardship, but they were unmoored by any context. There was no narrative to any of it, just hazy, painful vignettes.

"As I stood on that chair, with a noose of electrical wire wrapped around my throat, I realized that my life wasn't a failure, it was a vacuum. It was a gaping emptiness in every important respect, and it didn't make any sense. So I took the noose off of my neck and stepped down from the chair. I wasn't supposed to do that. I was supposed to hang myself.

"Here's another truth about vampires. Despair is how they kill their victims, the ones they don't turn. Despair so deep that you don't even try and remember what caused it. But I got lucky."

He reached up with both shackled hands and played with his goatee as his watery green eyes darted toward the ceiling. Fat teardrops ran past his trembling frown.

"I'm sorry," he muttered. "It's hard going down this road."

"You don't need to apologize to me," Dr. Vogel said.

The suspect gave the doctor a sad smile, then went back into his story.

"So I spent a lot of time after that just trying to make some sense of my existence or lack thereof. Walking cleared my head, so that's what I'd do all day, from dawn to dusk. For a while I was pretty sure I was insane, but the more I wandered around the city, the more I saw that I wasn't alone. The same emptiness that gripped my soul was prevalent all around. That kind of thing is invisible to your average Joe, most of us are so self-absorbed, but I had eyes to see. Maybe because I had no self to be absorbed in. Where others just saw junkies, or bums, or crazies, I saw that black void. I could tell what had happened to them.

"So I started watching these people, then talking to them. They were sad, interchangeable husks. Dead-eyed and hollow-voiced. None of them lasted more than a week after I'd spot them before sucking on a tailpipe or walking into traffic. Like I said, that's how the monsters kill. Vampires don't rip out your throat, they just point you to the gallows."

The man with no name reached up for his throat and wrung his fingers in strange patterns as if he were throwing up gang signs. Coarse, ugly sobs issued from his mouth, followed by a torrent of tears. His crying was unabashed and free of shame. It was the kind of therapeutic crying that Dr. Vogel wished he himself was capable of.

"Perhaps we should take a break and meet again tomorrow," Dr. Vogel suggested. The suspect nodded and mumbled a thank you.

Dr. Vogel sat at his desk, looking over his notes from yesterday's interview with the self-proclaimed vampire hunter and murderer of Courtney Waugh. The case still excited him, both as a clinician and as a man eager to cash in on a good story, but part of him dreaded seeing the patient again. Criminals didn't get under his skin. Over the course of his career he'd dealt with killers, rapists, and even child molesters. Some of the atrocities those animals had committed made the single torture and murder that this guy was accused of seem vanilla in comparison.

Despite all this, the doctor considered faking a stomach bug so he wouldn't have to look into the man's eyes. It wouldn't have been a complete lie. His head was pounding and he felt run down, but he'd definitely worked through worse.

What was it, he wondered, that bothered him so much about this guy that he'd consider going home sick to avoid his gaze? Emptiness, he supposed. When the suspect had described that vacuum in his spirit, he wasn't being melodramatic. There was something missing there—something conspicuous in its absence, and Vogel could make out the ragged outline of that void, just as it had been described.

There was a knock at his office door, even though it was open. The suspect stood in the threshold, shackled at the hands and feet, decked out in an orange jumpsuit, and escorted by a grim-faced corrections officer. There was some color to his face, and his features weren't quite as sunken. A good night's sleep seemed to have gone a long way for him. Seeing this change made Vogel feel a bit more at ease. He looked more human and less like a walking corpse.

"Good afternoon," the doctor said as his patient sat down and the corrections officer connected his leg shackles to the wooden chair. Once the suspect was secured Dr. Vogel dismissed the guard, who seemed happy to leave.

"Dr. Vogel," the suspect said, tapping on the doctor's nameplate as he spoke, just as he had done the day before.

"You look better today than yesterday," Dr. Vogel offered.

The suspect smiled. There was almost genuine happiness on his face, which was a huge difference from the last time they met.

"They let me talk to my wife last night. It was just a few minutes, but her voice—man, it's music. You know what I mean?"

Dr. Vogel offered a curt smile but didn't respond. The fact was he didn't know. He'd been something a romantic failure and had been alone for the better part of a decade. That wasn't something he was about to get into with a potentially insane murderer, though.

"Plus, she had some Duke Ellington playing in the background. You an Ellington fan, doc?"

Vogel was feeling angry with the man before him, and he wasn't sure why. Generally speaking, he was a man of patient temperament, but these simple, innocuous questions were getting under his skin. Perhaps, he considered, it was his headache making him grumpy.

"Yesterday you were going to tell me about Courtney Waugh and why you killed her. Do you think we can get back into that?"

"Yeah, um, that's why we're here, right?"

"Indeed." Dr. Vogel took hold of his pen in one hand, his pad in the other, then leaned back in his chair.

"So, I told you how I, um, I could spot people like me, poor bastards who'd had everything good cut out of their being by some evil creature. It's like I told you, most of them offed themselves within a week of popping up on my radar, but a few of them didn't. The ones who didn't take a bath with a toaster, they still walked around with that emptiness inside, but outwardly things started getting better for them. The darkness of the void in their souls was so intense I could physically see it radiating out, eating the light around them, but I guess I was the only one who noticed.

"One day you had a forgotten geriatric living under a bridge, the next they're a lawyer, or a rock star, or a trust fund playboy, and no one ever noticed the change. Except for me, that is. I could ferret them out, because that void from what had been taken from them had become a vacuous singularity that only I could see—a black hole that could never be filled. You see, the truth about vampires is, no matter how good they have it, they're never sated for long. There's nothing that can undo that original loss; no stolen thing quite the right shape to fill in that blank. So they feed and feed and feed, taking bits of anyone who will let them in, until they eat them all up."

"You said that once a vampire took something from a person, it's as if they never had it and the vampire always had," Dr. Vogel commented, tapping his pen against his pad. "But you could remember that this person who, let's say, is a rock star today was a vagrant yesterday?"

"Yes and no," the suspect answered. "It's, um, it's more feeling than memory, you know? Like the aftermath of a hazy dream or some cousin to déjà vu. But beyond that, I can see in them that same yawning blackness within my own heart but grown out of all proportion. And that's what I saw in Courtney Waugh."

"Tell me about that," Dr. Vogel urged. "How you met her. The course of events that led to her death."

"She was the, um, the common thread, you know? There was this old lady named Mary who I knew was a victim, just like me. I guess her name wasn't worth taking, so she got to keep it, but nothing else. Anyway, she lived under an overpass just outside of the city, and Courtney Waugh would drop her a dollar every day and spend a few minutes chatting with her.

"The same with some of the junkies outside of the methadone clinic. She'd come by with coffee and talk to the same two addicts every Thursday. Then there was the pigeon man at the park. Guy was a mute, just sat there making cooing sounds at the birds and feeding them scraps he'd dig out of the trash. Courtney would show up with a loaf of bread for him to share with the birds, and she'd just talk at him, even though he never said a word back."

"That doesn't sound like the work of a vampire to me," Dr. Vogel commented.

"Ah, but it is. You see, in the movies and the books they use their fangs to drain their victims, but the truth about vampires is they suck you dry by talking. Words are like magic to them. They tell you secrets and speak sorrows, and in exchange they take the good things from you. That's how it works, and that's what Courtney Waugh was doing.

"So I followed her. I watched her. She became the reason I got out of bed in the morning, and the reason I didn't open up my wrists. I know how that sounds—like I had some pervert obsession over her—but it wasn't like that. Courtney was the key to getting back some semblance of what had been taken from me. I knew I couldn't get my life back, but I could get a life back—someone else's.

"Finally, after months of stalking her, I broke into Courtney's home, and you wouldn't believe this place. Million-dollar artwork on every wall. A cellar full of fine wine. Hot tub on the roof. I can't imagine this all came from just one victim; it was like a hodge-podge of luxuries ripped from countless lives. She must have been doing this to people for a long time, you know? Maybe centuries."

Vogel was having a hard time focusing on the other man's words, and he found that his headache was being exacerbated by the sunlight streaming in from the window. He squinted and winced.

"Barnabas, can you, um, close the blinds?"

"Of course," Barnabas smiled, and for the first time his expression reflected genuine happiness. He turned and drew the blinds, leaving them to talk in the dim, filtered daylight.

"So, like I was saying, I broke into her house, and I waited, and for all the power vampires have, all those folklore stories about heightened senses and invulnerabilities are bullshit. She never saw me coming, and it didn't take a silver knife to cut her or a cross to burn her."

"Why, um, why did you want to hurt her?"

Barnabas sat back in his chair and fiddled with his cufflinks, casting a pitying look at the man across from him.

"Because I needed the truth, doc."

"Doc?"

"I needed the truth about vampires. The secrets of how they consume all the good things in someone's life and make them their own. The way they twist reality so it's like things have always been that way. And she told me, too. Each little phrase to utter, and what magic gestures to make with your hands.

"She taught me what truths to pass on in trade for those beautiful things in a person's life. Because there's a cost to the truth, you see? But I'd already paid it, so she had nothing to take from me. But you, you had a lot to lose. You dig?"

"Can you, um, can you repeat the question?"

Dr. Barnabas Vogel stroked his goatee and looked at the picture on his desk, a photo of him and his wife dancing at a jazz club in Chicago. He missed her, and he couldn't wait for the day to be over so that he might take her dancing, then make love through the night.

"I said, the purpose of these meetings is to determine if you are mentally fit to stand trial for the murder of Courtney Waugh. Do you understand?"

The nameless man shackled to the chair across from Dr. Barnabas Vogel's desk did not understand, though. He didn't know where he was or even who he was. He didn't know what was going on, and he didn't care. There was an emptiness in him, a black void whose ragged outline he could almost feel, and nothing else mattered but finding a way to end that pain.

She Hunts Dying Monsters

Autumn—she hunts dying monsters
And shades of dark legends long past.
She stalks dread fey, vampyr, and ghast,
Homunculi and werewolf curs.

Autumn—she grinds their bones to dust
And burns their skin and hair to ash.
With mortar and pestle she'll mash
Their dry remains with blood and lust.

Autumn travels giving tattoos.
Her grim tinctures serve as her ink.
From her needle magic does slink
Into poor souls she would misuse.

Autumn gives new life to old things
And births monsters in human flesh.
Two souls made one chimeric mesh;
A new generation of kings.

Autumn—she hunts dying monsters,
But through her art their life recurs.

Beneath the Emerald Sky

1

It's funny, the little things that stick with you—a phrase that brings to mind fond memories or a scent that triggers bygone trauma. The way a particular shade of green can cause your fingers to tremble and your eyes to grow wet with tears.

I vividly remember the smell of the woods where I spent the worst night of my life—the heady musk of forest compost and the crisp scent of cold air. It felt strange and alien. Before that drive to my grandparents' cottage, my idea of a "clean" smell was fabric softener or fresh-scent chemical sprays. I found the wholesomeness of the wilderness unnerving.

I was barely fifteen that December, and my few excursions outside of New York had been family vacations to other sprawling cities—Paris, Havana, Hong Kong. I'd been to Iceland once before. My grandparents usually came to the U.S. to see us, but we had visited them in Reykjavik when I was little. This was our first time traveling to them since, and the lonely country roads we drove down were a far cry from the bustling streets of the Icelandic capital.

After getting my first iPhone at the age of ten I don't think I ever looked up from a screen during a car ride, up until that day. The brownstones of Long Island and the skyscrapers of Manhattan were mundane to me, but these vast woods demanded my attention. Pale birch trees lined both sides of the road, their narrow trunks piercing through the ice-encrusted earth. The charcoal asphalt stretched on forever beneath the cloud-mottled sky.

Dad smirked at me in the rearview mirror of our rental car. He was happy to see my eyes diverted from my phone for once. Being the little shit I was, I shot my gaze back down to my screen and pretended to scroll through some mindless nonsense. In truth, I didn't even have a signal. After a few moments I looked up again. Dad's eyes were back on the road, so I went back to looking out the window.

Nikki snored in the seat beside me. I nudged her, not wanting her to miss out on the scenery, but she grumbled and pulled her hood over her face. She'd become increasingly lethargic over the past year. I'm not sure if it was the antidepressants, the hormone blockers, or the weight she'd gained since starting on both, but she couldn't keep her eyes open for even a short drive anymore, never mind the long expedition we were on.

"We're almost there," Dad said, turning off the two-lane highway onto a dirt road. "When I was a kid, my parents would take us out this way every Christmas. We'd stay at the old cottage through New Year's and go hiking around Hallormsstaðaskógur."

"It's certainly quaint," Mom replied, her signature cynicism bleeding through. "Personally, I'd prefer to spend the holidays someplace a bit more . . . cosmopolitan."

I looked at my father. The smile evaporated on his face as he nodded in slavish agreement with my mother.

"Too bad Amma hadn't been more accommodating about where she wanted to spend her last Christmas. Right, Mom? I mean, how selfish is that old bat?"

Dad grimaced and his hands tightened on the steering wheel, as he waited for the backlash from Mom. She whipped her head back and glared at me. I refused to look away, which only pissed her off further.

"You do not speak to me like that, Kimberly Eldon-Fischer."

I'd come to understand Mom's playbook over my lifetime. She was like a chess player who'd learned a single opening from one of those ——— *for Dummies* books and stuck with it for life. Intimidation was always her first move—white bitch to D4. She used it on co-workers, family members, and unfortunate waitstaff with an effectiveness I never understood, given her five-foot, hundred-pound frame.

"No, Dad and Nikki don't speak to you like that."

Her eyes widened and a red twinge radiated from her cheeks. I couldn't help but smirk.

"How dare you! Erik, are you just going to sit there and let her speak to me like this?"

"Kim . . ." Dad started, but Mom interrupted him straight away and went for her standard follow-up maneuver—the guilt trip.

"I only get six weeks off each year . . . six weeks out of fifty-two . . . and here I am, giving up my precious time, not to mention the chance to spend the holidays in London or Prague, so you kids and your father can see your grandparents, who, for the record, hate me."

Mom turned away and stared out the window, careful to make sure that I could see her in profile as a single crocodile tear rolled down her cheek.

"So excuse me, Kimberly, if I vent my frustration. I'm only a human being, just like you, so maybe consider treating me like one."

Dad ate up the act, as he always did. He reached out for Mom's hand and gave it a gentle squeeze. She choked back a well-practiced sob. I sighed and turned my attention back to the boundless sea of birch, aspen, and ash trees. I took special care to appreciate the beauty, as much as an act of rebellion against my mother as for the genuine value of the experience.

My father turned on the radio to drown out the uncomfortable silence. He'd made sure to get a rental car with satellite radio so he and Mom could listen to the news in English. They were both addicted to the twenty-four-hour news cycle, and the more tragedy, outrage, and indignation that got packed into the airwaves, the better.

The sadomasochism of news junkies always grossed me out—the way my parents and their friends would get excited about terrible events around the world. There would be a report about three kids shooting up a school in Massachusetts and my mother would light up with the chance to express her anger. A reporter would detail the last moments of an unarmed man at the hands of police, and my father would spark to life and pontificate about the failings of the system. They called it "being informed," but the pain and loss of others was like a drug for them.

While I found their relationship with the news morbid at the time, I think I get it now. Life was mostly easy for us. My parents liked to use the word "privileged" as a pejorative, but that's what we were. Dad always said we were "comfortable." I think the word "wealthy" left a sour taste in his mouth. Being comfortable meant you voted blue and drove a Tesla. Being wealthy meant you voted red and wore Armani.

Whatever label you wanted to throw on our financial status, we never wanted for anything. Our family faced very few hardships, aside from Nikki's health problems and depression, and when life is too easy you go looking for vicarious problems. I suppose it's part of our DNA to seek out struggle and conflict. Some people look for it in action flicks or horror novels. Others watch CNN or Fox News. Little did we know that tragedy, genuine and intimate, awaited us just down the road.

My grandparents' cottage was something from a fairy tale. The outside walls were made from wide boards, weathered and gray, set upon a fieldstone foundation. Grass clung to the steeply angled roof, like pale green shag carpeting.

A white goat poked its head out from a second building, a small barn that stood a ways behind and to the side of the main house. It was built into a mound of earth that gave the impression that the forest was slowly trying to reclaim the lumber and stone.

Amma and Afi—that's what we called our grandparents—had decorated for the holiday, but not in any way I'd ever seen. There were no multicolored lights on nearby trees and no garland around the window frames. The candles in the window burned with genuine flame, rather than artificial radiance. Straw goats stood on either side of the door, each decorated with strips of red ribbon.

Even the wreath on the door was different from what I was used to. Evergreen needles decorated the top half of the circle, while the lower arc was a tangle of exposed branches, twisted and woven together. There was a heft to it, and I don't mean just physically. It seemed to radiate something spiritual—an essence of the holiday—in a way that anemic New York City wreaths did not.

Two cars were parked in a clearing to the side of the cabin. One was an old VW from the '90s covered in faded bumper stickers—

undoubtedly Amma and Afi's car. The other one was a newer Toyota with a sticker from the same rental place we got our car from.

"Looks like your Aunt Siggi beat us here," Dad said, pulling in behind the Toyota.

"Siggi on time for something?" Mom asked. "That's a first."

Nikki was still curled up, sleeping with her head against the window. I shook her. She shrugged me off, but I persisted until she opened her eyes and sat up.

"Are we there yet?" she asked.

I snort-laughed in response. Nikki had become so quiet and withdrawn that I sometimes forgot her sense of humor and dry delivery.

"It wasn't that funny," Nikki smirked.

We got out of the car and unloaded the trunk, each of us carrying a bag or two. Mom and Dad shared a large suitcase, while Nikki and I each had smaller ones of our own. There was an extra bag filled with gifts for our extended family. Our presents for each other were back in New York. Mom and Dad hadn't wanted to pay to fly them to Iceland and back just so we could open them on Christmas day, so we planned on doing another mini-Christmas when we got back to the States.

Mom was the first to the door, already complaining about the cold and eager to get inside. She stopped for a moment, her lip pursed in horror and disgust. Dad looked back and forth between her and the door, trying to figure out what had evoked such a response.

"That's a white power symbol, Erik" she whispered, pointing toward the center of the wreath on the door. "I recognize it from the news."

The wreath framed an angular rune carved into the door. The symbol, a diamond set upon an inverted V, was painted a rusty red that stood out from the faded gray of the wood. I had never seen it before, but its very geometry stirred something in me—not hate or disgust but a sense of warmth and comfort.

"It's the Odal Rune," Dad said, placing his hand on my mother's shoulder. "It stands for home and hearth. The Nazis co-opted it and made it into something ugly."

"They stole the swastika too, but you wouldn't put one on your front door, would you?"

"My parents are kooky and eccentric, for sure. They're old-fashioned, in the oddest of ways, but they are certainly not Nazis, Rachel."

"Well, it's thoughtless at the very least. This has to be stressful for Nikki," Mom said, talking about my sister as if she weren't there. "That symbol is a reminder of all the bigots who think she shouldn't exist."

"I don't know, Ma," Nikki said, squeezing past Mom to run her fingers across the red, angular lines. "I think it's kind of neat-looking."

"You're right, Rachel, it's thoughtless," Dad said, caving into Mom, but following up with a plea in the most desperate and emasculated tone he could muster. "But please don't make a thing of it."

Mom gave him a dirty look but knocked on the door without further comment. A few moments passed with no answer. She shifted her weight impatiently, each breath ending in an exaggerated sigh.

The door opened, ringing a bell that sat above the inner frame. Afi greeted us, his broad shoulders and barrel chest taking up most of the doorway. He smiled, but his eyes were burdened with sorrow and age. He looked so much older than the last time I'd seen him. His face was weathered behind his white beard, and dark bags hung under his eyes. I'd always known him to have an impeccably shaved head, shiny and smooth, but a shag of thinning hair now sat upon his head. I found myself wondering if he was also sick, or if the stress of Amma's impending death had taken its toll on him.

"Come in! Come in!" he urged, greeting each of us as we entered. He took my mother's hand in both of his and thanked her for making the trip, then gripped my father by the forearm and pulled him in close for a one-armed hug.

"It's good to see you, Erik. Having one last Yule with all the family means so much to your mother."

"Of course, Dad."

Watching Dad and Afi together was always odd. They were alike in many ways. They shared the same deep, boisterous laugh and their faces bore sharp noses and cold gray eyes. The similarities made the differences starker, however. While both men were tall with large frames, Afi was hard and sturdy, his posture like that of a Viking Jarl. He looked as if he'd been carved from the same birch that grew in the woods around his home. Dad, on the other hand, spent most of his life behind a computer, and it showed in his pudgy belly, rounded back, and flabby arms.

"What's with the bell on the door?" I asked.

"It's for Amma," Afi whispered. "So I can hear if she tries to wander off."

Afi took me in his big bear arms and lifted me off the ground. I tried to suppress my laughter but couldn't, and Afi laughed back. I found comfort in his embrace—his strength, the warmth of his presence, and the mixed scent of turpentine and campfire smoke that always clung to him.

Afi placed me down and turned to Nikki. His expression hardened and he nodded at her. At the time I thought he looked cold or maybe even disgusted, but in hindsight, I think it was concern that I saw on his face.

"Nick, er, uh, Nikki."

"Hi, Afi," Nikki replied. Her expression was blank, as it often was, but I could read the anxiety in her eyes—the fear that Afi and Amma would turn their backs on her—the nervous knowledge that even if they did accept her, things wouldn't be different.

Afi hugged Nikki, but he was gentler and more reserved with her. Nikki hugged him back, burying her face in his flannel shirt. He patted her back and muttered something in Icelandic that earned an angry glance from my father.

I thought they might have words, or that Mom would jump in, demanding to know what had been said, but Aunt Siggi came in from the kitchen, announcing herself loudly and breaking the tension.

"Merry Christmas!" she shouted, wrapping her arms around my father. "Long time no see, baby brother."

Dad hugged her back and reminded her, as he always did, that she was his senior by only 16 minutes. Aunt Siggi retorted that her birthday was July 13, while his was the 14th, making her a day older, technically. It was the same back and forth as always. Siggi and my parents could never find much common ground, so this little game was how she and Dad bonded.

Aunt Siggi went on to hug us all. She always smelled like cigarettes and hair spray, but I didn't mind so much and neither did Nikki. Mom was a different story. Her body stiffened as Aunt Siggi embraced her. You would have thought a pee-drenched hobo was bearhugging her, by the look on her face.

Aunt Siggi acted oblivious to Mom's disgust, but I think she knew how Mom felt about her. I'm guessing she found a sort of humor in it, which is probably why she gave my mother the tightest, longest hug of all.

The sweet smell of pastries wafted into the front room, heralding Amma's presence in the kitchen. It was a distinct aroma associated solely with my grandmother, something that you wouldn't come across in any bakery in the boroughs. I dropped my bag in the corner and made my way into the kitchen.

"Is that Vienna Bread I smell?"

"Vínarbrauð," Amma replied, using the proper Icelandic term for the pastry. She sat at the kitchen table, across from my cousin Christian, sipping a cup of tea. Her silver hair was woven into elaborate braids and she wore a beautiful crimson dress, fringed with white lace that resembled snowflakes. A series of delicate black runes were embroidered down each sleeve.

I walked around the table, passing by Christian, who muttered a greeting with a mouthful of Vínarbrauð. I hadn't seen him in a few years, even though both of us lived in NYC, and he'd changed in that time. He was only a year older than me, but he looked almost like a grownup—tall with a patchy beard and arms that filled the sleeves of his shirt.

Amma struggled to stand as I approached. I told her to stay sitting, but she hushed me and rose from her seat. I'd remembered her eyes being a fierce, piercing blue set against fields of pure white. Now one was filmed over with cataract and the other was the same jaundice-yellow as her once-porcelain skin.

Dad had warned me her mind was slipping and she was prone to mean outbursts, but I wasn't prepared for how frail she looked. We hugged and I could feel tiny, constant tremors going through her body. Her breath came in labored gasps and I could tell she was in more pain than she wanted to let on.

"Merry Christmas, Amma."

"I'm so glad you all made it," Amma said, kissing me on the cheek. "All I wanted was for us all to be together again."

Amma and Afi's Christmas tree was decorated with ornaments of wood and glass. No strings of electric lights snaked through its boughs. No plastic tchotchkes sullied its branches.

We sat around the tree and exchanged gifts. None of us knew each other as well as we should have, so everything was pretty generic. Amma and Afi gave us all sweaters. Dad had picked up a bottle of wine in Reykjavik for them and Aunt Siggi. Christian was given Rangers tickets, and the rest of us got gift cards.

After the wrapping paper was picked up and all the thank-yous were said, Amma grabbed an old leatherbound book and urged us to sit by the fireplace. We were too old for story time, but if it made her happy, I figured I could sit there and pretend to listen.

"Like the wolf-mother, if what we love is taken from us, we shall not hesitate to take it back."

It was worse than story time, I thought to myself. She was reading us parables or prayers, or whatever neo-pagan hippies call their version of such things. Still, that was fine. I could ignore preaching just as well as I could ignore storybook legends.

Amma spoke the words in a trancelike state, her cataract eye looking through us rather than at us. Her voice was strong and she recited the ancient verse with passion. Afi smiled. Amma had been sick for a while, so I imagine it had been nice to hear some life in her voice, rather than exhaustion and consignment.

"Like the bride of the flame, we must let go of what we love, in order to keep it."

I'm not sure if those were her exact words. As I confessed, I wasn't paying much attention, but that's the version I found later on, long after the terrible events of that Christmas.

I stared at my phone, futzing with the settings and trying to find Wi-Fi to steal but feigned engagement whenever Amma took a pause. Christian sat beside me with one earbud in, his music loud enough for me to hear the monotonous bass and rhythmic whispers of someone rapping about *bitches and money*.

Looking back, I feel bad for ignoring Amma while she tried to share something she found important with us. Maybe things would have gone differently if we'd just sat and listened . . . if we had shown her more respect and consideration. But we didn't. At least Christian and I had an excuse. We were teenage assholes, at the age where adults were mostly bores and bothers.

Mom, Dad, and Aunt Siggi, though, knew how much these old traditions meant to their dying mother, and they ignored her as well, and more blatantly. Aunt Siggi dozed off in the corner while my parents held a conversation in whispers.

"And if I am to fail and fall, let me be like her with the heart of ash, and rise thrice from the flames."

Nikki, unlike the rest of us, was enraptured by the recitation. She'd always been interested in stuff like that—magic, myth, and fantasy. Mom must have noticed how enthralled Nikki was with the story, because I overheard her whisper to Dad, saying something about Amma filling our minds with nonsense. I looked up and saw Afi staring daggers at my parents, silently reprimanding them for their disrespect.

Amma stopped. I don't know if she'd heard what Mom said, if she suddenly realized that most of us weren't listening, or if a wave of dementia-fueled confusion had swelled up inside her. When I looked up from my phone she was staring at us, each in turn. Her lips trembled and her eyes were glassy with tears.

"Ásdís, are you okay?" Afi rose from his chair, knelt beside Amma, and took her hand.

"Ásdís, are you with me?"

Amma squeezed Afi's hand and continued shifting her gaze between the rest of us. We sat quiet and uncomfortable, save for Aunt Siggi who snored in her chair.

"Einar . . ."

"Yes . . . yes, it's me. And our whole family, just as you wanted, Ásdís."

"We failed."

"No. No, everyone is here."

"We failed them," she sobbed. "Our children—our grandchildren—our ancestors . . ."

Amma stood up. Afi tried to coax her to sit, but she swatted him away, a look of anger replacing the sadness on her face.

"I'm sorry," Amma said, running her hand through Christian's hair. "We should have raised your mother better . . . taught her to respect herself enough to wait for a decent man. You should have had a proper father."

"Yo, what the hell?" Christian exclaimed, waking Aunt Siggi. Amma did not get angry, she simply hushed him.

Afi took Amma by the shoulders and ushered her away. She stared into Nikki's eyes as they walked toward their bedroom and Amma broke into sobs. She pulled away from Afi and fell to her knees in front of my sister.

"I'm so sorry for what they're doing to you," Amma muttered, stroking Nikki's cheek. "It's all our fault. If we'd been better parents, maybe you'd have better parents."

Afi spoke gentle words that I could not understand and helped Amma to her feet. His eyes were red with the tears he was holding back. He led her to their bedroom, consoling her, unsuccessfully fighting to suppress the quiver in his own voice.

Christian shook with anger. Nikki cried beneath her hood. Dad let out a drawn-out sigh, while Mom fumed.

"What the hell just happened?" Aunt Siggi asked, breaking the silence.

"I'll tell you what happened," Afi's voice carried into the room seconds before he appeared. "You couldn't just listen to her. No, you had to be staring at your screens and listening to your headphones. You couldn't just be present for a dying woman's last holiday."

Afi was furious. I had never seen him like that. His warmth had turned to burning anger. His thick arms and barrel chest seemed like a threat, rather than a promise of safety.

"Dad, you can't expect teenagers to be interested in fairy tales," My father said. "They aren't little kids anymore."

"Also, Eric and I have heard all this stuff a thousand times," Aunt Siggi added.

"Well, you won't ever have to hear it ever again," Afi said, turning his back on us and storming out the front door. "You can count yourself lucky, I suppose."

2

The rest of the night was awkward. Mom and Dad made small talk with Aunt Siggi, but it turned into a passive-aggressive competition. Mom would make jabs at Christian for being on probation. Dad would tell Siggi that she could be around more for him if she started making her money work for her instead of the other way around. Aunt Siggi would counter with a question about Nikki's mental well-being or the side effects of her meds. All this was done with fake smiles and under the guise of offering helpful advice.

I tried to talk to Christian, but he mostly ignored us after learning that none of Nikki's meds would get him high. Nikki wasn't much company either. Maybe it was the shortage of daylight; maybe it was the drama with Amma and Afi. Either way, she stayed curled up in her hoodie, quiet and sad.

I decided to get some air. The northern lights shined in the sky—a gorgeous display of cool, shifting colors. It made the bright lights of Broadway and Times Square look sad and cheap in comparison.

Afi was outside as well, chopping firewood in the cold and the dark, sweating despite the frigid night air. I watched quietly from the doorway. He split each log with a single swing of his ax. The power of his strikes amazed me. In the snow and among the trees he reminded me of some buff, angry Santa Claus, taking out his aggression at the naughty list upon log after log.

Afi slammed the ax's edge into a tree stump and wiped the sweat from his brow. He let out a puff of air, then sat down on the edge of the stump. A quiet groan issued from his lips as he massaged his right shoulder with his left hand.

"Blowing off steam costs a bit more at my age," he muttered. "When I was a boy, I could chop wood for hours."

"Sorry," I said.

"Not your fault. It's the way of the world, my dear. Nature provides and nature takes away."

"No. I mean I'm sorry about the thing with Amma. I shouldn't have been on my phone. I should have paid attention to her."

Afi placed his hands on his knees and stood with a groan. He smiled and beckoned me with his hand. I walked toward him and he hugged me tightly.

"I'm not mad at you. You're a good girl, Kimberly. It's not your fault that you were brought up in a world of shallow distractions—a world of flash without substance."

I nodded, not knowing quite what to say to him. I was insulted, but I kind of thought he was right. Everything in my life came in quick, snack-size bites: 15-minute dinners, 30-second videos, one-sentence status updates.

"I understand that the world will always change and some people and some things will be left behind. I'm sure it is for the best in many cases, even if I'm too old to understand it." Afi gave me a gentle squeeze before releasing his hug. "But there is value in ancient stories and ancestral traditions, and you'll be a better person if you learn the patience to find that value. I promise you that."

We went to bed early that night. It seemed a waste to me, to come all that way just to go to bed before nine o'clock, but everyone was still upset about Afi blowing up, and we were all suffering from the flight. Better to get some rest and start over in the morning. That's what Dad told me at least, and that's what I intended to do.

The room that Nikki and I were staying in possessed a more profound darkness than any place I had ever been. I don't think I truly understood the concept of darkness before that day. The lights never went out in New York City and there was no halting its intrusion into even the most secluded corners. The color-shifting glow of traffic lights crept into apartments past the edges of blackout shades. The blue radiance of a million televisions, phones, and tablets permeated every bedroom. Streetlights pierced through grates and into subway tunnels. But here, in this little room, in this house deep in the woods, it seemed that the light was afraid to enter.

I rested in that deep blackness, taking in nature's soft nocturnal song. Without sight to distract me, I found myself focused on the sounds of nature, which were so alien to a city girl like myself. Branches creaked like the groans of storybook witches. Nocturnal rodents scurried outside the windows, or maybe inside the walls. Owls let out slow, rhythmic calls as they scouted the snow for signs of fur and flesh.

"Do you think they hate me?" Nikki asked, pulling me from the trancelike peace I found myself slipping into.

"What?"

"Amma and Afi . . . Christian and Aunt Siggi . . . do you think they hate me? Because, you know . . ."

"No!" I blurted out, fueled more by an instinct to protect her feelings than out of any sort of conviction. "Of course not, Nikki!"

"Afi keeps acting like I'm broken, and Amma—the look she gave me . . . it was like I was a ghost or something. Every time I lock eyes with either one of them it seems like they're in mourning."

"They're old, Nikki. There are just things they're not gonna get."

"Maybe. But Christian hates me for sure. He wouldn't talk to me except to try and score drugs. Even then it was like he didn't want to look at me."

"Christian's a wannabe alpha asshole. He probably thinks he'll catch your queerness."

Nikki laughed, which made me laugh. I reached out blindly and found her hand. We laid there for some time, our fingers intertwined, listening to the night.

At some point I fell asleep, only to be awakened by the sound of the bell over the front door. It rang sharply, but something muffled it quickly. I figured it was Christian going outside to sneak a cigarette or one of the grownups in need of some fresh air, so I closed my eyes again.

Sleep settled over me once more, but something startled me awake shortly after. It wasn't the door this time, nor any other sound. It was the opposite. The world had succumbed to a deathlike silence. No night birds hooted. No wind whistled. I couldn't even hear my own breath.

I whispered Nikki's name, but it seemed to vanish as quickly as it left my lips. I found myself wondering if I had spoken at all, or if it had been in my mind. There was a moment when I considered calling out to her again, but I decided not to. The fear that my voice would be swallowed by the consuming silence was too great. Instead, I closed my eyes and prayed for sleep.

The next time I woke up, it was to my grandfather's cries. His voice bellowed through the cottage, calling my grandmother's name. The creak of panic in his tone struck a chord of deep unease within me.

I shot out of bed, stumbled through the darkness, and opened the door to the hallway. Light from the living room filtered down the corridor, along with Afi's voice. Dad opened the door across the hall. He stood confused and concerned.

"Is everything all right?" my father called out to Afi.

Afi stepped into the hallway, his hair disheveled, dressed only in flannel pajama pants. His hands quivered and concern had robbed his already fair complexion of any color.

"The front door is wide open and your mother's gone."

Dad rushed to the front of the cottage and I followed. A frigid breeze blew through the open door and a snowdrift had built up in the entryway. Dad gripped the door frame and leaned outside, calling for Amma.

I pressed up against Dad and looked past him. My eyes fell upon the footprints that dotted the snow and my heart sank. The prints were made from a bare foot. Amma was wandering shoeless out in the cold and the dark. Who knew if she was wearing anything that might remotely protect her from frostbite or hypothermia? If she'd gone out there with no shoes it stood to reason she hadn't bothered with a jacket, hat, or gloves.

The sound of the bell on the door and its sudden muffled silence played in my mind, and I found myself awash with guilt. I'd heard her leave. That's why the bell was there, and I'd ignored it.

This is my fault. The thought looped in my mind.

"What's going on?" Nikki was standing behind me, along with Christian and Aunt Siggi. Mom followed in after them, rubbing sleep from her eyes.

"Amma," I gulped. "She wandered off."

Afi laced up his boots, still dressed in just his flannel pajama pants. Dad slid his feet into his shoes as well. I stepped outside, barefoot, unconcerned about the biting cold of the frost-glazed earth. My mother called after me, demanding that I get back in the cottage, but I ignored her and followed the footprints.

The trail turned toward the barn, and I broke into a run. The layer of ice encrusting the snow broke with each step and my feet stung. The chill of the night air penetrated my sweatpants and T-shirt, sucking the warmth from my body as sure as if I'd been naked.

"Amma!" I yelled, but my words fell dead as quickly as I said them. My voice didn't project or echo off the legion of trees. The words died out, the same way the bell above the front door had gone mute after a moment's ring.

My legs stiffened as I approached the barn. The double doors were open, framing an utterly black veil. It seemed even darker in that barn than it had been inside the room Nikki and I shared at the cottage. I told myself it was just because the light in the living room had wrecked my night vision, but still I shivered, afraid to move forward. The dense shadows within the earthen structure were almost tangible.

I cried out for Amma again, reluctant to cross the threshold. My voice cut short as if the night itself were snatching the sound from the air.

While it was too dark to see, and though sound seemed reluctant to travel, my sense of smell was unimpeded. A mixture of odors, wholesome and putrid, emanated from the barn. Blood and piss and campfire smoke. Death and rot and incense.

Swallowing my fear, I took a step forward. The black emptiness within the barn had weight and density. Pushing through that viscous darkness, I stepped into something that felt like wet sand. I recoiled, unnerved by the sensation.

A hand touched my shoulder and I flinched. Afi stood behind me, offering words of comfort. He shined a flashlight into the depths of the barn, but the shadows swallowed the light.

Afi nudged me aside and stepped across the threshold. He vanished for a few seconds, both he and the glow of the flashlight lost to the darkness, then both reappeared. He scraped his boot against the floor, where his light now revealed a curved white line, bisected by the toe of his shoe.

"What is that?" I said.

"Salt."

Afi brushed a bit of the salt away with his foot and headed deeper into the barn. It was still dark inside, but the shadows seemingly thinned. His flashlight penetrated the veil of black and I could make out the vague shapes of tools and animal pens. A smoldering hunk of wood or coal sat aglow in the center of the barn. It was the size of a fist and its orange radiance pulsed with a slow rhythm.

I followed Afi deeper into the barn, keeping tight to his back. I peered past his shoulder as he shined his flashlight on the ember, which I now saw sat upon a slab of stone inscribed with runes and splattered with gore. It was a charred thing in the shape of a blackened human heart pumping with magma.

"Is that . . . ?" I asked, unable to complete my question, but Afi understood. He licked the tip of his index finger and jabbed it at the heart. A smear of soot coated his fingertip.

"No. It's wooden." Afi answered. "But that's real."

He shined his light around the stone slab, revealing the blood-slicked bones and hastily discarded skin of a goat on the floor. I recoiled and grasped onto Afi's arm. He muttered something in Icelandic, but all I could make out was my grandmother's name.

3

The scene in the barn had left everyone shaken. Afi urged us all to stay in the cottage. He blabbered on, like some end-of-days preacher, about death, doom, and evil spirits. He went around the outside of the house, carving runes along the frames of the doors and windows, and painting those symbols red with a finger he'd knicked with his knife.

Dad and Aunt Siggi weren't content to wait around while Afi worked his old-world magic. Their mother was out there, probably freezing to death, and they weren't going to hide inside because of their father's superstitions. Afi fought with them for several minutes in Icelandic. Finally he let out a defeated sigh.

"Jesus Christ, Dad!" my father finally shouted in English. "We aren't going to find her by reading tea leaves or casting runes! This is the real world and she needs real help!"

Afi glared at my father and slammed the heel of his hand into the wall so hard that the whole room seemed to shake. Dad flinched and took a step back. The rest of us just watched, afraid to speak.

"You have no idea what's going on here, Erik."

Afi turned his attention away from my father and over to Nikki, Christian, and myself. "If your parents want to be stupid, fine, but don't you children think of leaving this house."

He left the room, but his anxiety lingered in the air. It was contagious and seeped into each of us. Mom restarted her phone, desperate for some connection to the outside world. Nikki sunk deeper into her hoodie and retreated to the corner. Christian hung out the window, a cigarette trembling between his lips.

I begged Dad and Aunt Siggi to let us go with them to look for Amma. Mom wasn't having it. She was right not to let us go. I see that now, but I didn't at the time.

Once my aunt and father left to look for Amma, Mom shifted her focus to Nikki. She sat in the corner beside her and put her arm over her shoulder. I could hear her saying and asking all the things that Nikki's therapist and a dozen online forums had told her she should say.

While Mom treated Nikki as if she were made of glass, I may as well have actually been. I was that see-through—not quite invisible but like a window that you look right through and almost forget it's there.

A twinge of jealousy formed in my gut, along with a sense of guilt over that envy. I loved my sister, and it wasn't her fault that Mom favored her, but I couldn't help the occasional sense of resentment from surfacing. Angry at my mother, envious of Nikki, and worried about Amma, I decided to sneak off and chase after Dad and Aunt Siggi.

"Christian," I whispered, "you wanna get out of her and help find Amma?"

"Naw, I'm good."

I couldn't believe how casually he declined to help.

"What do you mean, you're good?"

"It's freezing out there and everyone told us to stay put, so that's what I'm doing."

"Since when do you care about the rules? Amma's out in the cold. She needs us."

"Not to sound like a prick, Kim, but I'm not risking hypothermia for some old lady I barely know, blood or not. I mean, I can literally count the number of times I've met her."

An unintentional sound escaped my lips—a squeak of indignation that did not begin to express my disgust with my cousin. Christian didn't care what I thought. He went back to his cigarette and I snuck out into the night, unnoticed by mother.

I was dressed this time, bundled up in several layers, when I went into the frigid night looking for my grandmother. The cold gnawed at me nonetheless and the relentless wind brought tears to my eyes.

Dad and Aunt Siggi's footprints were easy to follow, but Amma's stopped at the barn. I wondered if they had noticed some sign that I hadn't or if they had just picked a random path. I suppose that's what I would have done, but maybe they knew something I didn't—some nearby patch of woods or a little pond that was close to Amma's heart.

The crust of ice on the snow hardened further the deeper I followed, and Dad and Aunt Siggi's tracks grew less and less pronounced. Eventually they stopped altogether. My shoes weren't even breaking through the ice now, and I moved through the forest without a trace. Looking back toward the cottage, I could see that I hadn't gone far, but I could barely make out the lighted windows through the snow-bent boughs of trees along the path. If I went much farther, I'd have risked getting lost.

"Dad!" I called out. "Aunt Siggi!"

No one answered. I yelled into the night once more, this time for Amma.

"Kimberly . . ."

It was like a whisper in my ear, or maybe in my mind. I'm not sure that I heard my name called as much as I had felt it, but I edged forward.

"Kimberly . . ."

"Amma! Stay there! I'm coming!"

I couldn't tell where the voice came from, but I found myself drawn from the path and into denser woods. Amma's voice called to me, echoing off every tree, creaking in harmony with the stressed ice beneath my heels. A feeling of vertigo overtook me, and I swear that the trees began to move and nudge me forward.

The landscape before me, so uniform in its winter palette of white with aurora-colored highlights, was violently interrupted by a splash of crimson. The frozen snow sucked up the blood, taking on the appearance of a cherry-flavored snow cone. Scraps of clothes, my father's clothes, littered the scene—blue strips of nylon cloth and goose feathers—shredded denim, stained deep red.

"Dad!" I called, my voice cracking with fear.

"Kimberly."

It was undoubtedly Amma's voice. I knew, this time, that it was not in my head. She spoke to me from the dark cover of birch and ash trees.

"Amma, I'm scared."

"Don't be frightened, girl."

Amma materialized from the night. She was cloaked in shade, but the white lace of her dress stood out in the darkness and her braids glittered like woven moonlight. She stepped forward, her crimson dress dragging against the snow, sucking the blood from the stained ice and leaving it white and pure in her wake. The runes embroidered on her dress were darker than the night, blacker than space—delicate lines of oblivion, stitched into the cloth.

"Where's my father?"

"I'm so sorry that he failed you children so." Amma reached her hand toward me. Her fingers were smooth and unwrinkled, as was her face. Her belly was swollen beneath her dress and her pale skin, no longer jaundice-yellow, took on the same emerald hue as the Northern Lights above. "I'm so sorry that I failed him."

"Wh-whe-where . . ." I stuttered.

"Where is your father? Don't you worry, Kimberly. He's safe, and you'll be safe as well."

Amma's voice was her own, but there was a hollowness to it. Her tone was deadpan—haunting even. She stood with her hand extended and the black runes on her dress began to bleed down her wrists, marking her porcelain flesh with angular slashes.

I turned and ran. I could see the lighted windows of the cottage. I hadn't wandered too far, and I was so close, but the trees crowded toward me. Branches slashed my clothes and roots grabbed at my feet. I stumbled and crashed into the icy ground, bruising my face and hurting my hands. Tree roots entangled my legs, keeping me from getting up.

The pale, narrow birches parted as Amma approached. She walked across the ice and the uneven earth with terrifying poise and unearthly grace.

"I'm afraid this is going to hurt a smidge."

Amma made deliberate, sophisticated gestures and black runes flowed from her fingertips, painting the air. The trees responded to her magic. Branches and roots constricted around my limbs like coiling serpents, and white bark turned red as it ripped my flesh.

Amma hushed my screams. She strode toward me, her expression like that of a patient mother trying to calm an overreacting child.

"You're a good girl, Kimberly, but this evil world has filled your mind with poison."

Something slithered out from under her dress, long and sinewy, pink and glistening. It stretched across the forest floor, melting winding trails in the snow as it sought my open wounds. My skin blistered at its acidic touch and my stomach lurched. I tried to beg for my life but found myself muted by terror and agony. If she understood my wordless pleas, she ignored them.

Amma looked down at me. I was convinced of my doom at that moment. Her cataract eye glowed and pulsed like a dying star, while the other was an obsidian pool. Death lingered behind her gaze. No, I think it was something deeper than death, something more profoundly terrible.

When she stumbled back and that pink worm retreated beneath the hem of her dress—when the roots and limbs released their grip on me and blood spurted from Amma's chest, I could only stare in disbelief.

"Get up, girl! Run!"

Only after hearing Afi's voice did I notice the ax protruding from Amma's chest. It hung there, lodged firmly between her breasts. Amma staggered and fell. I looked at her, lying still in the snow, and I yelled her name in grief, despite the horrors of only moments ago.

"That is not your Amma," Afi said, his voice coarse with anger and grief. "It's a shadow of her sickness—a sad cutout of her disappointment, her anger, and her fear."

Amma gasped. The trees trembled and the earth quivered. She struggled to her feet despite the ax stuck fast in her chest. It was impossible, and yet . . .

"This whole family has succumbed to shadow, Einar. I'm here to bring us out." Her words dripped with venom and creaked like the January wind. Her swollen belly rippled and pulsed as if something were trying to escape from inside. Gripping the ax handle, she pulled the blade from her chest and tossed the weapon aside.

"Run! Get in the house and stay there!" Fear and heartbreak were written across Afi's face.

I did as I was told and crawled away on my hands and knees, over rocks, ice, and tree roots. Finally I was able to rise to my feet and make a proper break for the cottage. Behind me I could hear my grandparents fighting: Afi, shouting angrily in a language I didn't know and the words falling dead from the air—Amma screeching in no language at all, but her voice echoing and resonating through the woods. I didn't look back.

The forest seemed so much denser now, and the night so much blacker. I followed the lights of the cottage, but it was hard to see. The wind whipped my hair across my face and tears welled in my eyes to further blind me, but somehow I made it back to the house. Throwing myself at the front door, I pounded and screamed for help.

Mom opened the door and I fell over the threshold. She took me in her arms and let off a barrage of questions, none of which I could answer. I simply shook and muttered a single word, over and over.

"Amma . . . Amma . . . Amma . . ."

Nikki and Christian rushed to my side. Mom shouted commands at them, but I don't remember what she said. Soon enough they came back with a first-aid kit. Nikki washed my wounds and Mom wrapped my shredded wrists and ankles with gauze.

Christian stood in the doorway, yelling into the night for Aunt Siggi. Amma's inhuman cries were still audible from the woods, but Afi had gone silent.

She got him, I thought. *She got him, and Dad, and Aunt Siggi.*

"Close the door!" I shouted at Christian. He turned and shot a look of annoyance my way, then went back to calling for his mother.

"Close the goddamn door!"

Nikki tried to calm me down. She told me to take deep breaths and tell her what had happened. Mom wasn't so patient or curious: she'd seen enough. Snatching up her keys, she turned to Nikki and told her to get me in the car.

"Where are we going?" Nikki asked. "What about Dad and Afi, and Aunt Siggi?"

"We'll send help, but right now we have to get away from whatever's going on here."

"But Ma . . ."

"I said get your sister in the car, Nicholas!"

There was a moment of tension where no one spoke. Nikki stood, lip trembling, tears in her eyes. Mom took a deep breath and tried to compose herself.

"Nikki, I'm sorry. I didn't mean to—"

"Didn't mean to what?" Christian interrupted. "Didn't mean to use is his real name? I can see his dick through his PJs, for Christ's sake. Dude ain't fooling anyone, so can we cut the woke bullshit for a second and focus on reality? Something out in those woods just seriously messed up your daughter. My mom, our grandparents, and your husband are still out there with it."

Mom's face was red with anger. She was protective of Nikki and had very little patience for behavior she saw as bigoted. More than any of that, however, people simply didn't talk to my mother in that way, and for all her social justice rhetoric she couldn't stand the idea of a person of "lower status" talking down to her.

"Christian's right," Nikki said, wiping her tears on her sleeve. "We don't have time for this right now. It's not important."

Mom grabbed Nikki's hand and locked eyes with her. "It is important, Nikki! You're important! Your identity is important!"

There was so much passion in my mother's voice. It made me love her for how much she loved Nikki, and it made me hate her because she never once looked at me that way—never once spoke about my importance.

Jealousy is petty, I know. Nikki was having a harder time of life than I was, probably harder than any of us could grasp, and she needed more attention and support. I feel guilty for my anger toward Mom and my foolish envy of my sister, but I was just a kid.

"Ma, it's fine. I'm fine," Nikki said. "You're right. Let's go find help."

Mom squeezed Nikki's hand, then walked past me, not so much as glancing at the strips of blood-soaked gauze around my limbs.

"I'm going to start the car. You three get ready."

"I'm not going anywhere without my mother," Christian said.

"Then stay here," Mom replied. "Frankly, Christian, I don't give a rat's ass."

I tried to tell her not to go outside. I wanted to beg her to stay in the cottage, but I couldn't. Maybe it was the trauma or maybe it was exhaustion, but the words wouldn't form.

Nikki put on her shoes and her jacket, then helped me to my feet. She whispered reassurances to me, telling me that my wounds probably looked worse than they were and that Mom was going to get us somewhere safe. Christian got dressed as well, cursing my mother under his breath.

I heard the rental car turn over and started toward the door. Nikki stopped me, telling me that we had to wait for the car to warm up. I argued that we didn't have time for that.

"What's out there, Kim?" she asked. "What happened to you?"

I couldn't answer. The only sound I could make was an ugly breed of sobbing. My knees gave out. Nikki sat on the floor and held me. She hushed me and told me that everything would be okay. I don't know how long we sat like that waiting for Mom to come back. Not much time could have passed, but my mind shut down from the pain and the stress and I fell asleep in my sister's arms.

4

I woke up to the door slamming and my mother screaming. "It's gone!" She was pacing and pulling at her hair, like some madwoman in a horror film.

"What's gone, Ma?" Nikki asked, her voice subdued, twinged with anxiety.

"It's gone! It's just—it's just not there."

"What's gone?" Christian lit up a cigarette before opening the window and poking his head out. "The cars? They're both out there. Yours is running." He said the last part with an incredulous tone.

"Not the damn cars!" Mom walked over to Christian, snatched the cigarette from his hand and took a long drag. I hadn't seen her smoke since I was a little kid, but she sucked in those burning carcinogens with relish.

"The road!" she said after blowing out a large puff of smoke, "The fucking road is gone!"

"What do you mean, the road is gone?" Christian asked.

Christian tried to calm my mother, though his approach was aggressive and condescending. He shouted at her to settle down and to stop acting hysterical. They yelled back and forth, Christian telling her that she must have gotten turned around and that roads don't just disappear and she insisting she knew what she saw.

Nikki helped me sit up, then headed toward the door. I whispered, begging her not to go. She hushed me and promised she'd be right back. Mom was so busy arguing with Christian that she didn't even notice Nikki leaving.

A new torrent of tears ran down my cheeks as I watched her touch the doorknob. My hands tensed into fists and I waited for that pink, slithering rope to reach into the cottage and grab my sister. I waited for tree branches to slice and impale her. I waited, but nothing happened. Nikki stood at the threshold, shining the flashlight of her phone into the night, then she took a step back and closed the door.

I breathed a sigh of relief, but my fear resurfaced when she turned. Nikki's complexion had always been pale, the consequence of a lifetime spent behind screens and books at the cost of sun and fresh air, but now it was absolutely pallid. Her mouth hung open and her lower lip quivered.

Mom and Christian stopped fighting and shifted their attention to Nikki.

"What is it?" I croaked, my voice hoarse from crying and screaming. "What's out there?"

"Trees." The word was barely a whisper and contained far more dread than it had any right to.

"Trees?" Christian asked. "Well, no shit."

"No," Nikki said, her voice soft and deadpan. "Just trees. No road. No paths. I can't even see the barn. It's like the forest moved in to surround us."

"She can command the trees," I muttered, looking at the stained bandages on my extremities. "She's here."

"Have all you bitches gone loco?" Christian blurted. "Who do you think is here?"

"Kimberly." Amma's voice floated by each of us, a whisper carried a preternatural distance. "Nikki."

"Amma?" Christian asked, pushing past Nikki and heading for the door. I rushed over to him and placed my hand on his shoulder. I pleaded with him not to open it. He shook free of my grasp, then turned the knob.

Our grandmother stood at the treeline, which was now much closer to the cottage than it had been earlier. The crisscrossing branches obscured her face, though I could see the tear in her dress where Afi's ax had struck. The wound in her chest looked like a black chasm.

"Chriss—tee—annn . . ." He recoiled at the sound of his name, the way she broke it into syllables and dragged them out one at a time.

"Is—is my mom with you?"

"She is. Let me take you to her." Amma extended her hand but did not move forward.

Christian backed away. He was an asshole and a thug, but growing up in Hunt's Point had left him with good instincts.

"Ásdís!" Mom shouted, coming toward the door. "Where's Erik?"

Amma ignored her and called out again to Christian.

Mom nudged past us and walked out the door. She shouted at Amma, demanding to know where my father was. A wave of panic washed over me and I found myself whispering *no* over and over, rather than reaching out to stop her. I wonder what would have happened if I had acted. It doesn't matter. The fact is, I didn't stop her. She crossed that threshold and strode toward Amma, asking rapid-fire questions without waiting for answers.

Where is my husband?

What happened to your chest?

Where the hell is the road?

Mom approached the woodline and Amma's hand shot forward, stopping just before my mother's lips. She pinched her fingers together and drew her hand back. My mother's breath was visible in the frigid air and Amma pulled at it like a thread, one hand over the other.

"Hush, Rachel." Amma's voice was like a storm wind. "You've done enough damage to my family. I won't suffer you any longer."

Mom gasped and clutched at her throat. Her eyes bulged and her face contorted into a hideous purple mask. She staggered and collapsed as Amma coaxed the last bit of air from her lungs.

I leaned against the doorframe and blubbered, paralyzed by cowardice and disbelief, as my mother died before me. I don't know what Nikki did at that moment, nor Christian for that matter. Maybe they screamed or cried. Everything on my periphery ceased to exist. There was only the grim visage of my mother's still form. I stood, fixated on her, looking for the rhythmic rise and fall of her chest. There was none. In my mind and all at once, I prayed and cursed, willed and begged for any sign of life.

"You can save her if you like." Mother's final breath spiraled around Amma's fingers like a serpentine phantom. "You can return the air to her lungs. Just come and take it."

I wanted to save her. I wanted to rush out into the night and pry my mother's life from Amma's grasp, but I didn't. No, I slumped to the floor and wept. Amma flicked her wrist and Mom's breath dissolved into the night.

"I agree, she wasn't worth it."

Christian had pulled me away from the door and slammed it shut. It was locked now, but Amma lurked outside. She scratched at the doorframe while tree branches clawed at the windows. She called our names making promises and threats.

I'll bring you to your parents, my loves.

I can make our family whole again.

Come out or I'll knock this house down on your ungrateful heads.

The three of us sat in silence for a long while. What was there to say? Nothing made sense, so we waited. For what? For someone to come and save the day, I suppose—for an adult to swoop in and fix everything. In my heart I believed that someone would come. I'd seen Mom die, but Dad was still out there, and maybe Afi and Aunt Siggi were too. That's how these things always worked in the movies. If someone didn't die onscreen, then they'd be back. I guess I was still young enough to believe that real life was the same—a sensible narrative where the good guys prevailed.

"Why doesn't she just come in and get us?" I asked.

"Maybe she forgot her keys," Nikki said, her delivery dry as always.

Christian didn't get the joke, or maybe he wasn't in the mood for gallows humor. He just glared at her as if she were an idiot, but I let out a laugh that morphed into a sob.

"For real, yo. I watched her rip out your mother's soul, like some video game wizard bitch. She can't just magic her way inside or bust through a window?"

"The runes," Nikki said. Christian and I stared at her, neither of us understanding what she was talking about.

"Afi carved runes into the frames of the doors and windows. I think they're holding her back, like a cross with a vampire."

"So you think our grandmother is like a Dracula or something?" Christian asked.

"That's not our grandmother, Afi told me so, and she's sure as hell not human," I said.

Christian went to the kitchen and came back with a can of cooking spray and a lighter. "Vampire or ghost or crazy, senile bitch, I'm betting that fire will do the job." He flicked the lighter and sprayed the can into the flame, creating a stream of fire.

"Slow down there, Simon Belmont," Nikki said, grabbing my hand and pointing to the blood-stained bandages on my wrists. "Do you see my sister's wrists? Did you see what she did to my mother?"

"I think I'm a little tougher than two rich girls from Long Island, and I'm definitely tougher than a rich—whatever the hell you are."

"Christian, you absolute prick, listen to me! The trees are alive, as if we're in the Lord of the frigging Rings or something, and they listen to her! She just waved her hand and they tried to rip me apart. And that's only part of it. She has some kind of slimy pet monster with skin like acid. We can't fight her."

"There was this Haitian kid in juvie. He was a thief and a schemer, but people let him get away with all sorts of stuff because he was always threatening to cast voodoo curses and hexes and crap. I don't know if he was legit or not, but none of that helped him when I ground his face into concrete for stealing my cigarettes."

"Amma, or whatever the hell that thing is, is not some punk-ass kid. Afi put an ax in her chest and she's out there talking shit and clawing at the door. You think you can just whoop her ass with a ghetto flamethrower?"

"Amma killed your mother. She probably killed my mom, your dad, and Afi too. So no, I don't think I'm gonna whoop her ass. I'm gonna burn her like the witch she is."

Christian threw open the front door. Amma stood mere paces away. The trees had drawn closer again, but their jagged branches ignored Christian, opting to claw at the runes on the door frame. Orange embers burned at the tips of those probing tree limbs, the cottage's protective seals having left them scorched.

Christian eyed Amma, sizing her up. His breaths came in quick huffs as he shifted his weight from one foot to the other. He shook the spray can and flicked the lighter.

"Don't," I said.

"Do," Amma commanded. Her dress rippled around her swollen belly. A hollow whistle issued from the black wound in her chest. The eerie colors of the aurora sky burned beneath her cataract eye.

Christian swallowed hard; his posture stiffened. For a moment he stood frozen, then he slammed the door. He cursed himself as a coward and tossed his makeshift weapon across the room.

We decided to try and outwait Amma. It was Nikki's idea, and neither Christian nor I could think of anything better. We didn't know what she'd become—a witch or a monster or both—but maybe she'd burst into flames when the sun came up, or at least run away from the rising dawn. It seemed to make about as much sense as anything had that night.

We feared that she would find her way inside before daybreak, of course, and she threatened as much. The nights were long during the Icelandic winter, and this one seemed eternal.

"You think your Afi's runes will hold?" Amma asked. "Magic is not the province of men, and even Odin's skill paled next to that of the daughters of Utgard."

Nikki was curled up under a blanket, reading through Amma's book of myths and pagan practices. She was sure that some clue of what was happening was held in those pages. Christian scoffed at her, insisting that the only answers to be found would be in violence.

I was too tired to mediate their fight. I lay on the couch, my eyes and nose raw from crying. I shifted in and out of consciousness, bouncing between terrible dreams of Amma's inhuman gaze and the waking terror of her presence just outside.

Time crawled. Nightmares felt like hours, but each time I awoke, only minutes had passed. I tried to keep my eyes open, afraid that the next time I dozed off I might never wake. At the same time, never had I been so profoundly tired. I yearned to close my eyes and wake up on the other side of sunlight and sanity—to wake up to my parents, Aunt Siggi, Afi, and Amma . . . my real Amma.

My eyes sagged and my head lolled. When I looked back up, the cottage had given way to forest—an endless maze of trees, each decorated with chimes made from tiny bones. I stood in a clearing and my father waited at the edge of a dense patch of woods. He motioned to me, nodding his head toward the trees. He called my name, but his voice was the creak of an old woman.

Dad stepped into the forest, pushing aside one of the macabre windchimes, and vanished among the white trunks and snow-covered evergreens. The hanging bones knocked against one another, but the sound was wrong. They didn't make a clink or tink, as I'd expected, but rather rang out like a bell. The sound was snuffed out, mid-ring. There was something familiar about it—something like . . .

. . . the bell on the door. I sat up with a start, fully awake in my panic. The door was open and Nikki stood outside, naked and trembling. She held her arms out to her sides and raised her head to the shifting, emerald sky.

Tree roots erupted from the frozen earth, coiling around her ankles and climbing her calves like ivy on a pillar. Gnarled wooden fingers reached down to her from the forest canopy.

Amma stood just beyond her, once again drawing black runes upon thin air.

"Nikki!" I cried.

She looked back, her face wet with tears but a smile on her lips. It was the first time in years I had seen her smile so sincerely.

"It's okay. I want this." Her voice rang true and clear. I have no doubt that was Amma's doing. She allowed me to hear Nikki's words—she gave them wings and carried them to my ears.

I darted across the room, but the trees were quicker than I. Branches slammed the door closed and held it firm. I threw my body into it, trying with all my might to break through and save my sister, but I was too small and too weak.

Christian stirred in Afi's recliner and cast a groggy look my way. He wiped the drool from the corner of his mouth with one sleeve and rubbed his eyes with the other hand.

"She has Nikki . . ." I said.

Christian grabbed his aerosol can and pulled the lighter from his pocket. He strode toward the door. I stepped out of the way and he kicked out with his size 12 Timberland. The door shook in its frame. He kicked it again. It gave way and swung open to reveal Nikki hefted in the air by sundry branches, her head tipped back in silent agony as a pink and ropy monster burned acid trails along her flesh.

Christian's expression darkened. He raised his makeshift flamethrower, and his eyes narrowed into a severe gaze. At that moment he reminded me so much of Afi—strong, dangerous, and bullheaded. Problematic and narrow-minded but fearless and driven by love, even if he would never admit it.

Like some B-movie hero, he ran out into the night, bounding over churning roots and shrugging off the slashing tree limbs. Amma raised her hand and began to say something—perhaps an incantation to stop him in his tracks, or maybe an idle threat. Either way, it didn't matter. Christian lunged forward and blasted her with his torch.

Amma fell to her knees, screeching, but Christian didn't let up. He kept the flame on her until she stopped moving and screaming. The trees retreated and dropped Nikki to the ground. Christian turned his back on Amma, dropped the spray can, and scooped Nikki into his arms. He ran with her, past the gauntlet of writhing birches, and into the cottage.

Christian was surprisingly gentle as he placed Nikki on the couch, considering how cruel he'd been to her with his words. Her arms and legs bore deep cuts and abrasions and her skin was striped with pink burns.

She sobbed, digging her nails into her palm. Christian clasped her hand in both of his and brought his face close to hers.

"We're gonna get through this, Nick. I promise."

He let go of her hand and began ripping a slipcover into strips of bandage, since we were out of gauze. I sat next to her and brushed her matted hair away from her face.

"He's right, Nikki. Everything's gonna be okay." The words tasted like a lie.

"No!" Nikki shouted. "Things will never be okay!"

"We're safe. Amma's dead now."

Nikki sobbed so hard that I feared she was having a seizure. She slammed her fists against her head and bit her lip until it bled.

"Nikki, calm down."

"No! You fucked it up! Amma was going to fix me! She promised!" Nikki screeched, pointing to her groin in disgust. "She was going to remake me, unbroken—the way I was supposed to be!"

"Nikki, you don't need fixing."

"Oh, screw you, Kim! You don't know what it's like. All I am to you is an Instagram prop—a way for you to be queer by proxy without all the inconvenience. Same thing with Mom and Dad. I'm just proof of how goddamn progressive they are—but this isn't fun or cool for me! I hate my voice. I hate my body. I look in the mirror and my skin crawls."

"Nikki, I'm—I'm sorry that you . . ."

"Don't Nikki me! Amma was going to fix everything! She was going to make me whole." She turned to Christian, eyes red with rage. "And you killed her!"

She pushed me aside and ran into the bathroom, locking herself in. I put my ear to the door and could hear her ugly sobs. I tugged on the knob and asked to open the door. Nikki had a history of self-harm, and I feared that in her current state she might do something terrible.

"Fuuucck," Christian interrupted. The word came out as a slow exhalation. I turned to find him staring out through the broken door, his shoulders fallen and his arms limp, as if all the fight had drained out of him.

Tree limbs reached down and helped Amma to her feet. Veins of orange heat crisscrossed her charred skin, and the glow of the Icelandic night stained what was left of her silver hair with jade highlights.

Fire danced across her dress, rapidly turning the fabric to ash. Amma ripped the scraps of the dress away and tossed them into the snow. Despite her newfound youth, Amma's naked form was horrific beyond anything I'd ever imagined.

Hands and faces moved across her distended belly—captive souls pressing against her from the inside, yearning for release. Worse still, I recognized the faces. I tried to tell myself that it wasn't my family crying out from within Amma's belly—not my father and not my aunt—but there was no denying it.

"Why do you fight?" Amma asked, her blackened skin healing and growing paler with each step forward. A knotted tendril, wet with mucous, hung from her vagina, like a serpent creeping out from a cave.

"This is all for us—a second chance for this family—an opportunity to undo all the mistakes I made with your parents and all the injustices they inflicted on the three of you."

"And what about Afi?" I screamed.

"Afi didn't love you enough to do what must be done."

An orange glow was creeping up between the trees, separated from the shining aurora by a veil of black. Amma glanced back at that first hint of sunrise, then toward us again. Her monstrous eyes were unreadable, but something in her face betrayed a sense of anxiety.

"Please, children, I promise this is for the best." That wormlike thing between her legs—that grotesque vaginal tongue—slithered across the snow and toward the cottage, but stopped at the runic wards around the doorway.

"Holy crap, Nick was right," Christian said. "She's afraid of the sun and she can't get past whatever this stuff is that Afi carved around the door. We just need to wait her out."

"You think you can wait me out, boy? Your generation has no patience. You come from an age without will."

"Bull! I saw how you looked at that sunrise." For the first time that night I felt a ray of hope. "You're running out of time and you're scared shitless."

Amma threw her head back and wailed. The aurora cracked in the sky. Spiderwebs of unlight stretched across the color-shifting sky. The whole cottage shook as if it were being ripped from its foundation and into the gravity of Amma's rage. Trees uprooted themselves from the ground and battered the outside walls. Windows shattered and wooden floorboards splintered beneath us.

The doorframe gave way to trees that hit it like a battering ram. The entryway collapsed, but pale birch limbs reached in and held it open. With the wards Afi had inscribed now destroyed, Amma crossed the threshold and entered the cottage.

Christian ran at her, fists raised. She nodded her head and tree roots burst through the floor, entangling his feet. Carried by his momentum, he fell forward and smashed his face.

Amma turned toward me. I backpedaled, imploring her to leave us alone. She reached out and grabbed my breath, just as she had with my mother, and began to pull it from my lungs. I gasped and choked. She hushed me and the monstrous tongue that hung between her legs sought out my flesh. Its touch was like fire. I wanted to scream, but I had no breath with which to do so.

"Me first." Nikki stepped out of the bathroom, razor-blade slits up and down her arms. She walked past me and locked eyes with Amma. "Please," she said, nodding in the direction of the door outside, toward the rising sun. "In case we run out of time."

Amma released her grasp on my breath and retracted her slimy, serpentine appendage. I tried to argue—to tell Nikki to run—to demand that Amma leave my sister alone—but I had no words, only pain.

A smile crossed Amma's face, and it was as hollow as the black hole wound in her chest. Nikki's skin sizzled and smoked as Amma's acidic tendril wrapped itself around her neck and forced her to the ground. Amma's vagina opened to an unnatural width, like the maw of some alien beast. Bile rose in my throat at the sight.

She drew Nikki toward her, eager to take her into her womb—to nurture her in some grotesque chrysalis and rebirth her. Christian fought to get up and stop her, but the roots had spread across his entire body, holding him in place.

"I'm sorry," Nikki said, then sliced through Amma's tendril with a razor she had hidden in her palm.

Amma stumbled back. Nikki pounced on her and drew the razor across her throat. Black ooze poured from the wound, like boiling tar. Nikki charged her, driving her shoulder into Amma's obscenely pregnant belly, and pushed her out into the coming day.

The first rays of sunlight pierced the treeline and fell upon Amma's naked back. She twitched and convulsed. The stump of her vaginal appendage writhed between her legs. Swirls of the fading emerald aurora and the golden glow of dawn on the horizon were siphoned into the endless void of Amma's black-hole eye, into the chasm of her chest, and the dripping emptiness of her slashed throat.

My father and Aunt Siggi, or what was left of them, screamed in silent agony, pushing their faces against Amma's pregnant belly, trying to break free from the impossible womb-world she had condemned them to. Amma clawed at the ground, let out a final gurgle, then went still. Her stomach fell flat, like a deflated balloon and dark sludge poured from between her legs.

I watched her belly, looking for my father and my aunt—waiting for them to burst out of her, like the climax of some surrealist horror film, but I knew they were gone—miscarried in Amma's final moments.

5

We spent days answering the questions of the Icelandic authorities. I was so tired, nearly catatonic, but I understand why they grilled us. There were dead bodies and missing persons, trust funds, and life insurance policies.

I can't imagine anything we said made sense. Christian and I formulated a paper-thin lie. I don't remember exactly what BS we came up with—something about a home invasion, I think. Nikki told them exactly what happened, however—every impossible detail. I'm surprised they didn't lock her up in the nuthouse right then. They probably would have if we'd been back in the States.

They didn't hold us for too long, all things considered, probably because Nikki and I were wealthy and American, and our family was well connected. The inquiries didn't end in Iceland, of course. Everyone from the attorney general to the insurance investigator to the *New York Times* tried to pry the truth from us. There was no rational way to explain any of it, however, and we were all kids, so with a little bit of palm-greasing and political navigation from Mom's side of the family, the whole misadventure got swept under the rug.

I probably had the easiest time of readjusting, once things settled down. Bubby, our other grandmother, took Nikki and me in. She and I got along fine. I withdrew into my studies and into myself, so I was easy. Nikki was another story.

The trauma of that Christmas changed us, but Nikki most of all. She couldn't forgive us for saving her from Amma—couldn't forgive herself for saving us at Amma's expense—and she took it out on everyone. She and Bubby constantly butted heads. By the following summer, Nikki had run away.

I didn't see her again until my third year of college, when we were old enough to claim our shares of the trust Mom and Dad had left. She was dating a thirty-year-old "filmmaker" named André who had paid for her top surgery. She never took off her sunglasses, but I could see the purple and yellow edges of her black eye.

Nikki never got her bottom surgery. Andre nearly beat her to death when she tried. He claimed the money wasn't hers to spend—that she owed it to him as repayment. They both died in a house fire the next Christmas. Firefighters discovered two melted gas cans beside their bed.

Christian ended up tracking down his dad. Aunt Siggi had always told him that she didn't know where his father had run off to. It turned out he'd only made it as far as Hoboken. He let Christian move in, but they never really formed a relationship beyond sharing the occasional joint or six-pack. Once he was eighteen Christian moved out and tried to make it as a mixed martial artist. It didn't pan out, so he did odd jobs for small-time mobsters. I don't know if he saw something he shouldn't have, or if he slept with the wrong mafioso girlfriend, but his body turned up in the Hudson a week before his twenty-third birthday.

I was haunted by nightmares after Nikki's death, and they only got worse when I heard about Christian. Amma would come to me in my dreams and utter accusations in a voice like the creaking of trees in the wind.

This is your fault, Kimberly. I could have saved this family.

As my nightmares grew in intensity and as they came more often, I decided that I needed to face the truth of the past. I needed to understand what had happened.

I spent years studying Northern legends. I read countless books on witchcraft and folklore. I learned Icelandic and became an expert on runes, all in hopes of making some sense of that one night.

Afi was right about that witch in the woods—it wasn't Amma but a shadow of her resentments. In her concern for our family, she sacrificed her mind and her soul to channel a sliver of the dark and primal mother—the bride of flame—the thrice-burned—dread Angrboða.

It's been thirty years since that Christmas in Iceland. I'm a mother now and my children are nearly the same age as I was then. My husband died when they were young, and I fear that I've screwed everything up since. Some women are matriarchal rock stars who can work and date and raise children on their own. Even with the cushion of my trust fund, I wasn't up to the task.

My daughter, Nicole, has already been to rehab twice—once for alcohol, when she was thirteen, and once for pills, just a few months ago. Paul, my boy, is a nervous wreck—debilitatingly introverted and terrified of the world. I can't imagine any future for him that includes love, adventure, or success. I know that's not what a mother is supposed to say, but it's true. The future isn't going to be kind to my children, and I can't leave them to such a fate.

In all the years since that Christmas, I haven't celebrated the holidays. Every string of tinsel and cheap, gaudy light fills me with dread, and forget the idea of bringing a tree in the house. Maybe it's time to embrace tradition, however.

As I said, I fear that I've done a terrible job with my kids, and I'm beginning to understand Amma's position. The cottage is gone, but there are other places to stay deep in the Icelandic wilderness. I think this year we'll make the trip—Nicole, Paul, and myself. Maybe there, beneath the emerald, December sky, I'll find a way to undo my mistakes. Maybe, if I say the right words and pray to the most ancient of matriarchs, my family will find a second chance.

A Wordless Hymn

A small town sits on a plateau, overlooking the sea. Alongside Cedar Avenue, the road that leads to the town, a stake light shines up from the soil, illuminating a sign reading *Dove Cliff, population 600.*

The night is still and quiet, save for the baying of dogs, and the faint hint of a whistled song on the wind. Cedar Avenue is lined with light posts, but they are few and far between and the mercury vapor light does little to alleviate the darkness of the tree-lined thoroughfare. Each casts only a small cone of light beneath it. Their narrow radiance makes the black of night seem even starker by contrast.

Houses begin to crop up along the road into town, before Cedar Avenue branches into the numerous streets of Dove Cliff. Incandescent lights shine in empty windows. Doors, each marked with a cross in gray ash, have been left wide open to breathe in the night air and exhale the sounds of radio plays and variety shows.

Dogs howl and whine in their yards for their absent masters. Mosquitos scout the night for blood while flies swarm around pitchers of Kool-Aid and the spilled remnants of overturned beer bottles left on picnic tables and stoops.

Deeper into town, the occasional storefront breaks up the residential monotony. A barber's pole spins in an endless red and white spiral while clumps of hair and discarded scissors lay on the floor inside. Circular Coca-Cola signs frame the words *Powell's Drug* beneath a green awning. Abandoned glasses of root beer and melted ice cream sit on the counter inside.

Around the corner and two blocks down stands St. Thomas's Methodist Church. It seems modest, at least as churches go, but it towers above the surrounding homes and there is a subtle breed of power and dignity to its simple architecture. The arch of its roof points heavenward. The clapboard exterior mimics the white cliffs that are the namesake of the town, claiming their beauty and grandeur for its own.

Candles burn within the vacant church. Their wavering light creates ghastly shadows and lends a ghoulish pale cast to images of saints and messiahs. On the pulpit lies a Bible. The book is opened to Romans, chapter 12. Faint pencil marks bracket off several verses.

Repay no one evil for evil, but give thought to do what is honorable in the sight of all. If possible, so far as it depends on you, live peaceably with all. Beloved, never avenge yourselves, but leave it to the wrath of God, for it is written, "Vengeance is mine, I will repay, says the Lord." To the contrary, "if your enemy is hungry, feed him; if he is thirsty, give him something to drink; for by so doing you will heap burning coals on his head." Do not be overcome by evil, but overcome evil with good.

Scraps of paper sit on the pulpit beside the open bible. A flowing script across the top sheet warns that opening one's heart to evil is more dangerous than opening one's home to it.

A cemetery lies behind the church. Several plots are marked by freshly excavated soil. Each of these graves is marked with a small headstone, commemorating the short lives of the recently deceased.

Bethany Hillstrom, 1945–1953
Deborah Oaks, 1943–1953
Mary Naughton, 1948–1953

There are other graves, not quite so fresh but also marked with the names of girls who died tragically young.

South of the church and the cemetery sits a secluded house. It's a small but handsome brick building with bay windows in the front. The door, like all the others in town, has an ashen cross drawn upon it and stands wide open.

The inside has been ransacked. Furniture lay tipped over. The stuffing from pillows and mattresses lies strewn about. The drawers have been torn from dressers and desks. Their contents litter the floor.

An esoteric mixture of books lines the walls of the study, from treatises on philosophy and spirituality to physics texts and books on mummification. Charred spines with strange glyphs upon them sit among the fireplace ashes, along with half-burned journals scrawled in a Cyrillic script.

Several scrapbooks lie open on the floor. One contains Polaroids of young girls. Their eyes are sewn shut, and each bears the lines of a Y-incision across their chest, the flaps of skin sutured together. Arcane, un-Christian symbols are painted upon their naked flesh.

An older scrapbook contains a magazine clipping about a young man who escaped the Vinnytsia Massacre in Ukraine by hiding among the bodies of a mass grave and sneaking away beneath the cover of night.

Gravely injured in a botched execution, young Ivan Chornyi remembers nothing after being shot and is convinced he was dead for several hours. Chornyi claims that it was "the great oblivion," the void of death which he had touched, which shielded him from Soviet detection and allowed him to escape across the Black Sea to Turkey and then immigrate to the West.

Another clipping pasted on the opposite page is about the same young man, where he talks about the detached calm of his would-be killers.

These men . . . they were not just comfortable with death, they had an intimate connection to it. They were eager servants of oblivion. The man who shot me, you could see it in his eyes—a sliver of the void expanding throughout his soul.

He whistled as he shot us into that pit. A wordless hymn floated from his lips, accentuated by the pop-pop of his rifle. By the time a victim had fallen onto the corpses of their friends and family, the executioner had already resumed his song.

The road away from the secluded house climbs eastward, edging higher and higher toward the oceanside cliffs. The whistling, first audible at the edge of town, is much louder here. Fine homes line the edge of the plateau, overlooking the dark and grim Atlantic. The houses are too small and cropped together to be called mansions but impressive enough that the residents of a little coastal town might consider them such.

Bald patches and flattened trails of grass mar the perfectly manicured yards that span the distance from the homes to the cliffs. A gnarled tree behind the largest house clings to the furthest edge of the plateau. Its roots dig into the earth and grow down the face of the alabaster cliffs, like thick brown ivy.

A dead man swings from a leafless branch that stretches out past the cliffs and over the ocean. His limbs are bound and his eyelids are sunken into empty sockets. A whistling song echoes from his breathless lungs. Maybe it's a trick of the wind, but maybe it's not.

A cat looks over the edge and mews, its hackles raised. The cliff face, a rough wall of white stone, stretches up from the ocean, more than a hundred feet over the water's surface. The ivory ridges take on an almost glacial hue in the moonlight. Streaks and splashes of crimson mar the obtuse portions of the cliff face.

The black ocean below laps blood from ruined corpses dashed upon the rocks. There is a nocturnal glow to the seafoam, which ebbs and flows in radiant contrast against the dark water. Spilled life adds a tinge of pink to the whitecaps, which shift and vanish like neon fog.

Men and women of all ages lie dead on the rocks and bob among the waves. An old man in oily coveralls lies folded over a rock jutting up from the water, while a young girl with a purple, concaved cheek is battered against the cliff face, over and over. A heavy-set woman floats, face down between two rocky outcroppings. The waves occasionally retreat to reveal deep lacerations across her face.

Some of the bodies already rest on the ocean floor, their buoyancy robbed by the water in their lungs. No seaside scavengers molest the dead. The crabs and gulls, who are well known to dine on rancid flesh, give the corpses a wide berth. Sea-strewn kelp wilts as it catches on their motionless limbs.

A number of the dead drift in the riptide, past the ivory cliffs and toward rocky beaches to the south. Some drift out to sea. Others wash up on shore.

Between corpses strewn on the sand, briny water puddles up in footprints leading out of the surf. The beach gives way to brush and forest and a wordless hymn echoes from the black shadows beyond the woodline.

A Grave at the End of the World

Two clocks counted down, one on a ticker high above the war room reading minus eleven hours and fifty-eight minutes. The smaller clock ticked away in the corner of a computer monitor. It was at T-minus five minutes.

General Adams cursed. There was less than half a day before the extinction event if the Norns were right. They always were.

Adams watched video streaming from a test lab in another part of the facility—a place unofficially known as the Black Box. There were four men in the room—criminals he'd snatched from a military prison. Each had a number spray-painted across his bare chest. They sneered and howled from plastic cages set in each corner. Some smashed their heads against the plexiglass. Others beat upon themselves with balled fists. No humanity resided behind their eyes—only drug-induced madness.

In the middle of the lab, equidistant to each cell, stood a teenage girl named Providence. Adams had known her since she was a child, and looking upon her still chilled his blood every time. She looked mostly human, almost beautiful in fact, save for the obsidian ram horns crowning her head. Her pale skin and platinum hair glistened with sweat and her orange jumpsuit was soaked through.

A bespectacled figure with bulbous eyes and a tweed suit sat at a computer to the side of the general. Adams watched him type in a series of coded commands. None of it made sense to the general, but he pretended it did.

The man in the tweed suit, Dr. Wallach, pressed a button on the microphone by his monitor. Feedback squelched across the speakers before he spoke.

"The Norns predict that one of these men has a fixed destiny,"

Wallach said into the microphone. "One of them is supposed to die tomorrow when the event happens. We want you to kill them all right now instead. Do you understand, Providence?"

"That's not possible, Dr. Wallach. The Norns are never wrong."

General Adams winced. She was right. The artificial intelligence network that ran the facility, or the Norns as it was nicknamed, created an algorithm for predicting the future. It had never been wrong. In his time on this project, Adams had concluded that free will was a delusion.

General Adams killed the microphone. "What's the point of lying to her?"

"I want to overtax her abilities, General. Force her to trust her instincts and go against preconceptions. She can't change the future if she doesn't learn to question it."

Dr. Wallach clicked on an icon marked "open." A siren wailed in the test lab, accompanied by flashing amber lights. The men in the cages howled and screamed. Providence closed her eyes and envisioned the night sky—a sight she had never seen with her own eyes. She floated in the cold emptiness of space, free from the sweltering concrete facility she called home. When the siren sounded again, Providence opened her eyes, centered and at peace.

The plastic cages opened, and the men charged at her with impossible speed. Providence extended her consciousness beyond her body and infiltrated the mind of the man tagged as Subject One. She could see the world through his drug-blurred eyes, could taste his foul breath and hear his gibbering thoughts. His body was hers to command.

Providence made him tackle the man to his right—Subject Four. Four clawed and bit in response. Providence abandoned her victim's mind, leaving them to fight among themselves.

Subject Two was a wild-eyed monster with a bodybuilder's physique. He rushed at her from his corner. Even as he charged, Providence could sense the last of the prisoners coming at her from behind. She sidestepped with calm and grace, then reached out with her mind and possessed the raging giant.

Two's thoughts were as muddled as One's had been, and his senses just as dulled. His body was hard to control—cumbersome, full of drugs and hate—but she managed to charge him head first at the last of the men—Subject Three.

Two's shoulder caught Three under the ribs, and the girl ran them both into the wall as fast as Two's big gorilla legs would carry them. Her consciousness snapped back into her body as the victim of her possession caved his own skull in against the steel wall.

The forceful return to her own flesh left Providence dizzy and out of sorts, but she was cognizant enough to note that Subject Three wasn't doing any better than Two. Some organ, or perhaps many, had burst inside him. Red gore drizzled from his nose and mouth. Both men slid down the wall into a lifeless heap of flesh.

"I told you this was a bad idea," General Adams said, watching from the war room. "You practically walked her down the path that the Norns predicted."

"Hush, General," Dr. Wallach said, watching the battle. "We aren't done here."

On the screen, Providence turned her attention back to One and Four. The men were still rolling on the concrete, savaging each other. They bit, punched, and gouged, each trying to dismember the other. Providence stood still and watched them, her chest heaving with each heavy breath.

"She looks spent," Adams commented. "We've been pushing her hard lately, maybe to her limits."

"Providence has no limits, General."

On the monitor they watched Subject One rip out Four's throat. He stood up, glistening with blood, and turned his attention to the girl.

General Adams lit a cigar. There was no smoking in the building, but the facility, the project, Providence—none of it even officially existed, so the hell with it.

"Smoke 'em if you got 'em."

Providence was afraid of this one. Not because of his gruesome appearance or the madness in his eyes, but because the others were dead. That meant he had to be the one destined to live beyond this moment. He was the primary target—the one the Norns had decreed would live to see the end of the world. The computer had made no such assurances about her, so far as she knew.

"What is stronger than destiny?" Dr. Wallach's voice asked over the speakers in the room.

"Providence," she whispered.

Providence launched her psyche into the last of the madmen. She took his body for her own and grew dizzy in his drug-addled psyche. His pounding heart echoed in her ears. She cringed at the copper taste of blood on his tongue. His arms held more power than she had ever imagined flesh and muscle could. She took a measure of joy in that strength as she pressed his calloused thumbs against his eyes.

Providence trembled with excitement at the idea that she might actually kill this man—that she might defy the Norns' flawless algorithm. She took a deep breath, readying herself for the pain she would feel as she pressed his eyes into his skull. Using the man like a puppet, she applied pressure with his thumbs, but a feeling came over her—a forceful intuition. She stopped.

"This man . . ." The words came out in stereo from her mouth and his. "This man is supposed to die right now, not tomorrow."

The general dropped his cigar and smoke billowed from his open mouth. A wide smirk crossed Dr. Wallach's thin lips. Both men stared at the timer on the monitor. Only one minute remained until the moment the Norns had predicted the subject would die. They were almost there.

"How do you know his destiny?" Wallach asked. "Do you think you are wiser than the Norns?"

"I don't care what the computer says." Providence's voice crackled over the computer speakers. "This man is supposed to die right now, just as the others were. I can feel it."

"Very good, Providence. The Norns did say he would die right now," Dr. Wallach admitted. "Can you prove them wrong?"

Dr. Wallach's tongue darted out as he clicked another icon. Subject One fell to the ground seizing inside the test lab.

"What the hell did you do?" Adams screamed.

"Induced a heart attack."

"You what?" General Adams yelled again, pointing at the counter on the computer screen, which now read T-minus thirty seconds. "We were almost there! We almost beat the fucking computer!"

"The world's at stake, General. We need to make sure she can do this when it matters."

The shock of the heart attack pushed Providence out of Subject One's mind. She stared down at the convulsing body. She cursed and bit her lip as she reached back into his psyche and embraced his pain.

She pushed through his mental fog of toxins and trauma so that she might navigate his neurons. She slowed his breathing and relaxed his muscles. She gripped his failing heart and sang it back into rhythm.

The subject stopped seizing. His breathing regulated. He was alive, despite what the algorithm had predicted. Providence had done it. She'd proven that destiny could be shifted with the proper leverage.

"How did you know that all the four subjects were destined to perish right then?" Dr. Wallach asked. "How did you know I was lying?"

Providence looked down at her can of Pepsi, her reward for finishing the experiment. She stayed quiet for a few moments, afraid to answer. She hated most of the people in the Black Box, but not him. She loved him, as best as she understood the concept, and she didn't want to disappoint him.

"I—I'm not sure. I just . . . knew."

Dr. Wallach placed a finger beneath her chin and raised her head so that she would meet his gaze. "You just knew?"

Providence stared into his bulging, emerald eyes and felt a twinge of shame. "Yes."

"And how did you stop his heart attack? How did you keep him alive when he'd been fated to die?"

"I, um—I took over his body and sang to his heart. I helped it find its rhythm."

"But how did you make his heart respond to your song? How did you break the hold of death?"

"I—" She couldn't explain this any more than she could explain how her heartbeat or how her hair grew. "I don't know. I just willed it, I guess."

Dr. Wallach took her hand and smiled. "That's excellent, Providence! That is what we want!"

"It is?"

"Yes, my dear!" he shouted, slapping the table.

Providence smiled then sipped her Pepsi. The sugar was nice, but it was the cold carbonation she loved. She was always so hot, always sweating and feverish, even when everyone else in the Black Box shivered and complained about the cold. The Pepsi cooled her, and the bubbles tickled her mouth.

"You have tapped into the infinite, my dear. You have the power to save the world—the power to do whatever you choose."

Providence looked into Dr. Wallach's eyes. She searched them for lies or sarcasm. She found only sincerity.

"Does this mean that I can leave now? Does this mean that I can see the stars?"

Dr. Wallach frowned, then ran his long tongue across his thin lips.

"I'm afraid not just yet. We only have eleven hours until the extinction event."

The girl stared down, past the lip of the can and into the Pepsi. The lights in the ceiling reflected off the dark surface of her drink, creating a microcosmic galaxy.

"But you said that when I mastered my talents—when I tapped into the infinite—I would be allowed to see the stars."

"That's not what I said, Providence." Dr. Wallach frowned.

"Yes, it was!"

Tears mingled with her sweat and dropped into her cola, sending ripples through the space-time of her soft-drink cosmos.

"No. Those were not my words, and I've told you the importance of speech—the importance of saying exactly what you mean."

Providence wiped away her tears, but they kept coming. How stupid had she been to think that any of her captors might be honest with her? Dr. Wallach was just another agent. He was just another man doing a job and she was just an asset. It was foolish to think otherwise.

"The event is coming. Everything changes in less than a day," Dr. Wallach said. "You decide how it changes, Providence. Not General Adams. Not the Norns. You."

"I saved one person's life! One! I'm not ready to save the world!"

"I think you're ready to do whatever you want."

"I'm not, and why would I even want to save the world? So I can rot in this hell forever? You're all liars and you're never going to let me see the stars!"

The can of Pepsi trembled on the table. Pinpricks of starlight pierced through the billowing fog that rolled out from the liquid's surface. Providence did not notice, but Dr. Wallach nodded in approval.

"I've never lied to you, Providence," Dr. Wallach said, wiping the tears from her face. "But I've guided you as far as I'm able. It's time for me to go."

The anger on the girl's face melted into panic and sorrow. "You're leaving? No!"

The can of Pepsi burst and dark liquid spread across the table, cold fog rolling from its surface.

"You're on your own now. It's your decision if the world is saved. It's your decision if you see the stars."

"I can't do this without you," Providence said between sobs. "I can't beat that computer, and I can't stay in this hellhole with no one who cares."

"The gods of fate don't rest in an algorithm. The Norns are a manmade monster. And this place is no Tartarus. It's just a grave waiting to be filled."

Providence reached out and gripped Dr. Wallach's hands. An armed guard, one of two by the door, raised his gun. Dr. Wallach glared at the man and he lowered the weapon.

"Please don't leave me."

Dr. Wallach leaned forward and pressed his forehead against Providence's hircine horns. He closed his eyes and gripped her hands.

"There's nothing else I can teach you, but if you need guidance there is one place you may look." He whispered the words. "There is a witch named Angrboða . . ."

Static squelched from a speaker in the ceiling and General Adams's voice thundered in the room.

"Lieutenant, get him out of there!"

Providence glanced at the ceiling, then all across the room. The guard raised his gun and came toward them. She didn't know why.

Dr. Wallach took her face in his hands and commanded her gaze.

"She is the weaver of destiny and the mother of tragedy." His words were rushed and intense. "Reach out into the world and find her."

One guard took hold of Providence, while the other knocked Dr. Wallach to the floor. The lieutenant aimed his rifle at Dr. Wallach and commanded him to shut his mouth.

"She will take you into the infinite and grant you all the power you need!" Dr. Wallach shouted, ignoring the guards and looking deep into Providence's eyes.

"Get him out, now!" a voice echoed over the speaker.

The guard kicked Dr. Wallach in the ribs. He groaned in pain. Providence screamed and tried to overtake the guard's mind, but she couldn't. This guard, like everyone else in the Black Box, had an Isa implant on the back of his neck—a piece of cybernetic hardware meant to neutralize her powers. A single vertical line of red light showed on the implant's display.

Unable to possess the guard, Providence broke off the tab of her Pepsi can and jumped onto his back. He flung around wildly, trying to throw her off as she jammed the small piece of aluminum into one of his eyes. Blood and tears drizzled down her fingertips.

Before she could take more than an eye from the guard, Providence heard the clicking of a stun gun from behind her. Electricity coursed through her body, sending her into convulsions. The world spun into silent darkness.

Providence awoke in a white, windowless room. Her captors called it her quarters, but she knew it was a cell. Nylon straps held her to the bed, and an IV dripped mind-numbing poison into her veins.

Sweat saturated her clothes and her sheets. Neither the drugs nor the blasting air conditioner helped much to cool her.

She glanced around, but her vision was blurred. Maybe it was the drugs, or maybe the stun gun had short-circuited something in her brain.

"You know that guard you maimed has a name."

General Adams sat on a chair beside her bed. He jabbed an accusing finger into her side. Afterimages of his hand stayed behind after each poke.

"His name is James Filmore. He has a wife and a little girl. Now he'll never be able to see them right again."

Providence looked up at the ceiling, dreaming of the stars secreted above the concrete layers of the Black Box. She imagined the absolute cold and quiet of that black place that would steal the breath from men like Adams and shut them up for good.

The general grabbed Providence by the cheeks and forced her to look at him. Anger burned in his eyes, but also desperate fear. As much as he tried to hide his terror, he couldn't. The end of the world was coming, and he wasn't ready for it. She needn't reach into his mind to know that.

"Where's Dr. Wallach?" Providence asked.

"Dr. Wallach broke the rules and has been sidelined from the project."

"Did you hurt him?"

"Not as much as I should have."

Providence wanted to reach into the general's mind and pluck out the answers she sought. If she happened to do some damage while rummaging for those answers, all the better. She couldn't, of course. He was protected from her.

"So what now?" Providence asked, too weary and high to argue.

"Your little temper tantrum cost us precious time. We have less than six hours. The Norns have narrowed it down to a small list of names who might trigger the extinction event. You're going to kill them."

"I can't do that if I'm drugged up," she said looking down at the straps and the IV. "And I don't think you trust me when I'm not."

General Adams leaned in close to the girl and patted her face.

"No, I don't. But I trust my tech," he said, tapping the implant on the back of his neck. "And I get the impression you care about Dr. Wallach. If you play any games—if you don't do exactly as I say—I'll put a bullet in his face."

Tears came. Providence had learned to keep from crying after a lifetime in the Black Box, but the drugs always shattered her resolve. A whispered curse escaped her lips.

"Save that anger for the bad guys, little girl."

The general shut off the IV drip then headed toward the door. Providence glared at him, but it hurt to stare so intently. The light of the room intensified into a gleaming aura around him, and his movements left drug-induced afterimages burned in the air.

"Sober up," he said without looking back. "We don't have much time."

Providence closed her eyes and let the drugs coax her back into sleep. She muttered to herself as she drifted away.

"Angrboða . . ."

Providence woke up in a blanket of snow. She lay still for a moment, embracing the chill, and looked to the heavens, hoping to see the stars at last, but there were none. The sky was a field of darkest blue, mottled with obsidian clouds. If alien suns did shine above her, their light was too weak to penetrate this place.

She rose, the frozen ground creaking beneath her. Cold winds blew upon her naked flesh, comforting her body and soul.

The world was tundra to the south and the west. Far to the east, the cyclopean walls of a dead, frozen city stretched high into the starless night. But it was to the north that Providence found her attention drawn—to a burial cairn on the broken cliffs that marked the end of the world.

Providence walked up the rising and narrowing cliff, her platinum hair dancing in the wind. She reached the piled stones and studied the strange, angular symbols carved into the monument. She had never seen them but she knew their meanings nonetheless. She spoke the name inscribed.

"Angrboða . . ."

The cliff trembled, knocking stones from the cairn off the cliff and into the nothingness beyond. White mist oozed from the spaces between the rocks, congealing into an incorporeal spirit, wrapped in a cloak of fog. Its face was obscured beneath the shadows of a spectral hood, but a single eye glowed in the dark recess.

"Who is this girl, to me unknown, that has called me back down this troublesome road?" the ghost asked. Its voice was hollow and husky, and it spoke in a tone that might have been musical in life.

"My name is Providence and I seek Angrboða, the wisest of witches and the mother of tragedy."

"You have read the name on the rocks," the ghost said, "and to you I have come. What wisdom do you seek, Providence—girl who would save the world?"

"What force will destroy my world and how do I stop it?"

The ghost stood silent and studied Providence with a single glowing eye. The hungry nothingness beyond the cliff sucked at the air around them, sending Providence's hair into a wild dance, and pulling at the wispy cloak of the specter.

"I shall speak no more."

Providence leaned toward the ghost, pressing her body against the cold stones of the cairn.

"Please," she whispered. "I was told to seek you out. I was told you could guide me."

The ghost let out a disgusted huff. "I don't know your game, but you are no girl, and your name is not as clever as you think."

Providence ran her fingers over the runes on the cairn, but the feel of the engravings did not match the sight of them. Smooth rock lay where inscriptions could be seen, and rough lines where the stone looked even.

"And you are not Angrboða," Providence said, realizing that the name she saw on the stones was an illusion. "You are a dead and jealous thing, who would see everything follow it to the grave."

The frigid nothingness sucked at the specter and its hood flew back revealing the face of an old man. His skin was marked with lines of age and lines of battle. Crimson gore stained his white beard. One eye glowed with anger and wisdom, while a black hole filled the other socket.

"Ride home, little witch. Sully no more my grave," the ghost spoke, its voice now changed. It was no longer husky or hollow, but deep, musical, and commanding. "Ride home little witch, back into the darkest pit of Hel where you belong."

Providence woke up in the sweltering confines of the Black Box. She could no longer feel the sedatives, and her head did not pound with the after-effects. A medic stood above her, removing the needle of a saline drip from her arm.

Three soldiers trained their assault rifles on her and urged her out of bed. She rose without complaint and let herself be led from her cell. The guards and the medic stayed behind Providence, their guns aimed at her back as they marched her to another part of the facility—a room nicknamed "The Pool."

Providence was sure there was something below these particular corridors. It tugged at her soul, like a hungry singularity devouring light. It called for her to burrow through the ground so that she might merge with it. The girl slowed upon this sensation, but only for a moment before the muzzle of an assault rifle urged her forward.

"What's below us?" she asked, realizing she had been too afraid to do so in all her years.

"Below us?" one of the guards answered, nudging her forward with his rifle. "The darkest pit of hell. Now shut up and walk."

She fantasized about letting her consciousness fall back through her body, and into one of the guards. A snippet of gunfire and bloodshed played out in her mind. How easy it would be if they were not shielded by those implants. She could bounce between their minds forcing them to fire on one another, leaving each of their wives widowed and their children orphaned, all in a matter of seconds.

A few more twists and turns through the labyrinthine halls and they arrived at the Pool. The room housed a sensory deprivation tank that looked, as the name implied, like a small pool. Wires, tubes, and sensors stretched out from computer workstations where three hunched technicians monitored and controlled a number of variables.

General Adams stood by the tank. His back was straight and his face cold as stone, but his eyes were bloodshot and a day's growth of stubble marred his face. Cracks were appearing in his stoic façade.

"The Norns have identified three figures from around the world who may be responsible for the extinction event. You're going to find them, possess them, and kill them."

"How much time do we have left?" Providence asked.

"Just under four hours."

"If they're far away, in another country or on some other continent, that won't be enough time. It takes too much out of me."

General Adams put his hand on the girl's shoulder and looked deep into her icy blue eyes.

"Wallach says you have no limits, and I don't care what it takes out of you. I don't care if it kills you. You will find these men, you will end them, and you will save the damn world."

Providence didn't argue. She disrobed, letting her orange jumpsuit fall to the floor, and walked up the plastic ladder of the sensory deprivation tank. Concentric circles rippled through the water where she breached the surface tension, and Providence sank until she was shoulder deep. She lay back and floated upon the surface, the water filling her ears and dulling the noise of the world.

The water was frigid—salinized so it could be kept below freezing. Providence found comfort in that cold. It was a release from the intense, enervating heat that plagued her existence.

Muffled voices spoke commands and affirmations. The medic closed the lid. For a moment all was cold and dark. These were Providence's favorite moments—the solitary emptiness just before a mission.

A video screen popped to life on the lid above her. Pictures and video clips flashed across the display. They were all of one man—an Asian dictator with the cocksure arrogance that comes from inherited power.

Providence closed her eyes and let the dark and cold carry her consciousness away. She rode upon waves of black aether and after a few moments could feel herself dissolving. Her essence thinned and she became increasingly intertwined with the void. Higher thought stretched to dissolution, and comforting oblivion set in. As a shadow she stretched across existence, omniscient without thought, all-seeing without vision.

Some fragment of her psyche found the despot and instinctively summoned the rest of her mind. Her consciousness reformed, bits of her essence snapping back unto itself.

Providence opened her eyes to a lavish office on the other side of the world. She cursed at the bright lights from the overhead fixtures.

She looked at her hands, but they weren't hers. They were the wrong color, size, and shape. Fat, stubby fingers wiggled where she was used to seeing long, graceful digits.

Providence turned and caught her reflection in a glass door leading to a balcony. The face staring back at her, imperfectly reflected as it was, confirmed that she had found her target. She walked to the sliding doors and stepped out to the night-cloaked balcony.

The skyline of a gleaming metropolis greeted her. Skyscrapers designed with a utopian aesthetic shone in the night and stretched to the sky. To some it must have been impressive, but Providence was not moved by the urban thrall. Instead, she turned her gaze to the sky.

The stars above were blurry and dull, as they always were through another person's eyes, but there were also so few. The balcony was so high that Providence thought she should be able to stand up on her tiptoes and run her finger across the welkin, but as close as she was, so little starlight shined. She looked out at the skyline, shining with the fire of a million electric lights, and she cursed it. Not just the city, but the very light itself—that fraudulent, manmade illumination that blocked out the gleam of the heavens.

"Someday . . ." she uttered to the muted night sky.

Providence gripped the railing of the balcony, ready to throw herself off so that she might be done with this mission when she felt the phone in her pocket. She pulled it out and examined it. A number pad appeared on the screen and Providence ripped through her victim's mind for the code. She punched in the numbers, opening the phone's menu, then pressed a microphone icon.

"Who is Angrboða?" she asked, in the despot's voice.

Search results came up in foreign characters that she was able to comprehend after manhandling her target's psyche a bit further. Blood ran down her nose and from her ears as she scrolled past one result after another, each describing myths of a terrible giantess.

The wife of Loki.

The Bringer of Sorrows.

The mother Hel, who dwells in Jotunheim.

A mere legend . . .

Providence dropped the phone.

A children's story . . .

She looked to the few stars in the sky.

Nonsense . . .

She heaved herself over the ledge.

Providence awoke within the cold darkness of the sensory deprivation tank. She breathed in, cherishing the few moments she might steal for herself before the lid was opened.

The monitor flashed back on, blinding her for a moment, and casting back the merciful darkness. Another series of images and videos played out across the screen above her. This time it was of an older man with white hair and pale skin. In the media that played across the monitor, he was most often seen standing in front of the flag that all the soldiers and officers from the facility wore on their uniforms—a series of red and white stripes beside a field of blue mottled with white stars. She had grown to dislike that flag, as she had grown to dislike most of the people in the Black Box, but she appreciated the design. Streaks of blood upon white snow, and stars shining in a dark, blue sky. It was all she wanted from life—the embrace of the cold, the freedom to paint the ground crimson with her captors' blood, and escape into the heavens themselves.

Providence licked her lips and she could taste the coppery flavor of blood. Her nose was bleeding from the exertion of the last mission, and Adams did not plan on giving her a break.

"I'm bleeding," she said. "I can't do this."

"You can and you will."

"Sir, her vitals are stressed," another voice cut in from the background. "We may lose her if we push that hard again."

The speaker cut off with a squelch. Providence let her head fall back into the water and wept. She knew that General Adams didn't care if she died. He saw her as a tool to be used until she broke.

"I can't do this without you," she muttered to Dr. Wallach, even though he wasn't there.

"You have forty minutes, girl," Adams said over the speakers.

Providence closed her eyes and let sleep overtake her as she floated in the darkness.

"Hello, Providence," Dr. Wallach said, gazing at his reflection in a pool of toilet water.

You're alive. Providence's voice echoed through Dr. Wallach's brain. She hadn't even realized that she was in his head until she heard her own words.

"For now. And how fares my sweet Providence?"

They removed your Isa implant?

"No."

Then how am I in your head?

"How long did you think they could shackle you with trinkets of silicon and plastic? You're not a child anymore."

Providence took control of Dr. Wallach's body, more out of instinct than intent, and scanned the surroundings. He was in a cell, less hospitable than her own. Her prison at least kept up the pretense of being "private quarters." Dr. Wallach was quite plainly incarcerated.

There is no Angrboða. She's a myth. Why send me chasing ghosts?

"It was my final gift to you, Providence."

How is that a gift?

Her voice bellowed through Dr. Wallach's mind, eliciting blood from his nose and ears. Providence felt his pain and was immediately ashamed for hurting her only friend. Dr. Wallach was not upset, though. He laughed, then ran his tongue up over his lip to catch a taste of the blood.

"How is it not a gift, my dear? I gave you all you need to tap into the infinite—all you require to take the reins of fate."

You gave me nothing.

"Exactly! You sought the wisdom of a witch who doesn't exist, to save a world you do not love, from a monster that no one knows."

I don't understand!

"You will, Providence. And when you do, you *will* see the stars."

Providence tired of Dr. Wallach's riddles, or his insanity—whichever it was on display. She tore into his mind, ready to pluck out the secrets he hid, no matter how much she might hurt him. He was surprisingly strong—stronger than any mind she had invaded—and she could only grab snippets of thought.

The taste of wine and calamari—a favorite meal.

Naked men and women dancing on a snow-covered beach in the moonlight.

She dug deeper, tossing aside these unimportant bits. Dr. Wallach screamed and covered his bleeding ears.

A monstrous array of networked computers and monitors below a digital clock—the Norns.

She was getting closer. She tore deeper into Dr. Wallach's mind as he thrashed about his cell.

An ice sculpture in her image, but grown and weathered with age.

"I'm sorry, Providence," Dr. Wallach said, "but I can't let you cheapen this."

He threw himself back toward the toilet and gazed down at his reflection. Crimson streams ran from every orifice, but his eyes showed no sign of anger or fear.

"I love you, Providence."

Without hesitation, Dr. Wallach shoved his face into the water and inhaled deeply. Providence tried to stop him. She tried to force him to stand, and cough up the water, but she was evicted from his mind.

Providence awoke, gasping for breath. She could still taste the toilet water and feel it in her lungs.

"No!" she screeched, banging on the lid.

"What the hell is wrong with her now?" General Adams's voice echoed from the speakers in the sensory deprivation tank. "We don't have time for this."

Providence thrashed in the water and screamed for Dr. Wallach, knowing full well he was dead or dying. She slammed her fists against the lid, shattering the video display.

"God damn it! Sedate her, but nothing too heavy!" Adams growled through the speaker.

The lid opened and two men grabbed Providence. She thrashed against them as they dragged her from the tank. Blood dripped from her nose and between her legs.

She couldn't outmuscle them. Instead, she closed her eyes and concentrated on Adams. She conjured his terrible, gravel voice and the chemical smell of his aftershave in her mind. She imagined his stoic expression and troubled, bloodshot eyes. She thought of his cruel indifference and his threats against Dr. Wallach.

Her spirit reached out for his and her power shorted out the implant on his neck. She could feel it burning the flesh on the back of his neck and the electrical tingle that ran through his spine.

Providence allowed Adams to retain his awareness. She wanted him to experience what was about to play out. She wanted him to feel it all.

Adams was powerless as Providence forced him to pull his sidearm. She manipulated his body and put slugs into the heads of the three technicians, all in such quick succession that none of them realized what was happening. A moment later she forced him to shoot the medics who stood by her tank. Their blood contrasted beautifully with the white plastic. It reminded her of their striped flag.

A moment of confusion set over the room. Guards watched Adams, unsure what was happening or what they should do. He tried to warn them. He tried to command them to shoot him before it was too late, but no words came forth. Providence smiled with his mouth and aimed the pistol at the first guard.

She fired and a slug caught the man in the throat. Arterial spray gushed from his neck and his body slumped to the ground. The second and third guards each fired their assault rifles into the general's torso. The pain was incredible, but Providence only experienced it for a moment before jumping out of Adams's mind, leaving him alone with his suffering.

Adams collapsed and tried to utter a command for the men to kill themselves before she could take them, but only scarlet effervescence came from his mouth. Through the eyes of a guard, Providence watched him gurgle on his own blood.

The senior of the two soldiers took cautious steps toward the general, his rifle trained on him. The other, now possessed by Providence, stayed behind and fired into his comrade's back.

The possessed soldier watched his own hands bring the muzzle of the M4 assault rifle under his chin. Providence could have spared him from this fear. She could have put his consciousness to sleep and killed him with mercy, but she chose not to.

General Adams lifted his pistol, his hand trembling violently. Crimson bubbles oozed from his mouth, bursting as they rolled down his chin. Providence regarded him with a cool expression and strode across the room.

Adams tried to shoot, but Providence was in his mind again, keeping him from pulling the trigger. She knelt beside the general, unconcerned about the pool of blood around him, and plucked the gun from his hand, along with the security badge from his jacket.

"No bullets for me. No bullets for you. We both deserve to see how this ends, General."

Providence tossed the pistol away, far from Adams's reach, then left him to his final, painful moments. The door to the Pool opened as she approached. Two more guards stood on the other side, each aiming their rifles into the room. Providence reached into the minds of both men at once, frying their implants and forcing each to fire on the other.

Stepping over the dying men, she made her way to the elevator. There was still some time before the end of the world, and she wanted to see what lay in the darkest pit of hell—that place the one-eyed ghost had told her to return to—that place at the bottom of the Black Box to which she had always felt drawn.

She swiped the security badge she had stolen from Adams over the elevator's sensor and the doors opened. She stepped inside and pushed the bottom button.

Providence made her way down, deep into the lowest reaches of the facility. The elevator stopped with a soft bounce and the doors opened to a massive laboratory. Directly across the room was a wall of networked computers and a dizzying array of monitors—the same ones she had seen in Dr. Wallach's mind. This was the Norns.

Cables ran from network hubs, all tying into a massive glass tank that stretched thirty feet to the vaulted ceiling. Entombed within the tank, floating in liquid, was a titanic figure with probes stabbed into her naked flesh—a horned giantess with Providence's face.

Two technicians lay dead on the ground, strangled with cables. Four more techs, the ones still alive, threw themselves to the ground. They kneeled and groveled as Providence stepped out of the elevator and into the lab.

"Brother Wallach said you would come," one of the men said, his forehead pressed to the floor.

"He said you would lead us into the infinite," another added.

Providence ignored the men and walked over to the giantess suspended in icy liquid. She pressed her hand against the glass and reached out for the mind of the creature who wore her face. She found only emptiness.

"She's dead," Providence whispered.

"No," a feminine voice said over speakers in the corners of the room. "Not entirely, at least."

Providence looked around the laboratory, finally focusing on the array of monitors. Three faces rendered themselves, pixel by pixel, across the screens. A girl of youth and beauty, a motherly figure, and a gray hag.

"This is Angrboða?"

"That is our mother," the youngest avatar replied.

"What happened to her?"

"Man, in his hubris, chained her and thought to steal her wisdom," the avatar in the center answered.

"But no, man is not meant to wield such magic, no matter how cunning or ruthless he may be," added the crone. "It is but a recipe for their end."

Providence turned her attention back to the giantess and stroked the frigid tank. Perhaps it was arrogant, given how much they resembled one another, but she was stricken by Angrboða's beauty—the sharp angles of her features, the hypnotic spiraling of her obsidian horns, and the way her white hair billowed around her. She seemed at such peace, floating in the embrace of cold and death. Providence envied the dead witch.

"We saw this time coming," the Norns spoke in unison as the doomsday timer counted down to the end of the world. "The hour when our mother would awaken and enter the infinite."

"There's nothing inside her. She's dead," Providence responded. "Whatever there was left of Angrboða, I'm afraid it's gone."

"You're looking in the wrong place," the crone said.

Providence looked upon the face of the titanic corpse, then at her vague reflection in the glass. Dr. Wallach had been right: she finally understood. She turned her back on the Norns and stepped past the groveling computer techs.

"If you'll excuse, I finally need to see the stars."

Providence stepped out from the blast doors that separated the Black Box from the outside world. The arctic air steamed against her blood-splattered flesh. She left no living soul within the facility, save for her cultists in the deepest depths of the facility and General Adams, who she hoped was still in agony. They too would soon be dead.

Providence walked out from under the concrete canopy of the Black Box, crimson footprints trailing behind her, a cold Pepsi in one hand. She looked up and let out a silent gasp. The night sky, seen through her own eyes, was as gorgeous as she had imagined. No—not as she had imagined—just as gorgeous as she remembered from another life. All the men she had possessed over the years—none could see more than a limited scope of light, and even that they viewed with weak, blurred vision. Now she looked out upon a cosmos, bathed in starlight, painted in radiation, and teeming with dark matter.

Providence opened her can of Pepsi. It made a satisfying hiss as she popped the tab. She took pleasure in the carbonation, the cold touch of the aluminum, and the sweet taste of the cola. Even now, seconds away from Armageddon, it was important to appreciate the little things.

Inside the facility, the Norns counted down the final seconds before the extinction event. Outside, Providence tossed her empty can into the snow. She ran her middle finger against her bloody sex and painted her chest with forgotten runes, now remembered. The symbols merged into one another, centering around a triangular vortex.

She spoke her own name, not the one the project had given her but that name which was older than mankind. Her magic stripped away the atmosphere above and silence overtook the world. The snow around her melted then boiled into gas. Providence rode the water vapor into the sky, then out into the stars.

Inside the Black Box—that grave at the end of the world—the clock had struck zero.

Acknowledgments

"Angrboða," first published on Patreon, 2020.

"Beneath the Emerald Sky" is original to this collection.

"Elvis and Isolde" is original to this collection.

"Everything Smells Like Smoke Again," first published in *Wicked Haunted: An Anthology of the New England Horror Writers,* edited by T. Scott Goudsward, Daniel G. Keohane, and David Price (NEWH Press, 2017).

"A Grave at the End of the World," first published in *Penumbra* No. 2 (2021).

"Great-Uncle Bendix," first published on Patreon, 2019.

"The Green Man of Freetown," first published in *In Darkness Delight: Creatures of the Night,* edited by Andrew Lennon and Evans Light (Corpus Press, 2019) as "The Greenman of Freetown."

"The Happiest Place on Earth," first published in *One of Us: A Tribute to Frank Michaels Errington,* edited by Kenneth W. Cain (Bloodshot Books, 2020).

"Monsters Have No Place in the World That Is to Come," first published on Patreon, 2020.

"Orphan" is original to this collection.

"The Rye-Mother," first published in *Doorbells at Dusk,* edited by Evans Light (Corpus Press, 2018).

"Secrets of the Forbidden Kata" is original to this collection.

"She Born of Naught" is original to this collection.

"She Hunts Dying Monsters," first published on Patreon, 2020.

"Thurisaz in the negative aspect," first published on Patreon, 2019.

"The Truth about Vampires," first published in *Penumbra* No. 1 (2020).

"Vermis Paranoos" is original to this collection.

"Waspqueen Sestina" is original to this collection.

"White Night and Black Stars," first published in *HWA Poetry Showcase, Volume VI* (2019).

"The Witch of Rock Hollow" is original to this collection.

"A Wordless Hymn" is original to this collection.

"You and I and the Envious Nothing," first published in *Cosmic Horror Monthly* No. 24 (2022).

Thanks to Christine and Tristan for their patience and support, S. T. Joshi and Derrick Hussey for their belief in my work, Joshua Rex, Rebecca Clegg Dunski, Robb Kavjian, John Chesnut, and Jason Nugent for being my sounding boards, Joe Morey for his kindness and wisdom, Jared Collins for sparking my obsession with *The Nothing*, and all my readers and Patreon supporters.

CPSIA information can be obtained
at www.ICGtesting.com
Printed in the USA
BVHW050804170522
637193BV00007B/113

9 781614 983651